Widow

The Virgin Widow

CAS SIGERS

URBAN BOOKS

http://www.urbanbooks.com

URBAN SOUL is published by

Urban Books
1199 Straight Path
West Babylon, NY 11704

ISBN-13: 978-1-59983-091-9
ISBN-10: 1-59983-091-4

First Printing: January 2009

10 9 8 7 6 5 4 3 2 1

Printed in the United States of America

For my parents, thanks for always allowing me to be me! I love you.

Chapter 1

Blushing Bride

1 ounce peach schnapps
1 ounce grenadine syrup
4 ounces champagne

Pour the peach schnapps and the grenadine syrup into the bottom of a champagne flute. Fill with the champagne, stir, and serve.

In a perfectly square boutique painted in perfect pale pearl, I stood among a sea of satin, silk, and lace dresses, ranging from shades of luminous white to dirty beige. I was in a brilliant white, satin-silk combination with a fitted, strapless bodice and a full Cinderella bottom. It had tiny handmade silk roses along its edges. Inside each rose were three pearls, which matched the three pearl clusters on the matte satin bodice. Except for the four pounds of crinoline scratching my three-day-old shaven legs, this dress was absolutely perfect. I wore a diamond and pearl tiara, as opposed to a long veil, because I wanted to look like a princess, and princesses didn't wear veils; they wore crowns. I continued to stare in the three-sided mirror and practiced saying my vows.

"I, Isabelle Trotter, take thee, Carlton Trace, to be my lawfully wedded husband. I promise to honor and keep—"

Suddenly, my sister, Satchel, walked up behind me and interrupted my pledge with her ornery, raspy voice.

"Your boobs look full, and your waist looks tiny. You're the black Cinder-freakin'-rella. Now get your ass out of that dress and let's go."

I gave her a squinty-eyed look and glanced down at my dress and smiled. "I don't want to take it off."

"Well, you're going to look crazy serving drinks tonight in a big, fat wedding dress."

I whimpered the entire twelve minutes it took Satchel to unhook all twenty-eight hooks and eyes on the back of the bodice. But finally, I got the dress off, paid for it in full, and left the store.

Satchel and I grabbed lunch at Luckie and talked about the final plans for my big day that coming Saturday. I was so excited to become Mrs. Isabelle Trotter-Trace that I could hardly take it. The mere thought of me saying I do nearly made me faint with excitement. Satchel went over the list.

"Okay. You have something old?"

"Mom's diamond necklace."

"Something borrowed?" she asked.

"You said I could wear your shoes," I responded.

"Okay. Something blue?"

"My garter is blue," I answered.

"And something new?"

"My dress," I replied.

"And your cootchie," Satchel smirked.

My sister, though crass, was right. I would be walking down that aisle carrying something most brides didn't have, my virginity. I was a twenty-six-year-old virgin, a rare thing for a *Sex and the City*, modern woman. Not that I was judging, but it was amazing how quickly girls gave it up these days. One or two dates and they were already serving up the goodies. Me, I chose to wait. I had given great consideration to the law of no pre-marital sex, due to my devout Catholic upbringing and my current Southern Baptist Sundays. Yet this was not why I was still a virgin. During my teens, when all my friends were experimenting with sex, I was working with my mom as an office assistant. An ob-gyn, she constantly warned me about the dangers of frivolous sex. She'd come home with pictures of infected vaginas just to prove her point. It was very disgusting, and truthfully, it frightened me.

But once I became twenty-one, I was no longer scared, and I figured I would hold out, because I realized that I had something special. It was a distinctive thing I had, something that most people had lost. After college I knew I'd enter a serious relationship, and it would be wonderful to say that I was a virgin. I felt precious and pure. Honestly, I didn't know anyone who could say the same thing. Besides, after hearing all the details from my sister, Satchel, who had lost her virginity at the tender age of eighteen, I realized that living vicariously through her sexual escapades was good enough.

Of course, I considered doing it a few times; after all, I was made of flesh. The first time was with Theo James. My freshman year, I was his Sigma sweetheart, and, man, was he a cutie-pie. He stood only five feet six, but he had these huge dark brown eyes and lashes like those of a supermodel with a mascara contract. His eyes were mesmerizing, but after spending more time with him, I realized that he sometimes went days without bathing. Something, I later learned, many men did. But at that time it was highly disgusting to me, and I couldn't imagine his dirty skin rubbing against mine.

After Theo, there was Curious Lattimore. He almost got the booty on the name alone. He was tall, bald, and gorgeous, and put you in the mind of Chris Webber, the basketball player. He sported a beautiful smile and a light beard that never seemed to grow past its five o'clock shadow. Boy, he was sexy. But right before I decided to sleep with him, I found out that Satchel, who had met him the year before, had already ridden that horse. I couldn't let her sloppy seconds be my first, so he was definitely out. Finally, along came Carlton. Our situation was different. There wasn't an initial attraction like with the others. We started off as friends, and I never considered him to be the man I'd spend my forever with, partially because I never thought he'd consider me.

Carlton, or Carl as I called him, was the owner of the Shelby, the hotel that housed Ciel, where I bartended. He was eight years my senior and worth a load of money, and honestly, I thought he was out of my league. I was a worker bee, a cute one, but still on the payroll. Yet most evenings when Carl came into Ciel, the French word for "heaven," and ordered two vodka shots, he headed to my station. He said I was his favorite bartender. We did shots together while he would vent about the pressure of possessing the only black-owned hotel in Atlanta, the city where African Americans came to invest, own, and conquer. He would discuss the stress of making sure that his business didn't succumb to the stereotypical pitfalls like the businesses of many of his ethnic compadres.

The Shelby was more than a business, because Carl's father had purchased the land beneath it and died before ever breaking ground on the building. He was continuing his dad's legacy. I told him my sister practiced law because she was following in my dad's footsteps, but that I had always wanted to own a bar, and bartending was my way of stepping closer to my dream. I admired him for his tenacity and dedication to his career. When he built the Shelby, Carl was involved in everything from the architectural design to the paint colors in each of the themed suites. It was one of the nicest hotels in the city. A lot of actors stayed here while filming, and after Diddy went on record saying it was one of the best places to host a party, it became the hotel for any and everyone in the urban entertainment industry. From Patti LaBelle to Jay-Z, everyone had stayed at the Shelby.

Eventually, Carl's venting sessions about the hotel became pleasant conversations about movies, spirituality, and love. Carl and I had lots in common, and we continued this over-the-bar courtship for a year before he asked me on a date. First, we went to dinner, sat up all night talking, and had breakfast, and then we took a flight to Destin, Florida, and went fishing off the pier. Our rendezvous lasted forty-eight hours. When I returned to Atlanta, I was in love.

Now, I used to sport the big *V* like I was Virgin Girl, a superheroine fighting for women's rights all over the world. However, with Carl, I was afraid to mention it. I had never been with a man like him before, and I didn't know if he'd understand. More importantly, I didn't know if he'd still want to date me. He had his pick of many women. They would come into the bar and cross-examine the bartenders about his likes and dislikes. I figured once he knew I was a virgin, he'd probably dump me for one of the long-legged beauties that would give up any and everything on the first date. True, he acted like a gentleman with me, but you never knew with guys. Yet, when I told him, he was elated. He gave me a grin and a look of relief, a look that said, "I found her." I knew then what I'd been holding out for. It was Carlton, and when we were together, he made me feel like one of the most precious women on earth. Exactly one year after our first date, he proposed. *Ebony*'s most eligible bachelor was officially off the market. I even got a call from *Upscale* magazine, asking for the details of the proposal, but I denied it. First of all, I was extremely private. Secondly, the special evening in Maui was as valuable as our relationship, and I didn't need to share that with the world to prove our bond was real. I was the calm in the midst of Carl's stormy life, and he was my knight. I continued to work at Ciel once we were engaged for two reasons. I didn't want to sit around and do nothing while my man made all the money, and secondly, I loved my job. Carl knew this, and he never asked me to stop serving. I found pleasure in meeting new people and counseling my regulars. Ciel was owned by a private investment group, but Carl promised to buy it and give it to me. It was going to me my wedding gift. He said I could continue bartending, manage the bar, or have someone else run it. It was going to be mine. Not only was I getting a dream husband, but he was also making my dreams come true. I figured I was kissed by God to be so lucky.

It was five days until the wedding ceremony, and I was at home, going over my checklist. The hotel had taken care of the caterer and decorations, the rooms were reserved, and the flight arrangements were good for our families. Our ceremony was taking place in Villa Dorez, off the coast of Cozumel. It was a gorgeous, tranquil spot, and I'd always wanted a wedding by an exotic beach, but the arrangements had literally given me migraines. If I had to do it all over again, I might have eloped. But then again, I was crazy about my beautiful white gown, so maybe not.

While I was fixing lunch that afternoon, I heard keys opening my front door. Knowing it was my future husband, I rushed to the entrance, jumped into his arms, and wrapped my long, thin legs around his waist. He kissed me with so much passion, I nearly got woozy. I wanted him; I wanted all of him. He walked through the house, with me hanging on like a baby marsupial.

"Let's do it!" I whispered in his ear while I nibbled on his lobe.

"All this time you made me wait, and now

you want to do it?" he said. "We have to go to the lawyers."

"Just to do it?" I joked.

Carl placed me down and softly kissed my lips. "I am so glad you picked me to be your husband." I began kissing him, but he pulled away. "Seriously, we have to go."

"Okay. Let me get my purse."

We left the house and arrived at Klein, Klein, Jordan & Murdock around 2:00 p.m. As soon as we walked in, I was handed a large stack of papers.

"What's this?" I asked Carl.

"It's some paperwork I want you to go over."

I perused the stack of papers and quickly realized it was the deed to his house.

"I want you to know how much I consider us to be partners. What's mine is yours," said Carl.

I continued reading all the legal jargon, and it seemed simple enough, but I had to let Satchel look over it. She was a legal eagle and would kill me if I signed anything more than a receipt without her permission. "I have to let Satchel see this," I told him.

"I understand, but, baby, it's just a deed."

I agreed to get everything back to the lawyer this week. Carl had a business meeting to attend, and so he dropped me back off at my house and left. This was still a bit overwhelming. I knew I loved this man and wanted to spend my life with him, but the wedding was now in a few days, and for the first time, I questioned if I could spend my forever with him. Carl was a high-powered business mogul, and I was simple, possibly too simple for this lifestyle. He loved jet setting to Vegas for the weekend and high-profile parties.

I loved quiet country getaways and hated getting dressed for parties filled with pretentious people. I called my sister, frantic.

"I don't like Vegas," I said before she could complete her greeting.

"And?" she responded.

"I don't know if I can marry him. I love him, but forever? That's forever . . . as in for an eternity, until I die."

"Yes, it is, Izzy. So what happened?"

"He wants me to sign this paperwork."

"What paperwork?" she screamed. "Did you sign anything? It's not a prenup, is it?"

"No. He wants to put my name on the house. I have everything with me."

"Bring it over right now," she demanded.

An hour later, Satchel was going over the deed. "It all seems legitimate. Talk about a come up," she said, with a smile.

"I'm not marrying him for his money," I quickly replied.

"I know. I'm just saying, if you were, this would be a good come up." Satchel continued looking at the paperwork.

"But . . ." I paused long enough for Satchel to look up and question me with her perfectly arched brows. "I'm going to have to be his other half. People will be looking at me like I'm sort of a big deal."

"You are my sister. You are a big deal," Satchel boasted as she pinched my cheek.

"You know what I mean. I don't know if I have enough allure and glamour."

Satchel pushed the paperwork over to me, leaned on the desk, and stared into my pupils. "If you don't want to marry him because you don't want him as your husband, okay. But if you are having doubts because you're scared that you are not glamorous enough, you're cuckoo."

I sat quietly and looked at the various degrees and profile articles on my sister's wooden office walls. She was smart, high profile, and had charisma popping from every pore. She seemed more his type, and yet he had fallen for me. He'd given me the ring, and he wanted to make me his partner. A smile crept across my lips. The smile turned into short spurts of laughter. "I'm going to be Mrs. Isabelle Trotter-Trace."

Satchel matched my grin and responded, "Yes, you are." She paused. "Is this house paid for?"

I shrugged my shoulders and glanced at the paperwork.

Since our ceremony was taking place out of the country, we were officially getting married Thursday afternoon at the courthouse. So technically the paperwork related to the deed wouldn't be official until then. Satchel kept saying I had three days to change my mind, but I was ready. It was just jitters. I went ahead and signed everything with my hyphenated name, and Satchel agreed to drop everything off at the law office after the ceremony. I left her, made two more stops, and then went home.

That evening Carl and I went to dinner at Wisteria, one of my favorite little eateries downtown. Of course, all I wanted to talk about was the wedding, but he seemed distracted. Naturally, I assumed it was work.

"You're going to enjoy our honeymoon, because you need a break. You work all the time," I said.

"I may have to fire Adrian," he blurted out.

Adrian was Carl's older, less responsible brother. He was the general manager at the Shelby. But in no way was he dedicated like Carl. I think Carl had only made him the general manager to keep an eye on him, which in turn would keep him out of trouble.

"He's stealing," Carl added.

"From you?" I asked.

"I think he's gambling again. I hired a detective last year to watch him, but he didn't come up with anything concrete."

"So maybe . . ."

"No, my CFO and I have gone over the records, and money continually comes up short at the end of the month. Money Adrian has in his possession."

I knew Adrian, but we weren't that close. In truth, Carl and Adrian didn't act like brothers. Sure, they worked together, but they never visited each other and didn't spend much time outside of work together. My sister and I saw each other almost every day. In my eyes, that was normal, so I would surely not call Carl and Adrian's relationship normal.

"Have you talked to him?" I asked.

"I tried this morning, but I think he knew something was up, so he quickly dashed out of the office, saying he had a meeting to go to. He's been on me about selling the hotel as well."

"Why would you do that?"

"I wouldn't. I'm sure he's gambling again. Probably in over his head."

I reached across the table and caressed my man's hand. He reached down and gently kissed my fingers.

"Wait until we get back from the honeymoon," I suggested. "Who knows, maybe Adrian will come clean."

"You don't know my brother," Carl said, with a smirk. "But, I will wait. I have a few other odds and ends to address before we leave, and they need my full attention."

We finished dinner, and I went back to his house, but a few minutes after we arrived, Carl was headed back to the hotel. After we married, he'd be gone for twelve days, and he wanted to make sure everything was set to run without him. Carl had never taken more than three consecutive days off. I knew he wanted this honeymoon, but it was driving him insane that he'd be gone that long.

I had an early hair appointment the next morning, so I turned in soon after he left. Around midnight I heard a continuous, loud, syncopated tap. At first I thought I was dreaming, but then I realized someone was knocking on Carl's front door. I woke up, looked out the window and into the driveway, and saw Adrian's car. I rushed to the front door and yelled out, "Adrian, Carl's at the hotel."

"Let me in. I gotta piss," he said.

Wrapped in my robe, I stood at the door and debated whether or not I should let him in. I hated that I had even answered the door in the first place.

"Izzy, for real. I need to use the bathroom," Adrian pleaded.

Though it was against my better judgment, I opened the door and let Adrian in. He'd been drinking, though he wasn't drunk. He was slightly inebriated. He walked by me and winked.

"Hurry and go so I can get back upstairs," I told him.

"I can let myself out," he replied but motioned toward the bathroom. A few minutes later, Adrian walked out of the hallway bathroom and slowly approached the front door. He looked at me once he got to the door and murmured, "He doesn't deserve you."

"Go home, Adrian."

"No, for real. I love my brother and all, but . . ." Adrian stopped talking and gave me the once-over. His eyes stopped wandering when he focused on my ring. He lifted my hand and spoke. "You know he had this made from our mother's ring."

By now, Adrian was making me uncomfortable. Therefore, I opened the front door and motioned for him to leave. "Where's you wife?" I asked him.

"At home with our son."

"That's where you should be." I gave him a light push, told him to drive slowly, and closed the door. I stayed downstairs a few minutes to make sure he'd taken off, and I called Carl to let him know what had just happened. Carl didn't answer his phone, and it took Adrian at least five minutes to pull away. As soon as I got back upstairs, Carl called me back. He'd walked down to Ciel to grab a drink.

"I might be here all night," he said.

"No," I whined. "What if Adrian comes back?"

"Don't let him in. Get some rest, and I'll try to get back before morning."

I was wired up from my midnight visitor, so I turned on the television to calm some of my uneasiness. The last thing I remembered watching was an infomercial about a high-powered juicer.

Carl didn't make it home that night, so close to 6:00 a.m. on Tuesday morning, I stopped by the hotel to see him. I strolled through the lobby and spoke to Ndeeyah, Adrian's wife. I didn't mention to her that Adrian had come by, but I wanted to make sure he had made it home. She greeted me with a pleasant smile and commented on my early arrival.

"I wanted to see if Carl wanted breakfast," I said.

"He and Adrian are in the office."

Ndeeyah was sweet, quiet most of the time. She was younger than Adrian by a couple of years, I think. They had a son; he was six. She and Adrian had been married for at least eight years. Ndeeyah was originally from Africa, although I didn't know what part. Because her and Adrian's courtship and then marriage had happened so quickly, I asked Carl if Adrian had married Ndeeyah so that she could stay in the country, but he didn't know. He mentioned that Ndeeyah had been here at least three years before they married and that she'd worked in housekeeping at the Shelby. Of course, when they married, she got an automatic promotion to the front desk. She was currently a front-desk manager. Again, there wasn't much to say about Ndeeyah, because she was rarely around. Since Adrian and Carl never hung out, there was no opportunity to get to know her. I hoped to change that once we married, but I didn't think Carl cared for Ndeeyah. He barely made eye contact with her whenever she spoke. Carl could be pretentious at times. It had been his idea that Ndeeyah work the front desk, since she was family. It wouldn't look good for his sister-in-law to work in housekeeping. He adored his nephew, who hung out at the Shelby sometimes after school, but I honestly thought he looked down on Ndeeyah.

All of the hotel offices were on the second floor, so I took the stairs up and walked down the narrow corridor to Carl's office. As I approached, I heard Carl yelling at another man. I stopped in my tracks, because his tone actually frightened me. I'd heard Carl raise his voice only once, and that was when we'd got into a fender bender with a young woman. She'd accidentally hit us from behind while she was talking on her cell phone. Carl had jumped out of the car and gone into a tirade. It had been only a minor dent, but he'd just purchased the Jaguar. The woman hadn't said much; she'd only waited in her car and called the police.

I continued to listen as the heated conversation died down. I figured this was a good time to knock, but as I was about to hit the door, Adrian came down the hallway.

"I thought you were in there with Carl," I whispered.

"I had to do something first," he replied. "Yo,

I'm sorry about last night. I drank too much, and I was going to stay at Carl's."

"It's okay. I'm glad you made it home," I stated.

Just then, Carl's office door flew open, and Keith Carson walked out. Keith was one of my regulars. He quickly brushed by Adrian and me but didn't speak. Adrian looked at me for excuses, but all I could say was, "He must have had a bad morning." I didn't tell him about the argument. I assumed that if it was hotel business, Carl would inform him, and if not, he didn't need to know. Adrian and I both walked in the office. Carl looked exhausted. I immediately embraced him and softly touched his wrinkled, puffy eyes.

"You need to sleep," I said to him.

"I got a few hours last night," Carl answered.

"You want to get some breakfast? I have a couple of hours before my hair appointment," I said.

"I don't—"

"You never make time," I insisted before he could finish. "You have to take time for yourself."

"You mean time for you?" he asked.

"No, I have you the rest of your life. But if you don't take care of yourself, that life is not going to be long."

"Okay, breakfast. Come on."

Adrian cut in. "I need to holla at you about that Franklin account."

"Already taken care of," said Carl.

"No, some new developments came about last night," replied Adrian.

"Okay. Meet me back here in an hour or so. I need to talk to you, anyway," replied Carl.

Adrian nodded and left as Carl grabbed his

things. I snuggled against him and said, "You're going to fire him before we leave, aren't you?"

"I have to. I don't know what he'll do while we're gone. Come on. We'll talk over breakfast."

While we ate, Carl explained how it was really bothering him that he couldn't prove Adrian was taking money. But last night he'd got a call from Jones, one of Adrian's seedy cohorts, and Jones had said that Carl needed to pay Adrian's debt. Jones was afraid of what might happen if Adrian didn't pay up. Carl's plan was to give Adrian the money to pay the arrears, which was sixty-two hundred dollars, but then to fire him. This was the third time he'd gotten Carl involved in his messy affairs, and Carl was tired of it.

"I heard you arguing with Keith this morning. Did that have something to do with Adrian, too?"

At first Carl didn't say anything, but then he decided to tell me everything. "I didn't want you to worry about all that was going on, but Keith is who I hired to follow Adrian, but like I said he claims he found nothing. Last night, when I talked to Jones, he said that Adrian had had the money but had to give it to some cop guy to keep from getting found out. That had to be Keith. I confronted him this morning. I'm just tired of everyone taking advantage of me."

"Okay, so now what?"

"Well, unfortunately, none of this is on the record, so it would be hard for me to prove Keith took a bribe. If I can get Adrian to admit what happened, then I can go to Keith's superiors.

But then Adrian would implicate himself. I just want them all out of my life."

"But he's your brother."

"He's my deadbeat brother, who I've been supporting my entire life. I'm tired."

There was nothing more I could say. Adrian had drained him. Maybe it would be best to cut ties. We finished breakfast and went back to the hotel. I could see the stress on Carl's face. I hoped that once we were husband and wife, I'd be able to relieve him of some of his woes. He had insisted that I become more familiar with the hotel business once we were married. I had no intention of stepping into Adrian's shoes, but I wanted to be able to help Carl run this operation, because right now, he did everything on his own.

That evening, close to six, Carl came home. I already had dinner prepared. He was bushed; he fell asleep on the couch while I was setting the table. Carl always carried two cell phones, because of all the calls he received in a day. They were vibrating, so I cut them both off. I nudged him to see if he wanted to eat, but he simply twisted around on the couch to find a more comfortable position and fell back asleep. I ate alone and let him rest. He finally awoke close to eleven and heated up his plate. I was on the phone with Satchel when I heard him moving around in the kitchen. I got off the phone and walked in the kitchen to join him.

"Where's my phones?" he asked.

"I cut them off and put them in the bedroom. Eat."

Carl gave me a stern look. "I don't like my phones turned off."

"I know, but you needed to sleep."

Carl retrieved his phones and turned them back on. He was scrolling through the missed calls as he entered the kitchen.

"It was only five hours."

"Five hours and eighteen missed calls."

"That's why I turned them off." I got his plate and pushed it in front of him as he continued going through his calls. I stood in front of him to demand a bit of attention. That was when Carl looked into my eyes and smiled.

"You love me," he said.

"With all my heart."

Carl put his phones down and took me into his arms.

"I know I'm a lot to put up with, and I haven't always been the best boyfriend, but I am going to do better. I promise to make you a great husband."

I embraced him as he leaned against the counter.

"We get to have sex on Thursday after the ceremony," I whispered.

Carl had a big, sneaky smile on his face. "I know. I can't wait."

"Your food is getting cold. Eat," I said, pulling away and motioning to his plate. Carl dug in while standing over the counter. I reached in the fridge for some juice. "What happened with Adrian?"

"I told him I knew about the gambling and that I knew he was taking money. He didn't deny it. He said he was going to pay it back as soon as he sold some bank instrument."

"At least he didn't deny it."

"No, but when I told him I had to let him go,

he went off. He said I had never cared about him, and he knew it would come down to this."

"Did you give him the money?"

"Nope. I will call Jones and take care of the debt. If I give it to Adrian, he may use it to get further into debt."

I knew Carl genuinely cared about Adrian, but how long could you help someone who didn't want to help himself? I meandered around the kitchen as he continued to eat.

"Did you take care of that Franklin account?" I asked.

"What?" he asked. His expression suggested he had no idea what I was talking about.

"Earlier, Adrian said you had to settle that Franklin account."

"Oh, yep, that's done. I was serious about wrapping up all loose ends before the honeymoon. I don't want to think about any of this while we are in Mexico."

This brought a big smile to my face. I walked up behind him and wrapped my arms around his waist. He had finished his food already and was putting his empty plate in the dishwasher.

"You were hungry." He agreed, with a nod, turned around, and lifted me on top of the counter. I interlocked my legs around his hips. "I'm gonna be your wife in two days!" I shrieked. "It's still so unbelievable."

"Well, I believe dreams come true, so it only seems right," he replied as I gushed.

One of his phones rang just as we were about to kiss. He picked it up, ignored the call, and kissed my cheek, my neck, and then my lips.

"Okay. For real, I want to do it tonight," I said.

Carl smirked but didn't respond.

"Seriously, there's no need to wait, and Thursday is going to be so busy with all of your friends coming in town. We should do it tonight. This way we can sleep in each other's arms, instead of doing it then and rushing off afterwards."

"Okay," he said calmly.

"Good." I hopped down from the counter. "And, I didn't want to say anything, but I don't want you having that bachelor party Thursday night. It's dumb. We'll already be married."

As Carl followed me to the bedroom, he explained, "It is already planned, and the boys are coming to town for it. We talked about this. If you hadn't moved the date from Friday to Thursday, it would have been before the wedding."

"But—"

"I don't ever get to see my boys. We're just gonna sit around, drink, and let off some steam."

"There's going to be strippers. Don't lie."

"Probably, but it's not like I've never seen strippers, and after we are married, I still may go to the strip club from time to time."

"You go to strip clubs?" I asked, completely surprised.

"Sometimes." He chuckled. I stared at my soon-to-be-husband and lightly slapped his chest.

"You are one big mystery," I said, giggling.

"And, you have the rest of your life to solve me."

I kissed him once more and pushed him into the bathroom. "Go take a shower," I said.

Carl went into the bathroom, and I rushed around the room, dimming lights and lighting candles. I wanted to create the perfect ambiance for our first time. My bags for the honeymoon

were already packed and in the other room, so I
rushed in there to find one of my sexy night-
gowns. I had purchased six for the honeymoon,
and I had to rifle through my luggage to find the
perfect one. Apparently, it took a little longer
than I thought, because when I returned to the
bedroom, Carl was out of the shower and asleep
on the edge of the bed.

"Carl," I called out. He didn't budge.

I moved closer and tickled the bottom of his
feet, but that still didn't work, either. He was out
cold.

"Oh well, tomorrow I guess," I uttered.

I slid underneath the covers next to him and
soon fell asleep.

Chapter 2

Wedding Bells Cocktail

3/4 ounce Dubonnet French vermouth
3/4 ounce gin
3/4 ounce cherry brandy
3/4 ounce orange juice

Place all the ingredients and ice cubes in a cocktail shaker, shake well, strain into a chilled cocktail glass, and serve.

Thursday morning, Satchel picked me up, and we went to breakfast. My good friend Mei Lu met us, and we gabbed with excitement about leaving for Cozumel on Friday. Of course, the conversation led to sex. It always did with Mei. She'd grown up in Gansu, China, a repressed society, especially for women. Mei had come to the United States right after high school and had married a guy in the army. They'd stayed married for only two years, and after leaving him, she'd made up for those many years of repression. She'd been with a few men of her own ethnicity, but she happened to have a thing for men of the Latin persuasion. We'd been bartending together over the last year, and her life read like a daytime soap on Telemundo. She brought me a lingerie gift for my wedding night tonight. I pulled out the dark red lace pieces and placed them on the bright red tissue paper. Between the strings, pieces of elastic, and snaps, I didn't know whether to put on this contraption or use it for a magic trick.

"What in the hell is this?" I asked her.

Though I urged her not to, Mei quickly demonstrated how to wear the lace ensemble.

"I can't wear that," I protested. "It doesn't cover a thing. Besides, I already have my wedding nightgown. It's flowy and white—"

"I'm so sick of you and this white crap. So what? You're pristine clean. It worked. You've got your man. Now it's time to be a whore," Mei urged.

Satchel laughed as I snatched the strips of red lace from Mei and shoved them back into the Frederick's bag.

"I know you've got it in you," Mei insinuated.

"Yes," I answered. "But I'm not going all whore on the first night. We have the rest of our lives."

"Yes, don't unleash the whore all at once. Ration it out," Satchel concurred, with a chuckle.

"Whatever. I say you rock his world tonight, with this outfit, a few gels, chains and whips, and then go back to sweet, conservative Izzy once you get to Mexico. Just give him a taste," Mei insisted as Satchel and I gave her a sharp look. Mei then totally switched subjects. "I heard Adrian got fired yesterday."

"Where did you hear that?" I asked, pretending to be in the dark.

"Keith was talking about it last night at the bar," Mei explained.

"Keith? How would he know?" I asked.

"He and Adrian are friends. I guess Adrian told him," said Mei.

Satchel and Mei waited for me to respond, but I said nothing. I finished my breakfast in silence. Satchel paid the bill, and we left.

Outside of courtroom 121B, Mei, Satchel, and I waited for Carl. Many people stopped and spoke to Satchel while we waited. She'd been involved in this high-profile murder case a few years ago, and people talked to her like the case was still going on. Several people asked for her card; others congratulated her on her latest cases. Then this woman with dark glasses walked right up to Satchel, complimented her on her shoes, and then asked for her card. The woman looked at Mei and me before walking away. Her mannerisms were odd. Mei noticed it, too. Satchel had represented so many crazies that she was impervious to weirdos. But I felt it. She was about to do something that could lead to Satchel's next appearance on Court TV.

Two minutes before the judge called my name and Carl's, Carl and his close friend Evan appeared. They look flustered and glossy eyed. The first thing I asked was, "Are you drunk?"

Carl smirked and replied, "Drunk, no. A little buzzed, yes."

"Dammit, Carl," I said, hitting his shoulder. "This is our wedding day."

Carl kissed me and responded, "You are my

baby doll, my precious angel. I was happy to see Evan, we went for drinks, but I'm good. Let's go in there and get married."

Of course, this quieted me. I knew Evan was a party boy, and Carl worked hard most of the time. Besides, he was probably nervous, too.

Seventeen minutes later, I was Mrs. Isabelle Trotter-Trace. We all went to celebrate at Ciel. My close friend Cole gave the toast.

"To Izzy and Carl, may your love continue to flourish and be an example of God's blessing of true love. I wish you a lifetime of good times, good laughter, and good loving."

"Hear, hear!" everyone cried. We all toasted.

Cole pulled me aside and whispered in my ear. "At first, you know I disagreed, but I am happy for you. I love you, and if he ever gets out of line, and you need me to whip his ass, I'm there."

"I know," I whispered, lightly kissing his cheek.

Cole and I had worked together for six years. We'd started out bartending at Applebee's; then we both had moved to Ciel. Cole had never cared for Carl. This dislike had started years before Carl and I ever dated. I think it was over some woman, who'd apparently gone for Carl and not Cole. We'd never had any romantic interest; I was not his type. At first, though, I'd thought he was attractive, but I'd seen Cole run through too many women. He was the nerd guy who caught women off guard with crazy pickup lines. At first they'd give him a strange look, then smirk, and then smile. Next thing you knew, they'd be laughing out of their panties. I'd seen it work over and over.

Secretly, he'd been waiting for Carl to mess up our relationship, which would give him the perfect motive to fight him. Right after Carl and I got engaged, Cole and I talked. He'd said that he didn't think I'd be happy with Carl, but I'd convinced him otherwise. After that, Cole never said too much about Carl. Cole and I had shared our special moments. Though they hadn't been romantic, our quiet encounters had always been precious and meaningful. Over the last year, however, he seemed to have settled down with Marley, who was Brazilian. I didn't really know her too well. She'd come into the bar only a few times.

After a few more drinks, everyone was feeling good, and I was contemplating getting tangled in that red ensemble known as Mei's wedding-night gift. I was ready to leave the celebration, but this was our reception for those who weren't going to make it to Mexico, so I felt obligated to stay at least another hour. Carl had several friends who'd come to town to celebrate before heading to Mexico. Unfortunately, Carl's brother, Adrian, was not at the party. Carl hadn't spoken to him since the firing incident. Ndeeyah did come by and give her blessing, but then she went right back to work. Carl said he was glad that Adrian hadn't come, but I didn't believe him. Both of his parents were deceased, and Adrian was the only family he had left. It was bothering him much more than he cared to admit. Finally, it was time to leave. It was four o'clock, and Carl's stupid bachelor party was supposed to start around seven, which gave us time for a three-hour romantic interlude. I suggested we go back to the house, but Carl suggested we just use one of the rooms at the hotel.

"We're always at the hotel. Let's go home," I urged.

Finally, he agreed, and so we left the party and went to the parking garage. However, when we got to the car, we discovered that both of Carl's rear tires were flat. He hadn't been in his car since that morning, because he'd ridden to the courthouse with Evan. My car was at my apartment and I'd ridden to the courthouse with Satchel. As Carl knelt to inspect his rear tires, he realized that they had been cut.

"That son of a bitch," he yelled. Carl rushed back into the hotel, and I followed, still trying to figure out what was happening. Carl rushed to the front desk and approached Ndeeyah.

"Where's your husband?" Carl snapped.

"I haven't seen him, Carl," said Ndeeyah.

Carl didn't believe her. He rushed over to the security guard at the front door, but the guy on duty hadn't seen Adrian since yesterday. This meant nothing, because the hotel was packed. We were hosting an insurance convention. The lobby was packed with men in suits and khakis. Adrian could have slipped in and out without anyone noticing. Plus, he still had his garage key card; he didn't have to walk into the Shelby to get to the garage. I tried to calm Carl down, but he was pissed.

"That fucking ungrateful, selfish negro," he said.

I walked back to the office suites. Carl checked Adrian's office, which seemed to be untouched. He then went to his office and made a call to have the locks to Adrian's office changed. He continuously apologized to me and asked me just to be patient until he got this situation under control. He called one of the maintenance men, gave him some money, and asked him to take care of the tire situation. I went down to the front desk and got the key to one of the suites. When I returned, Carl wasn't in his office, so I went back to the lobby, but no one had seen him. I called his cell, but it went straight to voice mail. I was praying he hadn't gone to Adrian's house. I continued to call. Finally he answered. He was with security, looking over the garage tapes, and agreed to meet me in the lobby in ten minutes. I walked into Ciel and talked to Mei until he returned. She was cleaning up from the reception. She had to work that evening, so I helped her.

"Ain't this something? I'm cleaning up after my own reception," I grumbled.

Mei tried to stop me, but I wasn't doing anything but occupying my time. I told her about what was happening. By now, everyone knew Adrian had been fired, so there was no harm in it. She listened to me and then replied, "That seems like something a woman would do."

"I'd never do that."

"I would," she said quickly.

"Well, he's with security now." I looked up at the clock. It was now after five, and time was ticking. "Do you think he should have this bachelor party?" I asked Mei.

"I don't know. It's not hurting anything. Men feel like it's something they have to do."

"I guess," I said, wiping down the counter.

Carl walked up behind me and poked me in the side. "I'm sorry," he said. I folded my arms and pretended to be much more upset than I actually was.

"You have so much making up to do," I told him.

Just then the maintenance guy came rushing into Ciel. "Mr. Trace, I need to speak with you."

"What now?" I complained.

Carl motioned me to give him a minute, and then he left the bar. Moments later, he returned, with a somber expression.

"I don't want to hear it," I complained.

"I'm sorry. I have to go take care of this."

"What? What is more important than us?"

Carl pulled me to the side and whispered, "We are leaving tomorrow, and you will have my undivided attention for two weeks—"

"Twelve days, not two weeks," I interrupted.

"Fine. Either way, if I don't handle this, I'm not going to be able to stay those twelve days. Look, I'm going to hang out with Evan and the guys for a few hours, and then I'm coming home. The party is here, so I should be there by ten."

"But we just got married," I whined.

"Izzy, what do you want me to do?" His tone changed. "You know I have a lot of responsibility. I'm trying to be everything for everyone. I'm doing the best I can."

I piped down, but I was still upset. When Carl tried to kiss me, I simply pulled away. He kissed my forehead and left. I moped back to the bar and looked at Mei.

"Don't look that way," she said, trying to wipe the frown from my face. "At least you're married. You have done something thousands of women have tried to do, tie down a wealthy, successful, attractive man who loves them."

I simply shrugged my shoulders, propped my elbows on the counter, and placed my face in my hands.

"We could go out and celebrate. Have a mini bachelorette party," Mei suggested.

"I don't want to hang out. Besides, you have to work."

"I'll call in sick."

"You're already here."

"So? Paula will be okay. I'm going to the back to tell her now."

I walked back to the front desk and saw Ndeeyah staring at me. As I handed her back the key to the suite, she leaned across the desk and whispered, "Adrian didn't do that to Carl's car. He wouldn't. He's been at home. I just called him."

I just wanted to stay out of it all. I answered, "Okay," and went back to Ciel. Before I could enter, Mei was walking out.

"I said my cramps were killing me and that I just couldn't stay," said Mei. "I told her I'd be back. Let's go."

Mei and I left and went to my apartment so that I could change clothing, and then we met Cole and Satchel at a restaurant for dinner. It was rare for all of us to be out together. Since I saw Cole and Mei almost daily at work, we hardly ever went out to socialize. When we were off work, none of us wanted to spend time in a bar or anything like it. Though Satchel and I talked daily, we didn't see each other but once a week, because her work schedule was so hectic. I was enjoying my friends, but it still felt odd to be spending my wedding day without my husband.

Satchel tried to make sense of it. "You guys just went to court and signed the papers. The real deal is the ceremony, which is in two days. You will have all of his attention then. It's not easy to drop everything at work and keep it moving."

Of course, she understood. Satchel had been top in her law class and was the youngest person to work at the Cochran law firm. This had earned her such prestigious clients that she'd started her own firm five years ago, and she spent every waking hour defending those innocent until proven guilty. She'd settled, had had some plea bargains, but had lost only two cases since launching her firm.

We all hung out and drank until ten that night. My cell phone was dead, and my charger was at Carl's house. Therefore, I couldn't call Carl, but I knew it was best to just let him hang out and get it out of his system. Satchel took me to my apartment, because it was closer. Plus, I wanted to get my car and drive to Carl's. However, I obviously had some tension to release, because I drank a little more than usual, and I was actually drunk. I didn't realize it until Satchel dropped me off. As I was walking up the stairs to my apartment, I nearly tripped over my own feet. As soon as I walked in the door, I began stripping off my clothes. I stretched across the bed and didn't awaken until a few hours later. My head felt like it was stuck in between two clamoring cymbals when awoke. I looked at the time and saw it was 4:00 a.m. I was heated, but the anger only made my headache grow, so I tried to calm myself by taking a shower. I turned on my cell phone and tried to get a few bars, but it was completely dead. I stepped in the shower and tried to wash away some of my frustration. As soon as I turned off the water, I heard keys in the front door.

"'Bout time," I mumbled. I normally greeted Carl at the door, but I wasn't giving him the satisfaction. But then he didn't come to the bedroom, either. I wrapped the towel around my body and called out. "Carl?"

He didn't answer.

I continued walking. "How did you know I was home?" I asked. When I got to the living room, I didn't see Carl. I looked over toward the front door and saw Satchel. She looked as though she'd seen a ghost. "What's wrong?" I asked her.

Satchel didn't answer, so I slowly approached her. I could tell she'd been crying.

"Something happened to Mommy," was my first guess.

Satchel nodded no. That was when it hit me. I felt the weight without her even saying a word.

"It's Carl," I stated, staid and calm. Satchel looked up at me. Her eyes refilled with tears. At that instant my headache went away and was replaced with a throbbing knot in my stomach. I slowly slid to the floor and wept.

"I'm so sorry, Izzy," Satchel said, holding me in her arms. I recalled watching Carl walk through the metal doors at Ciel. He'd turned back and smiled at me, but all I could do was grimace. That was the last time I'd seen my husband alive. I should have at least kissed him good-bye.

Chapter 3

Lady Killer

1 ounce gin
1/2 ounce Cointreau triple sec liqueur
1/2 ounce apricot brandy
2 ounces passion-fruit juice
2 ounces pineapple juice

Combine all the ingredients with ice in a cocktail shaker, shake well, and strain into a champagne flute or long drink glass over some ice cubes. Decorate with mint and a cherry, and serve.

I was afraid to listen to Satchel. I immediately covered my ears and rushed to the bedroom. I knew he was gone, but I wasn't ready to hear it. Satchel followed close behind, trying to get me to listen.

"Izzy! Stop acting like this. I have to talk to you."

Finally, I turned to her and whimpered. "He's dead, isn't he?"

Satchel slowly nodded. Though I already knew it, hearing myself say the words made me woozy.

My knees buckled, and I hit the hardwood floor.
My next recollection was Satchel smacking my
face to and fro as she screamed my name repeatedly. I popped open my eyes, and they immediately filled with tears. If Satchel had allowed
them all to fall, my room would have doubled as
a saltwater pool. I cried until nightfall. It wasn't
until late that evening that I was actually able to
comprehend everything that had happened the
night before. By that time Cole and Mei were also
at my home. I was completely dazed as Cole lay in
bed next to me, and Mei at the foot of the bed.
Satchel sat in the chair beside the bed and recounted the events as told to her by Evan and her
police friend, Detective Crooms, who happened
to be one of the officers assigned to the case.

Dave, Evan, and the other guys had met Carl at
the hotel around seven thirty. They'd spent a
couple of hours at Ciel, and then they'd gone
into one of the three reserved penthouse suites.
The guys had drunk more liquor and had done
the normal talking-shit guy stuff. Close to nine,
the strippers arrived. However, thirty minutes
into the show, another stripper showed up, but
by now the men were so inebriated, no one asked
who she was and who had sent her. They assumed
she was part of the show. She was dressed in
black leather, face mask and all. She looked like
Catwoman.

She walked over to Carl and proceeded to give
him a lap dance. When she was down to her black
corset and G-string, she pulled a tiny revolver
from inside the corset and shot Carl in the groin.
Obviously, everyone went ballistic. While the
strippers tried to flee the scene and the men

attended to Carl, two photographers bum-rushed the room. They were trying to take pictures of Carl. Someone subdued the Catwoman stripper and locked her in the bathroom until law enforcement came. It was absolute chaos. However, once law enforcement arrived on the scene, she calmly came out and gave herself up. The infamous woman was Shanice Franklin. Her family owned the bookstore chain Franklin & Scott. They weren't national but had at least ten stores in the Southeast.

Now, apparently, she didn't just wait until my wedding night to go crazy and randomly shoot my husband in the groin. According to her recorded confession, she and Carl had been seeing each other for four years and had been acquaintances since college. Though he'd never promised to marry her, they'd had many wild nights in Saint-Tropez and Aruba. The affair had been very torrid, and when she found out he was truly going to marry me, she flipped.

I was a bundle of confusion: I was mourning my dead husband, who, I'd just found out, had not been faithful during our entire relationship.

"Did he ever love me?" was the phrase I repeated amid the whimpers and cries.

The incessant tears lasted throughout the night. The following morning, my lamenting was replaced by the constant ringing of phones. Newspapers, the hotel staff, television reporters, and everyone else wanted to know the details. Luckily, my cell phone was still dead. However, when we left the house, reporters were actually outside my apartment. Satchel and Cole had to create a human barrier to keep them from taking pictures of me. Mei ran interference by scaring them away with rude gestures and a tour de force of curse words. Satchel had already called everyone in the family and told them about the tragedy. Thank God we caught people before they had hopped the plane to Mexico. At the time, though, I decided that getting away on a plane would be better than suffering the media barrage.

"Is it too late to go to Mexico?" I asked Satchel. I went on. "The hotel is paid for. I know I missed the flight, but there was a death. Maybe they will give us a break. Let's go get my bags."

Cole turned the car around, while Satchel tried to convince me that a trip to Mexico was a bad idea.

"Your husband was murdered. It won't look good if you leave town," she explained.

"Why? It's not like I'm a suspect. I need to get away," I argued.

"It may be a good idea," said Cole.

"No, she has to make arrangements, make a statement. People are going to be looking for her," Satchel said to him.

It didn't matter what Satchel thought. I had to get away in order to put things back into per-spective. There was nowhere to hide in the city. Satchel made a few phone calls, and three hours later Mei, Cole, and I were in the air, on our way to Cozumel. Satchel stayed behind to take care of any legal issues that might arise while I was out of town.

The three of us stayed in the honeymoon

suite. Mei begged me to get another suite, but I was still hanging on to some odd romantic sentiment, as eerie as it was. Though I was walking emotional wreckage, the quiet time gave me a chance to reflect on my relationship with this man whom I didn't know. How could he have lied to me all those years? How could I not have known? Was I truly that naive?

I sat on the beach for hours, burying my toes in the sand, and with no cell phone service, I was left alone with nothing but my thoughts. I walked on the beach, talked to myself, talked to Carl's spirit, and questioned everything about him and us. The more I thought, the more depressed I became. How could he have lived a double life with some other woman? The questions were unremitting, and by the second evening, the peace and quiet was more of a nuisance than a relief. I had to get answers, and speaking to the ocean in hopes that my deceased husband would answer back was not working. I hurried back to the hotel and rounded up the crew. It was time for me to go home and face the church organs. I had a funeral to arrange, and I had to find out what had really happened. No more hearsay.

"I want to know what happened," I told Mei and Cole.

"Well, I'm sure Satchel has more details by now," Cole commented.

Mei agreed and walked out to get ice. Just then, it all hit me. Everyone had probably known. I was the dumb girlfriend that people gossiped about behind closed doors. My sorrow was hastily becoming rage.

"Cole. Why didn't you tell me?"

"What?" he said, with a culpable look.

"I know you knew he was cheating. Why didn't you say something?"

Cole was quiet. He stared across the room at the door to the suite. I looked curiously at him, but still he said nothing. I didn't know what possessed me to react in the way I did, but I leapt from the bed and flew across the room like a mosquito zooming in on fresh blood. I commenced to pound Cole in the chest, while ranting.

"Why didn't you tell me! Why didn't you tell me! None of this would have happened had you just told me!"

Cole simply took his beating like a man. My yells turned to shrill screams, then moaning, and finally wailing. I curled my fists close to my body and coiled into a ball in Cole's lap. Cole just took me into his arms and rocked slowly. At first, I imagined he was Carl, cradling me after our first sexual experience. A first time that was never going to happen. It just felt so good being in a man's arms, and I wanted so badly for it to be my husband, my faithful husband, who was still alive, but then this thought made me cry harder. Cole's shirt was soaked.

"I'm sorry," I whimpered. "I'm so sorry."

"Shhhh," he said, brushing strands of my flyaway hair away from my wet face.

I stayed in Cole's lap for almost an hour. I cried myself into a migraine. He finally admitted that he'd heard some things but had no proof. He said he'd tried to mention it, but I would not hear of it. He said I'd accused him of "hating," and so he hadn't mentioned it again. Of course, I didn't recall that conversation. A woman in love could be a fool, and I was proof.

Sleep was the only thing that was going to cure my aching head, but unfortunately, there was no cure for my heart. My God, it twinged; it pinched; it burned; it languished. At times I felt as though I couldn't breathe. I felt that going back home was all I could do. Yet I knew that it would only cause more pain, and I didn't think I could take any more.

My legs quivered as I boarded the plane and quaked as I exited it and found myself back on home soil. I'd called Satchel and told her we were coming back, so she was there to pick us up. As we walked to the car, I questioned Satchel.

"Where is Shanice now?"

Satchel ignored me at first, but after I stopped in the middle of oncoming airport traffic, she realized that she had to answer me.

"She's in lockup, downtown."

"I need to see her," I said.

Satchel vehemently discouraged me from paying this visit. It didn't matter. My mind was made up. I had to talk to Shanice.

The case was quickly becoming high profile, and it took a few favors to arrange this face-to-face meeting with Shanice. The next morning, Satchel called her ex-boyfriend in the DA's department and made arrangements for me to visit the woman who'd shot and killed my husband. Up until the last minute, Satchel opposed the whole meeting and urged me to change my mind, but she knew we shared the stubborn gene and there was no persuading me. At the prison I walked into the rectangular room with five square window stalls. Satchel waited for me outside the room. I had bailed out Mei once, when she got into a bar fight, but never had I been to the back of the prison, where they actually kept the criminals. I was as nervous as a farm-raised turkey in November while I sat, with my hand on the phone, waiting for Shanice to appear on the other side of the plastic pane.

"I have to pee," I whispered to myself as I looked around the room for a rest-room sign, but there was none. Only dull painted concrete walls and one door, which served as an entrance and exit.

When I turned back around, she was there. She peered and I gazed. Even in lockup, her beauty was striking. Her hair was pulled back into a tight ponytail, and her face was clean and surprisingly refreshed looking. If it weren't for that nasty gray jumpsuit, she could have been shooting a Noxzema commercial. I'd never felt so much ire that I wanted to kill someone, but at that moment it was present and alive. My anger boiled so that I began to shake. Finally, she picked up the receiver and spoke.

"I didn't mean to kill him. I only wanted to shoot his dick off."

I was stumped. How did you respond to that?

"You killed my husband," I bellowed. The guard moved in my direction. Therefore, I took a deep breath, tried to lower my voice, and got to the reason for my visit. "Uh . . . I want to know what happened. How long—"

"Four years," she interrupted. Shanice was very

forthright and looked me square in the eyes as she gave me details of their relationship. "It was four years off and on. He said he wasn't the marrying type, but we had our own kind of commitment. Carl was very passionate, and I thought what we had would last forever. But in the end, I just wasn't special enough to marry. Obviously, he preferred a virgin," she said, with an extremely bitter tone.

I slammed the phone receiver into the thick-paned window. My anger shocked me, but Shanice didn't flinch. I don't think she even blinked. The guard, however, walked over and addressed me.

"You're going to have to leave."

"No, no, no, please, please. I'll calm down," I said.

He made eye contact with the guard on the other side of the wall. "Two more minutes, and no more outbursts," he stated. This time he remained by my side.

I studied Shanice's face. She looked familiar. "I've seen you," I said. Then I realized she was the odd woman who had asked for Satchel's card that day at the courthouse.

"I know you will never forgive me, but I honestly didn't mean to kill Carl. I loved him, and he betrayed me." Shanice's expression remained impudent, but her eyes softened some. Her icy stare began to melt.

Surprisingly, my anger subsided. I was still very bitter, but I could see how Carl had betrayed us both. However, my questions still lingered.

"Why didn't you end it with him? If you knew about me, why didn't you tell me?"

"You didn't have anything to do with it. I figured you were a fling. But then, when he said

you weren't even sleeping with him, I got concerned. A fling I could take. They come and go.
When I asked him to leave you, he said he would
once he got bored, but he never did. Then,
when he got engaged, he tried to end it with me.
We went on one last hurrah to Aruba, but that
turned into a few more late-night visits and a
couple more trips. I just knew he would never
marry you."

"But he did," I added.

"And that's why I shot him. I wanted to embarrass him. I didn't know he'd bleed to death,
but you just can't fuck with a woman's emotions
like that."

She spoke very calmly as she stared directly at
me. Carl had pushed this woman over the edge,
and she'd snapped. It was plain and clear. She
was right: it had nothing to do with me. I was an
innocent bystander.

"If you had known about me, what would you
have done?" she asked.

"Maybe the same thing. Who knows. But . . ."

"Yes, virgin, I know you didn't know," she
smirked.

"Please stop calling me that. My name is—"

"I know your name. Isabelle Trotter . . . Izzy,"
she taunted.

"Trotter-Trace," I said, with a punch that held
absolutely no power.

Shanice broke eye contact for the first time
since she'd sat down. She glanced over at the
clock on the wall and then at the guard standing
against the wall. She turned back to me, but this
time she held her face down and whispered.

"I did love him."

"Yeah, me too," I responded.

"I'm sorry, again," she said just before the guard shouted "Time's up."

With a soulful expression, Shanice hung up and walked away.

I walked outside to meet Satchel, who was chatting it up with one of her lawyer friends. By now everyone was gossiping about this case. As soon as I approached, Satchel's lawyer friend began to snicker.

"What's so funny?" I asked.

"That must have been some really good dick," she replied.

I stood with my mouth agape. "That was my husband," I said, offended. I, of course, didn't see the humor in any of this. Satchel gave her friend a look of reproach, but I could tell even she wanted to laugh at her friend's callous comment. As I was about to give her a piece of my mind, my sister pulled me away and walked toward the car.

"How dare she say that," I snapped.

"I'm sorry, honey. But, honestly, you didn't even know him."

"I did know him. I loved him. So he cheated. That does not mean that we didn't have something special." I stormed off.

However, when I got to the car, I realized that perhaps Satchel's friend was right. The sex had probably been good, good enough to send this woman over the edge, and I had never got the chance to find out. I was suddenly angry. Shanice had got to know him inside and out. She'd even known about me. He'd at least been honest with her.

"He was playing me!" I yelled as Satchel got in the car and cranked it up. Over the last three days, I had reached the peaks and valleys of at least thirty different emotions, and they'd flipped on and off in a moment. I was exhausted. I was ready to bury Carl and this whole situation.

"You have to call Adrian and talk about the arrangements, and you have to hold a press conference about this."

"Can't you do it for me?" I asked.

"No, virgin, I can't," Satchel jokingly replied.

"Stop it," I demanded.

"Sorry, I'm just trying to lighten the situation."

Satchel stopped her teasing but insisted that I go to the hotel and start dealing with the specifics of Carl's death. I still had to get the copy of his death certificate.

With both of Carl's parents deceased, Adrian, his brother, was Carl's next closest living relative. When I got to Carl's office, Adrian was already there, going through files, folders, notebooks, and anything else Carl had left behind. Adrian greeted me with a tight embrace. He reeked of alcohol. I didn't have to ask if he'd been drinking. I was a bartender. I knew what kind, what brand, how much he'd had, and when he'd taken his last sip. His hug threw me off guard.

I was still reeling from my cheated-woman anger, and my first words to him were, "Stop pretending like you're so sorry for me. You knew he was cheating."

I was sure he was also in pain, but at the time, I didn't care. He said nothing as I walked to the desk and helped him go over the files. Though I had no idea what I was looking for, I pretended and kept flipping through papers. Adrian eventually spoke.

"I'm going to have my hands full getting this hotel business in order. I know Carl wouldn't want you to keep working, so I can arrange for you to get some sort of allowance after I sell this place."

"Allowance?" I asked.

"Well, I'm sure you weren't going to keep working at that bar once you guys were married. I just want to fulfill my brother's obligations to you. You know a lot of people are interested in buying this hotel."

"You can't sell this hotel."

"This was my brother's dream, not mine. I was the manager, but I'm not interested in the complications of owning this business. There are already offers coming in."

"You haven't even buried Carl, and you're making deals on this hotel? And, didn't he fire you?"

Adrian looked up as if I had secret information that I shouldn't have divulged. Just then Satchel walked into the office, carrying two martinis. She spoke to Adrian and then handed me a drink. She removed her shoulder bag, walked around the office, and flipped through the piles of papers scattered on the desk.

"I just checked Mom in her room. She's asking for you," said Satchel. She continued to look around the office. "It looks like a hurricane in here."

Adrian spoke. "Yeah, I'm just trying to get a handle on things. I just told your sister about offers coming in, and I need to get the deeds and have this property reappraised."

"You can't sell this hotel," I reiterated.

Adrian turned to Satchel and said, "Would you tell Isabelle that it's okay to sell it? In fact, it would be best for us all."

Satchel smirked and sipped on her drink. I could see a snide response forming on her lips. "Izzy is right. You can't sell this hotel."

"See," I added.

"You can't sell it, because it doesn't belong to you. It belongs to her," said Satchel. She took another sip and waited for him to respond.

"What?" Adrian and I shouted in unison.

Satchel took a folder out of her bag and handed it to me. "Carl had his will changed. He left everything to you, Izzy, his house, another house, his accounts, and this hotel." She looked at Adrian and smirked. She loved bursting bubbles; it was part of her lawyer spirit.

Adrian had no immediate response. He only looked at me, looked at Satchel, and then looked once again at me. Then he furiously began tossing papers all over the desk and snatching folders from within the file cabinets.

"I have an extra copy of the will," Satchel said very coolly and collectedly.

Adrian turned to me and scowled. "You . . ."

"Me? I didn't do anything. I didn't ask for this," I said, feeling defenseless.

He snapped his fingers at Satchel and asked to

see the paperwork. She agreed with a slight nod and bombastic grin. He gave me another bitter glance and charged from the office.

I turned to Satchel and griped. "I didn't ask for this, Chully." Whenever I got in a pickle, I always referred to my sister by her childhood nickname. I couldn't correctly pronounce *Satchel* until I was five, and the name Chully stuck.

Satchel whipped around. "Look here. Stop acting like the victim. You are the victor in this thing. Your husband is dead, and I'm sorry, but now you own this four-star hotel. You are a businesswoman, and you have to act like one. People are going to be coming at you from all ends, and you will not let them take advantage of you."

I was hearing her, but I wasn't taking it all in. For some obscure reason, my thoughts turned to Shanice. I realized that she was probably going to spend the rest of her life in jail.

"Do you think they might ask for the death penalty for Shanice?" I asked.

Satchel snapped her fingers at the top of my lashes before she responded. "Did you hear me?"

"But Shanice—"

"Fuck Shanice," Satchel interrupted. "Stop worrying about everyone else, and worry about Isabelle. Shanice wasn't worrying about you when she shot your husband." Satchel calmed her temper and softened her voice. "Izzy, we have to get to the funeral home, pay for this burial, stop by the lawyer's office, and then do this press conference. I know this is hard, but this is your responsibility. I'm sorry Carl is gone, and I'm sorry I'm not more broken up about it, but

I'm pissed. He fooled us all and took advantage of you."

"I know," I said, looking the other way. Satchel turned my face toward hers and sighed. But as soon as her sigh was complete, the tender moment was gone.

"Now, drink your martini and let's go."

Satchel stomped her stilettos, then marched out of the office. I gathered my composure and followed close behind. As I went to the front desk to call my mom's room, Mei came rushing up to me. She had an odd look in her eyes as she handed me a newspaper.

"You okay?" I asked her, but she didn't answer. She only flicked her eyes in the direction of the tabloid. I glanced down at the picture of Shanice in handcuffs. "Oh, damn," I said.

Mei looked at me as though I were crazed. She took the paper and held it up so close that my eyes crossed. I moved back and focused on the bright yellow headline, which read: FRANKLIN CONFESSES THAT BOYFRIEND TRACE BETRAYED HER FOR A VIRGIN BRIDE!

"Everyone's been coming to the bar, asking if you are really a virgin," Mei exclaimed.

Satchel quickly realized that I was no longer walking behind her, and so she turned around to determine the holdup. She snatched the paper from my grips and read the cover. "Oh great! I told you we had to hold a press conference. Now it's imperative. They are going to blow up this whole virgin thing instead of focusing on the real story. Call Mom and let's go."

Satchel damn near skated across the lobby

and exited the building in seconds. I scurried close behind.

We held the funeral two days later, and it was a press production. All the local officials came out, and the mayor spoke. Adrian took care of everything, and I simply hid between Satchel and my mom. I didn't have the energy to talk, lie, or pretend. I was comatose the entire day. I just nodded at everyone's condolences and made it through the day. We booked my mom into another hotel, and I hid out in her room for the next two days, until Satchel finally came and pulled me from my comfortable crevice. She told me we had an appointment with Carl's lawyers. She also informed me that Adrian was petitioning to get the will overturned. Carl still had him as the insurance beneficiary, but he wasn't satisfied. He wanted the hotel. Though I wasn't sure I had the energy to fight him off, Satchel had other plans.

We got to the lawyers' office, and they ushered us right in. I sat down as Robert Klein Jr., the second Klein of Klein, Klein, Jordan & Murdock, looked over a stack of paperwork as thick as an unabridged dictionary. Satchel went into her routine, subjecting Klein to a whirlwind of questions, a storm of statements, and thunderous clacking as she paced furiously beside his desk. Klein slid the stack to my side and gave a series of consecutive sighs. Satchel leaned over and separated the documents in the stack. After raking over the documents, she spoke to Klein in a very forced tone.

"These properties rightly belong to my client. We have word that the deceased's brother is petitioning to gain ownership of these properties. We want to make sure that this doesn't happen. I need to get an updated value on these assets, and I would like the properties appraised over the next week."

Klein took the first set of paperwork and flipped through it. "The properties actually were just recently appraised. The date is marked here," he said, pointing to the fourth stapled sheet. Satchel looked over the details. Then Klein continued. "What you should know is that Mr. Trace was in debt."

"How much debt?" I quickly interjected.

Klein didn't answer; he only turned and pulled out another stack of paperwork from behind his desk. "His accountant dropped this off earlier." He slid this stack over to my side.

I fearfully turned each page and looked at the highlighted figures. I couldn't make heads or tails of any of it. Satchel looked over my shoulder and grunted.

"What does this mean?" I asked, praying for any kind of positive answer.

"How much did he owe on the hotel?" asked Satchel.

"Well, Mr. Trace had two private investors when he built the hotel. They each put in one-third. However, he managed to make enough money in the first three years through other business ventures to buy their shares. Therefore, he was the sole owner, and the building itself was paid for."

"That's good," I responded.

Klein nodded. "However . . ."

"No, no, don't say *however*," I pleaded.

Klein went on. "Mr. Trace took out a generous loan eighteen months ago, using the property at five twenty-two Courtland Avenue, the hotel, as collateral. He was investing in a casino deal in Mississippi. The deal went sour. He lost most of the money and then spent the balance on hotel renovations. He was paying back the loan, but he was not current—"

"So how much does he owe?" Satchel interrupted.

"He . . . well, Mrs. Trace owes . . ." Klein handed Satchel a sheet of paper.

Whenever people couldn't say numbers aloud, it couldn't be good. I heard Satchel gulp. She was speechless, and this was not a normal occurrence for my sister. I quickly took the paper from her hand and looked at the numbers. Finally, my eyes zeroed in on the figure at the bottom of the paper.

"Three hundred forty-five thousand dollars?" I uttered. I looked up at Satchel, who gave me a disturbing look.

Klein continued. "That's the business loan only. He still owes on his home."

I could feel the tears forming. I couldn't pay that type of debt.

"How much was Carl worth?" Satchel asked.

Klein turned and pulled out another file. I felt as though I would vomit if he pulled another piece of paperwork out onto that desk. "Here are his current bank assets, his last year's profit/loss statement, and his cash assets."

Satchel paced the room, huffing and puffing

between the one phrase she kept repeating. "This isn't good. This isn't good."

"What about insurance?" I asked.

Klein nodded. "Mr. Trace had two policies. He had an old policy, which is worth only fifty thousand. However, the beneficiary of that one is Adrian Trace. He took out another policy one year ago for a million dollars. Mrs. Trace was the beneficiary of this policy."

"Oh, thank God!" I cried out.

Klein sighed. "However . . ."

"Not another *however*," I begged.

Klein cleared his throat, looked at me, and continued. "However, that policy lapsed two months ago, so it is no good."

I slammed my head down on the desk. This was a living nightmare.

Satchel furiously tapped her foot and grunted. She gathered up all the paperwork, and turned to Klein. "Are these our copies?" He nodded and she motioned for me to grab a stack while she grabbed her pile. "We will be in touch with you this week. You have my numbers should you need to make us aware of anything else."

I wanted to cry, but Satchel, as usual, had no sympathy for me. "I don't want this. I have good credit," I screamed once we were in the lobby. She simply gave me a frown and sped off.

That night Satchel and I went over everything. We weren't familiar with the other house Carl had owned, but according to statements, we could possibly get $150,000 for it. It was currently being rented. Carl still owed $240,000 on his home, which hadn't appreciated, so selling it was not going to bring in that much, if anything at all. Carl only had twenty-two thousand dollars in his bank account, and though the hotel was usually booked, the expenses equaled what it was bringing in. The only choice was to sell the hotel. Once Satchel left, I tried to make peace with the decision we had come to, but I felt trapped. If I didn't have money to pay off the loan, the bank would eventually seize the property, anyway.

It was about eleven o'clock when I grabbed my keys and went to Carl's house. I hadn't been to it since before his death. I stood outside on the porch and took several breaths before walking in. I stepped into the frigid house. Carl had kept the thermostat on seventy, but when I'd come over, he'd always push it up to seventy-five. I didn't have the guts to change it. I wanted everything just the way he'd left it: his running shoes by the door, his sweats tossed over the couch, even his half-empty bottle of water sitting on the coffee table. I went into the kitchen and placed my face against the cold granite countertop. I remembered him bringing the stone samples to me at the bar one night to help decide between Magma Gold and Tuscany. I then glanced at the two-door, stainless-steel fridge and recalled all the nights we ate pizza and watched movies. Then, with my face still plastered to the granite, I started thinking about Shanice.

"I bet she got pizzas out of that same fridge. I bet they did it on this countertop," I said aloud. I hastily lifted my face and harshly scrubbed the imaginary tainted love juice away with a sponge.

And then, like a possessed woman, I rushed to his bedroom and went through all his drawers, tossing clothing all over the bedroom. I wasn't sure of the cause of this tirade, for I already had the evidence. He hadn't been a faithful man. I was not looking for proof of that, but rather, proof that I had meant something more to him. Yes, I had the ring, the marriage license, and the properties, but that wasn't enough. I needed more, a memento from a date, a letter he never sent, anything that would say I was special. I wanted something to explain why he couldn't let go of her and why I wasn't enough.

"Anything!" I screamed in the middle of the bedroom.

I moved to the office and pulled out mounds of unorganized papers. He'd been a horrible bookkeeper. And then I found a safe. It was in the floor, underneath the rectangular moss green rug. It was a combination safe. Quickly, I began going through the variety of numbers that could possibly be the key to unlock my mystery husband. I tried his birth date, my birth date, and the hotel address. None of them worked. I even went online and found Shanice's birth date, and thank God that didn't work, either. I continued, trying his mother's and father's birth and death dates, Adrian's birth date, and his Social Security number, but to no avail. The safe was not opening. Carl hadn't been incredibly sentimental, but he had had a romantic side, so I started going through the dates of our special moments: our first date, when he proposed, and our wedding date. I refused to give up; again, I was a woman possessed.

I hunted through his office, looking for clues, that was when I discovered a tackle box filled with pictures. My attention quickly focused as I scattered the pictures on his desk. There were several photos of him and his dad fishing, golfing, and drinking, and a couple from his childhood. There were pictures of him and Evan, but none of Adrian. Toward the bottom of the stack were eight photos of him and Shanice. I laid them all out and studied them. She looked happy and he looked complacent, or at least that was my take. He wasn't smiling. He was just there. Okay, he might have looked a little more than content, but it wasn't a look of bliss. I looked at the digital dates printed on the bottom and the back of each photo. There was scribbling only on one of them, and it was a random phone number, with no name. It was an international number. Probably some other woman he met while he was vacationing with Shanice. Knowing about Shanice, I was convinced that there had to be other casual chicks scattered here and there.

I turned back to the tackle box and saw one last picture. It was of us. We hadn't taken that many pictures, so naturally I recalled this one. It was taken on the night he asked me to be his date at some big charity function the mayor was having. I was at work when he came down to the bar and told me I needed a dress for next Saturday. We'd been going out a few months, and I was already completely smitten. However, I sassed him and told him that he was not going to tell me where I was going, but would ask if I wanted to go. He smirked and tugged on my shirt, pulling me across the bar. We kissed. That was the first time we made our relationship public. Mei, holding true to a Chinese stereotype, always had a camera on hand. She snapped a picture of our kiss. She gave it to me a few days later, and I gave it to him.

I turned the picture over and looked at the back. There was scribbling. It read, "Damn . . . I'm in love." He'd even written a date at the bottom. That one statement summed up Carl. He'd loved me, but he'd always fought the fact that he had somehow got caught up. As if God had put down a huge rattrap and had used me as bait, and he had stumbled upon it and caught his legs. Honestly, Carl hadn't been the marrying type, and all the signs had been there. I had just ignored them. I looked at the date again and then glanced at the safe.

"Maybe . . . ," I said aloud.

I walked over to the safe and tried the date. Eleven, fourteen, six. One click and it opened. As I sat in the middle of the messy office, I felt so dumb. I knew Carl had loved me, and this was no more proof than the way I'd felt when he looked at me or the way he'd touched me as though I was his precious angel. His indiscretions were definitely unforgivable, but many times, love and commitment lived on separate sides of town, and they never visited one another. Would he have been faithful after we married? Who knows? But I had the sign I was looking for, so I was satisfied.

I removed everything from the safe. There was a couple thousand in cash, his passport, some bank statements, and more hotel drawings. These weren't architectural plans, but sketches. His dad's name was at the bottom of each. The pencil drawings depicted almost an exact replica of the Shelby. I knew his dad had wanted to eventually open a hotel, but I had no idea the Shelby was his dad's dream. I gathered everything and went into the bedroom. I picked up the clothing and tossed most of it back into the drawers. I kicked the remainder into the closet and closed the door. I sat on the bed and stared at the six drawings on the ripped pieces of manila paper. I sifted through the pictures again and pulled out one with a red Mustang. Carl was sitting on the hood, and his dad was standing to his right. They looked so much alike. The only thing on the back was the date 1979. I fell back onto the bed and stared at the ceiling. Suddenly I heard Carl's voice. It was him humming an unfamiliar tune. I didn't lift my body, but I surveyed the room with my eyes. Then I heard Carl whisper to me. It was spooky, as though he were lying in bed beside me, but oddly I felt no fear. He told me I couldn't sell the hotel. He said it four times, and then there was silence. I spent the remainder of the night in that very spot, although I didn't sleep a wink. It was as clear as top-shelf vodka. I couldn't sell the Shelby. I didn't know how I was going to do it, but this legacy was not going to be destroyed on my watch.

Chapter 4

White Cotton Panties

**1/2 ounce butterscotch schnapps
1/2 ounce vanilla vodka**

Pour the ingredients into a shot glass, and serve.

Satchel wanted me to keep the hotel, but once we discovered Carl's debt, she knew that it had to be sold. She didn't see how I could handle that type of debt. Needless to say, she was not pleased when I told her I couldn't sell the hotel.

"What's your plan?" she kept asking as I explained about the legacy and the sketches. She could care less. When I answered that I had no idea how I would pay off the loan, she ranted and raved. "You have to have a plan, and it needs to be selling the hotel before they take it."

I was determined to do it my way. The Monday after I made my decision, I went into Carl's office to discuss the dilemma with Adrian. Much to Satchel's dismay, I told Adrian about the debt. I wasn't going to sell him the hotel property, but

I was hoping he would help with the situation. He had acquired fifty thousand from Carl's insurance policy. I thought I could speak with him about how we could come up with the money to save the hotel, especially since he had got the insurance money. However, Adrian came into the office with a list of potential offers, and once he found out about the debt, he insisted we sell the hotel.

"That insurance money rightfully belongs to me. So does this hotel," he barked.

"Look. Carl didn't leave you the hotel, because he knew you would sell it. I know he went into debt to save you. You owe him something," I argued.

Adrian sat at his desk, stretched his legs across it, and reared back in his executive chair. As though he was making a big managerial decision, he said, "I will assist with the funeral and burial."

"What!" I screamed. "You got all the insurance money. The other policy lapsed. You can't expect me to cover all the bills."

"You'd be able to afford to and then some if you sold this place."

I had thought he might play hardball, and I'd saved my wild card just for this occasion. "I'm not selling the hotel, but once I sell the property located at four fifty McGill Street, then I will have the money."

"That's my house!" he yelled.

"Correction. That's my house."

"Carl gave me that home," he grumbled.

"Funny, he never changed the deed."

Adrian removed his legs from the desk, sat up, and crossed his arms. I stood firm. I knew I had his attention. Adrian tried to bargain. "I will pay all his funeral costs if you agree to sign the deed to my house over to me."

"So, basically you want me to give you one hundred twenty thousand dollars in exchange for twenty thousand dollars. That's not a good deal." I headed for the door. Adrian jumped from his desk and cut me off.

"Look. I know four investors that will pay a million for this property. You mean to tell me you will walk out on that kind of money for some stupid legacy that's not even yours?"

"It meant everything to Carl."

"If it meant so much, why was he about to lose it?"

"Because he had invested in some casino deal." Adrian was quiet.

"You had something to do with that, didn't you?" I hinted. Adrian said nothing. "Fine! Adrian, I will sell your house and Carl's house to pay off this debt, if that's what it takes. Keep the insurance money. You're going to need it to find a new place to live."

I maneuvered away from him and exited the room. It was a page straight from the book of Satchel, and she was as proud as a momma seeing her child walk for the first time once I called and told her what had happened.

I talked with the Shelby's night manager, Warren, who had been with the hotel since its opening six years ago. I didn't go into detail about the debt, but I made him aware that we had potential buyers and that I had no intentions of selling the hotel. He agreed, mentioning that Carl had risked a lot to keep the hotel afloat and that he would help in any way he could. Finally, I had a voice of reason. Satchel put me in touch with an outside accounting firm to go over the hotel's books. All we knew was that the hotel was bringing in more than was showing up in the business escrow account. Warren reported to the day manager, and every two days, Adrian collected funds from the safe and deposited them into the business account. Most of the money came from credit cards. However, the Shelby had a decent amount of cash transactions. Satchel and I suspected this was the cash Adrian was taking off the top. The credit card money was wired directly into the business account.

I truly didn't want to put Adrian out of his home, but it was an option I had to threaten to use to get him to cooperate. Anyway, the real estate market was in a slump. No one was buying. So even if I put both homes up for sale, it might be six to eight months before I got an offer. I had a little money in my savings, but nothing to brag about. Therefore, I had to keep working and pretend everything was as normal as it had been two weeks ago.

When I got to Ciel that evening, it was just in time for the ten o'clock roundup. This was a ritual we did every night at 10:00 p.m., where we gave away free shots to five of our customers. It had started as a marketing tactic, but it had become something we did weekly. I saw nine shots lined up on the black and gray granite bar, so I quickly poured my shot and jumped in line. Now, ten hands were holding the glasses, five from behind the bar and the alternating five from the front. From the far right end of the bar, I looked down the row of tiny glasses and shouted, "One, two, drink."

We each swallowed our shots, slammed the glasses down twice, and tossed our hands in the air. I grabbed my glass and the bottle of butterscotch schnapps. Cole snatched the vanilla vodka. We refilled the shots, and in passing, we poured into each other's glass. I went to the left end of the bar. This time Cole called, "One, two, drink."

We each swallowed our shots, slammed the glasses down three times, and tossed our hands in the air.

"I'm out," I yelled before removing my glass from the shot lineup.

Naturally, four more people followed my lead and also removed their glasses. I didn't always participate in this alcoholic rite, but after the week I'd had, I was due. At Ciel it was constant good times. People used it as an escape, but their getaway was my life, and it was perfect. I had never dealt with troubling issues well, which was maybe why I liked my job so because listening to other people's problems distracted me from my own. But on this evening at work, everyone kept bringing my issues to the surface, and I wasn't used to that type of attention. My regulars normally poured their hearts out to me, not the other way around. For example, Mr. Ty Linney—twice divorced, no children—could have an orgasm only if he was watching porn. Justine Greenstein was Jewish but had married a

Japanese man just to piss off her racist dad, who
used to beat her mom when she was a little girl.
And then there was Keith Carson. Fine-ass Keith
Carson was what the women at the bar called
him. He was the police detective Carl had hired
to follow Adrian. I had heard him spit so much
game to the women that came in here that it was
hard to believe he was an officer of the law. He
was more like a pimp with a badge. But it wasn't
just the regulars; it was everyone. When people
walked in a bar, it was like they left their defenses
at the door, and with each outpouring of liquor,
out poured their heart.

   Ironically, none of them knew a thing about
me, or about any of the bartenders who worked
here. The drink makers were cryptic characters,
with only first names, friendly smiles, and oc-
casional jokes. Yet this disaster had broken this
cardinal rule, and everyone was staring right
through me and studying all the parts in between. I got looks of pity and sorrow. I even got
a few dim-witted grins from those who had no
idea what to say and how to look. Normally, I felt
at home behind the bar. It was my safe haven, the
only time I ever felt sexy, dirty even. But now,
everything was muffed up. The only positive
thing I remembered about that evening was my
tips almost tripled. People assumed Adrian had
got the hotel and didn't know where I stood fi-
nancially. Many thought Carl and I were still engaged and had not yet married. They tipped
bigger as some sort of condolence for his death
and his infidelity.

   I stayed that evening until closing. Afterward,
I told Cole about Carl leaving me the hotel. He,

surprisingly, agreed that I should try and save it. It was good to have a friend on my side. He also reminded me that he was supposed to move into my apartment next week. I had another six months on my lease, and Cole needed a place to stay. Since I was supposed to be living with Carl, Cole moving in to cover my rent was ideal. He wanted to know if he could stay a couple of weeks until he found something else. I obliged, of course. I wanted the company. I didn't leave Ciel until two thirty that morning.

Satchel was asleep on my couch when I got home. I really thought she would have stayed at her place that night, but she'd been watching after me like a hawk. She had strongly suggested I go see a therapist, but I had refused. So, in turn, she had become my shrink. But as usual, Satchel had taken everything too far. While I was at work, she'd decided to clean my house and wash my dirty clothes.

When I shook her to ask why she was still there, she opened one eye and whispered, "Why do you have so many white cotton panties?" I looked by the laundry room and saw all of my sullied textiles in tiny color-coded piles on the bedroom floor.

"Have you lost your mind?" I rushed to the piles and began collecting the clothes and tossing them back into the hamper. Satchel popped up and followed me as though she hadn't been asleep moments ago. "I don't need help washing clothes," I moaned.

"But your hamper was running over. Sometimes, when people go through a mild depression,

they don't do housework, and that's normal,"
Satchel said, patting me lightly on the shoulder.

"It may be, but I'm not depressed," I told her,
putting the last pile away.

Satchel followed me around the house, yapping away about my underwear. I didn't know
what her obsession was, but after thirty minutes,
I finally engaged in conversation about underwear just so she would hush.

"I like my cotton panties, and dye from
colored panties can give you yeast infections,"
I told her.

Satchel laughed until she cried. "I can't believe
we are sisters sometimes. You aren't going to get a
yeast infection from colored underwear. If you are
concerned, get the kind with a white crotch. You
need some new panties."

"Why, Satchel? With everything that is going
on right now, how are new panties going to make
it better?"

"Because you will feel sexier and stronger,
more like a businesswoman, not a little girl."

"I don't feel like a little girl," I replied.

"Well, you sure dress like one. All you wear is
long floral skirts, jeans, T-shirts, and white cotton
panties. Do you even own a suit?" she asked.

"I bartend for a living," I said.

"Well, everyone knows sexy underwear makes
a woman feel prettier. If you feel prettier, you'll
be more confident. If you're more confident,
you can take on this business."

"That's stupid," I retorted.

"We're getting you some new panties," Satchel
restated and walked out of the room. She popped
back in seconds later. "There's some pasta on the

stove. Eat something." She went into the guest room and retired for the evening.

I gave little thought to my sister and her crazy theories. There was no way colored panties would make me a shrewd businesswoman. I ate my pasta, tossed my comfortable white cotton panties in the washer, and went to bed.

The next morning, I paid Carl's bills for the month and called my real estate agent to give her the go-ahead to place Carl's primary home on the market. I decided to wait before putting Adrian's home up for sale, but it was still part of the plan. Satchel suggested that I let Adrian and Ndeeyah move into Carl's home, let them pay Carl's mortgage, and then sell Adrian's home. I wanted to at least offer the suggestion. However, I was sure if Adrian had to go from paying no mortgage to paying twenty-two hundred dollars a month, he was not going to be pleased.

Afterward, I went to Ciel and checked the schedule, which I was not on. Immediately, I went to talk to Paula, our manager. She admitted she had taken me off the schedule after everything had happened, because she thought I needed the break to get myself back together. I told her I needed the money, and she put me down for three days later that week. Everyone who knew I had been willed the hotel had been sworn to secrecy, and I wanted to keep it that way as long as possible. Adrian was still trying to overturn the will, still coming into the Shelby as though he hadn't gotten fired. He was running the business as usual. I knew little about

the business, and I didn't want to admit that I
needed him, but I did. Plus, I knew people's view
of me would change if they knew I owned the
Shelby. They wouldn't care about the debt; they
would assume I was rich. Adrian liked that
assumption, but I did not.

Close to six that evening, I decided to pay
Ndeeyah a visit. Adrian was still at the hotel, and
I figured I could talk to his wife about the offer
to move. After two rings of the doorbell and no
answer, I began to walk away. However, the door
opened, and there stood Adrian's son, Oren. He
wore printed pajama pants and a ragged blue
T-shirt. His eyes were huge, almost bulging from
his head. I'd talked to him many times before,
but as I studied his face that evening, I had to
admit he was an odd-looking kid.

"Hi, Ms. Izzy. I mean Auntie Izzy."

"What did you say?"

"My mom said that you were my auntie now."

I couldn't hold back the smile.

"My mom said she would be here in a second,"
he added.

I smiled politely and walked in.

"Isabelle, come in," Ndeeyah said, with her
African accent.

Almost like we were strangers, Ndeeyah invited
me to sit at the kitchen table as she continued to
cook. I followed her into her bright yellow and red
kitchen and sat down. Given the years Carl and I
had dated, it was hard to believe that I'd never
stepped foot in his brother's home. It was nothing

like I would have imagined. It was very modest, especially for someone of Adrian's position.

Ndeeyah poured me a glass of lemonade, leaned over the table, and spoke. "I knew you might be coming to see me. Do you mind if I continue to cook? I like to have dinner done by the time Adrian gets home."

Ndeeyah seemed very timid. I felt bad, because she was family, we worked in the same building, and I hardly knew her. It was like Adrian kept her shielded from everyone.

"I'm so very sorry for your loss. Carl was a good man," she added, with a bashful smile.

"In a way . . . ," I said, shrugging my shoulders.

"You cannot judge him by his infidelity. Many men have ways of coping with life. Sometimes other women can offer something that wives or girlfriends cannot."

"You see things differently from most."

"In Malindi, Kenya, where I am from, it is not uncommon for a man to have many wives."

"We are not in your country, Ndeeyah, so I can't be as understanding as you," I said. Her calm, almost monotone voice was aggravating. I was sure it showed in my tone. I tried to change the subject. "How long have you lived in the States?"

Ndeeyah stopped stirring her peas and rice. "I came here alone as a maid to a wealthy family, but the man of the house insisted I be his mistress, so I left. When I left Malindi, I was only fifteen, so I didn't finish school. I had no money, and when I applied for a job at the Shelby, I was homeless. Carl allowed me to stay in the hotel for a month. That's when I met Adrian. But I'm sure you've heard this story."

"Actually, I haven't," I told her.

No one talked about Ndeeyah, not even Adrian. She was like a closeted skeleton. She was docile and subservient. Therefore, she had probably never demanded attention. Ndeeyah worked at her job, came home, and took care of her son. That was her life, and she seemed to be fine with it, so who was I to judge? Yet it still seemed weird.

"Have you gone to school at all?" I asked.

She shook her head shamefully.

"What about your family in Kenya?"

"I left because I refused to marry the man I was betrothed to. Therefore, I was written off. I talk to my mother twice a year, but she can do nothing without my father's permission."

Ndeeyah went back to the stove. The more I thought about it, the more I realized I'd only seen her a few times without her uniform. She worked days and I worked nights, so I didn't even see her that much at the Shelby. But as I studied her five-foot five-inch frame, it struck me that she looked so frail. She couldn't have weighed any more than 120 pounds. Her legs looked like two twigs. Her skin was beautiful, though, dark and smooth. That was the one thing that always stuck out when I did see her. Although she had no wrinkles, she still looked old, as though her experiences had aged her.

"You're twenty-eight, right?" I asked.

"Twenty-nine," she answered.

She looked older than her age.

I finished my lemonade and placed my glass

in the sink. She didn't make eye contact when I stood next to her.

"I need to talk to you about something," I said. "Did you know this was Carl's house?"

Ndeeyah shook her head and looked completely surprised. "What do you mean?"

"I mean Carl let Adrian stay here, but he never changed the deed. When he died, it became my house."

"But we've lived here for five years."

"Where did you live before then?" I asked.

"In another home, but . . ." Ndeeyah stopped talking.

"But what?"

"Well, we moved out. It became too costly, and we lived in a hotel for a few months before we moved in here."

I explained the rest of the situation and then told her about Carl's primary home. Even as I was speaking, I realized that Ndeeyah had no idea what was going on. She just lived in that home and followed Adrian's rules. I finished talking with her and walked toward the door. I had thought at first she might have had some influence over Adrian, but I knew that this entire conversation had been a waste of time.

Before I was out of earshot, she called out. "Are you going to kick us out?"

I didn't have the nerve to answer, so I pretended I had not heard her question and quickly walked out of the house.

That evening I prayed about the situation. I really didn't want to kick Adrian and his family out of the house. But seeing its current condition, I had determined it could essentially sell for at least one hundred thousand dollars, fifty thousand less than I had originally thought, but if I did repairs and upgrades, it could go for more. This wouldn't solve all of the financial issues, but it would put a big dent in the debt. I was conflicted, and I really didn't want to ask Satchel her advice, but she was my lawyer. However, I thought I would run it by my mom first, so I gave her a call. I was surprised at her insensitive answer.

"Adrian, Oom Foo Foo, and Oinga Boinga have to go. You are not responsible for Carl's kind heart. That's why he was in debt."

"Mom, please don't call her Oom Foo Foo. Her name is Ndeeyah, and she's family."

"Family? Baby girl, you barely knew Carl, and you don't owe anything to his family. I don't know what you're going to do about this hotel, but you cannot have that kind of debt hanging over your head. It will take a lifetime to pay that off."

We bantered back and forth for a few more minutes. She was angry about the entire ordeal. She felt I'd been taken advantage of and set up, as though Carl had left me the debt on purpose. I quickly ended our conversation, hung up, and called Satchel. She was surprisingly agreeable that evening.

"Izzy, if you really want to keep the hotel, you are going to have to start doing something besides talking. I have only about seventeen thousand dollars in my savings, and I have plans for that. The hotel has to get out of the red, and you have to start paying on that loan. So, what are you going to do?"

"I'm going to sell Carl's other home. Maybe I can get some money from that. And, I'm going to make some cuts at the hotel to save some money."

Satchel was curt. "It won't be enough. I have to go now. I have a date."

"What? We're in the middle of a crisis. How can you date in these troubling times?" I responded very dramatically.

Satchel ignored me and hung up.

I spent the remainder of the evening debating this house issue.

My phone rang at 6:30 a.m. the next morning, and it was Adrian. He was livid.

"You had no fucking right to come into my house and talk to my wife about this home."

His yelling immediately woke me up, but it also pissed me off, so I hung up the phone, turned it to vibrate and tossed it on the floor. I slept for another two hours and then went into work prepared, knowing I would have to deal with Adrian's irate temper.

Before I went to see Adrian, I checked with the realtor to make sure there was nothing else to do and to confirm that Carl's primary house was officially on the market, and it was. I was excited about the possibilities. It would be great to sell the home for three hundred thousand dollars, since only two hundred thousand was owed on it. Then I could pay off a significant amount of the business loan. I decided to play it by ear and see what kind of offers we got, if any. I had to spend many hours in Carl's office in order to keep the hotel running, and rumors had started spreading about my involvement with the Shelby. I knew I would have to make an announcement soon, whether I wanted to or not.

I'd forgotten to switch my phone from vibrate. Therefore, when I got in the office, I had three missed phone calls, from Adrian, Satchel, and Carl's lawyer. I returned the lawyer's call first. He informed me that Carl's business loan was in such default that the bank insisted his estate pay 55 percent of the amount owed, or the foreclosure process would begin. He didn't have a time frame for the $189,750 payment but thought I should move expeditiously if I intended to retain the property. I called Satchel next, and while we were speaking, I noticed a note on my desk, saying I needed to call the accountant. Though I knew it was important, I didn't need to hear any more bad news. Therefore, I waited to call. I finally dealt with Adrian, who had calmed down by then but let me know that he wasn't moving and he was willing to take me to court to prove that the house had been his residence for the last five years, and I had no right to toss him out. Knowing he didn't have a strong case, he did offer to pay a monthly rental fee. He had already had his lawyers draw up a lease, which he wanted me to look over.

I was working at Ciel that evening, so Warren and I went over the hotel details most of the day. I was getting an accelerated course in hotel management. I was so engrossed in my lesson that

I never called the accountant. However, just before four o'clock, he came by the office. He walked briskly to my desk, handed me three navy blue folders, and asked that Warren leave. Something was up. I could tell by his hurried step and upset expression. I would not have guessed, however, that he was about to show me two separate accounts that contained money from the Shelby. The primary holder of these accounts was Adrian Trace. Although Carl's name was originally on the accounts, it had been removed two days after Carl's death. A percentage of all the hotel's credit-card transactions was dumped into these accounts. Basically, this was proof that monies were being taken off the top. What we couldn't show was that Carl hadn't been aware of this, since his name had been on the accounts. After the accountant left, I called Satchel and told her about everything. She suggested we call Adrian in, have him explain, and if he couldn't, fire him. I agreed to do just that. I called Adrian, but he'd already left the office. Therefore, I left him a message, closed up the office, and went to work at Ciel.

As soon as I stepped behind the bar, I felt refreshed. I breathed easier, and I even felt lighter, as though my worries were no more. My customers and friends were back to treating me like normal, and I felt like Dorothy back in Kansas. My first customer was a regular, Dr. David Cosumei, an internal medicine specialist. He always came to the bar to have a few drinks before he went home to his wife and four children. He ordered his normal two whiskey sours. We talked for a moment, until the gentleman next to him got my attention and asked me to make him a mojito. I wrapped things up with Dr. David and walked over to Cole, with a disgruntled look. I hated making mojitos. It was an easy drink, but I despised the smell of mint. It was odd, but true. Mint made my nose itch, and I rarely touched it. I asked Cole to make the drink.

When I returned with the drink, mojito man struck up a conversation. It was innocent at first, but then his questioning became more specific and detailed. He was a freakin' reporter. Cole had mentioned that several had come by that week, but this was my first encounter with any of them. I did as Satchel had advised: I smiled politely and told him I had no comment. He ordered a second mojito. I had Cole make it and deliver it this time, and I moved to the other end of the bar.

About an hour later, Adrian came in and wanted to talk. It was the wrong place and time to talk to him about the accounts, but he insisted that I explain to him the urgency in my message. When I said the word *accountant*, he went on the defensive, insisting that there hadn't been a problem before I started running things and that I was not qualified to run any part of the hotel business. He became so belligerent that Cole and a customer had to escort him out. The reporter soaked up every ounce of the disturbance. But other than that, the evening came and went peacefully.

Adrian came by the office the next day to explain the accounts. This time he was calm. His temperament had become a roller-coaster ride.

I wasn't sure if this was common behavior for him, but I wasn't about to put up with his belligerent attitude. Adrian explained that Carl had asked him to start the accounts to put money aside for taxes. This sounded reasonable; however, the accountant had showed me that none of the taxes had been paid from these accounts. In fact, all the withdrawals from these accounts had been personal. Adrian couldn't explain that at first, and then he said this money had been for his and Carl's private investments. Apparently, they'd been so private, Carl had had no other record of them.

Because Carl's name was on the accounts up until the time of his death, the accountant was able to get a record of the withdrawals on my behalf. There were two checks paid out to some Logan Equity, which we could find no record of, and two other transactions were large cash withdrawals. Though the accounts currently had a total of $18,245 in them, the older bank statements showed balances as high as $40,000 in one and $120,000 in the other. However, proving that Carl had been aware of these accounts at one time was impossible, and we had no proof that Carl had known money was being withdrawn at all. The lawyers said it would be damn near impossible to prove Adrian had been stealing money, for Adrian could always say that his brother had approved of these withdrawals. My guess was that Carl had originally put his name on those accounts and had thought Adrian was using this money for taxes, investment, or savings. The accounts were three years old, and Carl had probably forgot about them. His plate had been full, and he couldn't keep track of everything he had going on.

The next morning I had the lawyers draw up the paperwork relieving Adrian of his duties. I thought we were going to have a problem ousting him, but once the certified paperwork was delivered, Adrian cleaned out his office and left the property. He exited so calmly that it left Warren and me wondering what he was up to. Adrian was not the type to be denied something that he felt was rightfully his. Maybe he felt like he had gotten away with enough and it was time to go away. But then again, maybe he left quietly only to return months later with a big boom.

That evening, as Cole and I were eating dinner, Mei came over, unannounced as usual. She was bursting with excitement, so much so that her walk was a wiggle and her step was a trot.

"I figured out your money issue," she exclaimed just before handing me an airport catalogue of stores. "Go to page twenty-six."

Cole stood beside me as I flipped to that page. We didn't understand, but that didn't end Mei's enthusiasm.

"Read it aloud!" she shouted.

I read the ad for Franklin & Scott bookstores, but before I could finish, Mei continued in her high-pitched voice.

"You can get the money from Shanice. Her family is rich."

I gave her an unmistakable look that said, "You've got to be kidding." She returned my look with an adorable grin that said, "No, I am not."

I glanced at Cole, and he said, "She is rich."

"You two are crazy," I said. "She killed him because of me. Why would she help me?"

"Because she feels bad, and this would be a way to make things right," Mei suggested.

"She doesn't feel bad," I countered.

"But," Cole said, "she is going down for murder, and she might be trying to bargain with God and willing to buy her way out of hell."

"That's right. People always find God in jail," Mei added.

"They find God in prison. Shanice is just in a cell downtown," I said.

"Well, maybe she's on the find Jesus express train. It's worth a try," Mei responded.

I continued to look at the ad. I couldn't believe I was considering this idea. Mei was crazy. I expected this from her, but Cole was actually backing her, and I usually valued his opinion. Maybe it was worth a try. I had nothing to lose by her saying no. The worse she could do was laugh in my face.

"Okay. I'll go see her this week," I said.

I hadn't realized Shanice snorted when she laughed, but I quickly found that out on Thursday morning, when I approached her with the proposal. In between the giggles and snorts, she thanked me for the joy and said it was the only time she'd smiled since the whole thing had happened. As I was rising to leave, Shanice was still chuckling. However, she knocked on the plastic pane to get my attention before I walked away.

"Hey, virgin," she called out.

I hated that she called me that. Gritting my teeth, I whipped around and gave her a frown.

"I'll help you," she said. "Call my brother. Take down his number."

My frown flipped to a tight-lipped pucker. This was too easy, and I didn't buy it. "So, you're going to give me the money?"

"Not the whole amount, but I should have at least seventy-five thousand dollars in assets and stocks that I can free up."

I walked back to the chair and peered at Shanice. I still didn't buy it. "Why?" I asked.

"I like your nerve. Plus, I know what that hotel meant to Carl. I hate to see it go down like this. I'm surprised he left it to you, though. I thought Adrian was going to get it."

"Yeah, so did he," I responded.

"I've come to learn that Adrian is an asshole. If I can help you, I'm sure it would piss him off even more, so I'll help. Of course, I want a share in the profits. This is an investment, not a loan."

"How is this going to work? You're in jail. If you get convicted, doesn't the state seize your assets?"

"No, not unless they were obtained illegally. But I won't get convicted, because this whole thing was a misunderstanding. I didn't mean to kill Carl, and I can prove it."

"Well, I pray you have one hell of a lawyer," I said.

"If I give you this money, I will."

I gave her a confused look.

"Your sister rarely loses. She's like Johnnie Cochran with a vagina. I want her to represent me.

When she agrees, I will have my brother put that money in your account."

Just as she was finishing her last word, the guard came over to take Shanice back to her cell.

"Tell her to come see me Monday," said Shanice as she was being escorted away.

I left the jailhouse knowing that I had three and a half days to do the impossible. How was I going to convince my hard-nosed sister to represent the woman who had killed her brother-in-law? My sister loved a great case, but this would be a media circus, and Satchel hated the tabloid press and the circus it brought with it, complete with tents, clowns, and caged wild animals. She would never agree. I had to persuade her otherwise. Come hell or high water, she was going into the jail on Monday morning as legal counsel for Shanice Franklin.

Chapter 5

Absolutely Screwed Up

**1 ounce Absolut Citron vodka
1 ounce orange juice
1 ounce triple sec
1 ounce ginger ale, or to taste**

Pour all the ingredients into a cocktail shaker, shake well, and strain into a chilled glass. Six of those and you will be wasted for the rest of the night.

Satchel had another date on Friday night. Therefore, I didn't get to speak to her until Saturday morning. I was going to cook breakfast, but I figured she wouldn't shout as much in a public place, so I asked her to meet me downtown. We arrived at Java Jive around 10:00 a.m., and the wait was fifteen minutes. During this time, I attempted to get the scoop on all this dating she'd been doing, but Satchel was a closet dater. No one ever knew whom she was going out with until it was over, or until she got very serious, which was a very rare occasion.

I only recalled my sister being in love once. It was with a man named Tony Hunter, who was completely not her type. She claimed that she had slipped up and accidentally fallen in love with him. He was shorter than her, not all that handsome, and couldn't dress worth a damn, but Satchel had been crazy about him. He was a lawyer, and they met working against each other on a case. It was mind lust at first sight. But after months, they were inseparable. I thought they were going to marry. Then Tony took a job working pro bono cases in South Africa. He wanted Satchel to go with him, but she was not leaving the comfort of the United States to help out the unfortunate abroad. It wasn't her cause. Satchel was against helping those outside the United States before fixing our own domestic issues. She would never adopt a foreign child nor raise money for some foreign cause. It just wasn't her. He felt she wasn't political enough because of it, and she felt he was ignorant about the problems in our own backyard. They had a huge fight, and it was over, just like that.

Satchel hadn't been in a serious relationship since, and that was four years ago. However, she'd been seeing this new man for a few weeks now, and I needed to know who he was. She told me nothing except that they were still walking in the shallow waters, and nothing would be revealed until they were ready to tread in the deep.

As soon as we sat down to have breakfast, I nervously popped the Shanice question, like a geek asking a woman completely out of his league on a first date. Satchel did exactly what a woman in that situation would do. She gave me a puzzled look, glanced behind her to see if I was directing the comment toward someone else, and then burst into spontaneous laughter.

"I'm serious, Chully."

She stopped laughing and simply responded, "Hell no." Satchel then perused the menu as if I hadn't asked her a thing. I waited a few minutes and then mentioned the issue once more. This time I explained the situation in detail.

"You have to do it," I pleaded. "She will give us the money. Not all of it, but enough. What's the harm in you doing it? It will be a high-profile case."

"First of all, I don't need a high-profile case, and right now I'm overloaded. I can recommend one of my associates at the firm."

"No. She said you. You win your cases."

"She murdered Carl in cold blood. She is going down for this."

"Well, just go talk to her. There may be more to the story. You have to help me."

Satchel said nothing.

"I'll clean your house for a month . . . two months," I added.

I was praying that she was considering the idea, because I didn't want to resort to desperate begging, but I wasn't above it. The food came, and we ate in silence. Just as Satchel was finishing her waffle, she looked up at me, puckered her lips, and said she would agree to visit Shanice.

"My sister loves me," I said, beaming.

She didn't respond. However, two days later Satchel was pacing in front of Shanice in a rectangular gray room with steel furniture. Her meeting had started at 11:00 a.m., and by 11:30 I was on pins and needles, hoping that Satchel had taken Shanice's case. Two hours later, Satchel came to the office to see me. She strolled in, with a sly smirk, and sat down. She said nothing.

Finally, as I was bursting at the seams, I yelled, "So, what happened?"

"She has a case, a decent one. She's pleading not guilty."

"How?" I asked. "She was there, with the gun."

"I can't go into it. Attorney-client privilege."

I leapt from my seat and hugged Satchel tightly around her neck. She quickly broke loose from my grip and spoke. "She said to call her brother. Here's his number."

I snatched the piece of wrinkled paper and looked at the seven digits.

Satchel went on. "This is a serious conflict of interest. I'm not sure how we're going to get away with this. No one can know you are getting money from her. Plus, she cannot go on record as a co-owner of this hotel. We have to figure something else out, at least until after the trial."

"When is the trial?"

"We go before the judge next week. I'll find out then."

I fumbled through a few pieces of paper on the desk as Satchel sat in silence. It was killing me. How was my sister going to stand before a jury and argue that Shanice was not guilty? What had Shanice told her, and what was her plan? Just before Satchel left, she handed me a schedule.

"What's this?" I asked.

"My housecleaning schedule."

I sat and looked at the detailed, one-page to-do

list with completion dates. I should have known she would take that offer seriously.

I picked up the phone and called Shanice's brother, Jonah. He answered on the first ring. I hurriedly explained who I was and why I was calling. After I finished, he was quiet for a few seconds. I thought he had hung up at first, and then he sighed heavily before speaking.

"My parents will have nothing to do with Shanice. They've been burned too many times," he said, sounding exasperated.

"I guess this is why she gave me your number," I said, with a quick chuckle. He didn't find it funny, so I stopped joking and got serious. "Shanice and I spoke, and she wants to help me out. She doesn't want me to lose Carl's hotel."

"Why? If she killed him, then why would she care anything about his property?"

"Change of heart?" I guessed. "It's what she wants to do with her money, and she said she put you on her accounts. You should go see her. She needs some support."

"Maybe," he answered. "I don't know how much money Shanice has, but I will see and call you back."

"Thanks, Jonah. You know, I always liked that name. In fact—"

He interrupted my senseless chatter. "I have to go." He hung up.

With little excitement, I sat and pondered this situation. I doubted this was going to be easy. Jonah had sounded like he was done with Shanice, and I wasn't sure how many hurdles I would have to jump in order to get this money. Unfortunately, I had never been good at obstacles. I didn't tackle tough challenges with zeal. That was Satchel's joy. I liked the easy route, and there was nothing wrong with that. Not that I would back away at the first sign of a hurdle, but I'd rather not jump over it when I could just run around it. I couldn't end the search for money here with Shanice. I would have to keep thinking, just in case this didn't work.

I grabbed the stack of mail and sifted through the bills and junk mail. After opening three of Carl's bills, I came across a letter stating that the property known as the Shelby Hotel would be seized and sold at auction in thirty days if a balance of $189,750.00 wasn't paid. I stared at those eight figures typed on the off-white linen paper.

"Oh, that's all. Well, then I shall simply write you guys a check," I said aloud before laughing. I laughed for a minute, and then the mirth turned to sorrow and tears fell. The stress hit me like a box of bricks, and, boy, did I cry. It was one of those ugly cries, with the gasps and loud outbursts.

I was so immersed in my distress, I didn't hear Warren knock on the door. It wasn't until he stood in front of my desk that I noticed he was in the office. When I detected his presence, I tried to stop sobbing, but I couldn't. In fact, the tears fell harder. I didn't want his pity, yet I did. I wanted someone to know that it was not good. Someone other than Satchel needed to know that I was on the brink of losing it. Poor Warren. He didn't know what to do, so he grabbed a bunch of tissues from the bathroom and then disappeared. This blatant abandonment sent me into a frenzy. I began knocking papers off the desk, kicking the trash can, and repeatedly slamming the phone receiver onto the desk. Cole came rushing into the office. Apparently, Warren had sent for him. Cole grabbed my flapping arms and held me still.

"Shhhh," he repeated over and over.

I quieted down, but the tears still streamed down my face. With one hand still holding me in place, he took his other arm and wiped the tears away.

"This shouldn't have happened," I uttered, trying to stop the cries.

"I know," he whispered moving closer to my face. He kissed a tear that fell from my right eye. I lifted my face and placed my lips on his, and we kissed. It was a salty-tears, stress-induced kiss, but it was nice. I relaxed my shoulders and gave into the impulse. The tears ceased. I just needed to connect with someone, and this was it. No, it wasn't going to make my problems go away. In truth, it could have added a whole new set of issues, but at that moment it calmed my nerves, and I relished that small token of affection the remainder of the day.

After I calmed down, I gathered my things and went to Ciel to see Mei. On the way, I saw Ndeeyah leaving work. She avoided direct contact by turning around and walking in the opposite direction. I wasn't sure how Adrian had spun his story, but she had an attitude. I hoped she didn't think I had fired him for no reason at all.

Mei and I talked for a little while, and as usual, her lighthearted spirit cheered me up. I told her about the kiss, and she enthusiastically requested details. I had none to give. The kiss had happened in such a distraught moment, I couldn't remember how it had gone down. I only knew that it had happened, and that it had been nice.

"Juicy, wet nice?" Mei asked. "Or was it sweet schoolgirl nice?"

"Nice," I replied. "Just nice."

Mei was highly disappointed. She told me about her latest rendezvous, and then I went home.

That night, while I was eating dinner, Cole started bringing his things over. I was hoping that it wouldn't be awkward. Perhaps he didn't remember the kiss at all. No such luck. He sat beside me while I was eating and stared at every bite I placed in my mouth. I looked at him, and he continued to stare. Finally, I asked, "Why are you looking at me?"

"You know why," he said.

I gave a bashful smile and stared at my plate. "I fixed enough for us both," I told him.

"I already ate," he replied.

He flipped on the television and eased back in the space next to me. We were quiet for a moment, but the tension was thick.

"Thanks for today," I said.

"I always have your back. You know that."

We both were quiet again, but I could feel him wanting to say more. The emotional female in me wanted to hear what was on his mind, though I already knew. We were both waiting for the other to mention the kiss. I felt nervous bubbles in my tummy.

"Say what's on your mind," I told him.

"What if it's something I want to do instead of something I want to say?" he asked.

I began to blush. Cole was such a flirt, and he was using this opportunity to reel me in.

"Behave," I told him. "You have a girlfriend, and I'm married."

"You're widowed," he murmured.

I'm a virgin widow, I thought silently. What a crazy title to have. This sullied the mood some. I glanced over at Cole, and I had to admit that he did look more attractive than I'd ever thought before, but I was an emotional wreck. I probably would have gone after the hunchback of Notre-Dame if he'd comforted me. I simply shook my head and looked away.

"Yeah, Marley should be here in a few," he added to change the vibes.

Cole's girlfriend, Marley, was a very sweet Brazilian sista, and I liked her. And though she was on her way over, that didn't stop him from staring at my lips and moving closer to me. All of that made me uncomfortable. Therefore, I took my plate, walked into my bedroom, and finished my food in there.

Sleep set in quick, and before long the movie I was watching was watching me sleep. However, sometime in the middle of the night, I was awakened by short, strident shrieks and heavy panting. I sat up in bed and looked around the room. I knew what it sounded like, but I was sure that it couldn't be the sounds of sex. I hopped from my bed and tiptoed down the hall to Cole's room. The noises grew louder. I placed my head to the door. It sounded like he was strangling, suffocating, and slapping her around all at the same time.

"What is he doing?" I whispered.

I was drawn in. Although I knew it was wrong, I

continued to listen. It was like my feet were glued to the floor, and I couldn't walk away from the door. Then he began to climax. I felt ashamed of my behavior, and it wasn't until the room went silent that I was jarred from my captivation. Then I heard footsteps coming toward the door. I hurried down the dark hall and quickly turned the corner to retreat to my bed. However, when I glanced over my shoulder to see if Cole had made it to the hallway, I ran smack into the wall and fell down onto the hardwood floor. The collision didn't knock me out, but it sure as hell stung. I was dazed. Cole must have heard the thud, because when I opened my eyes, he was standing over me. Though he was wrapped in a towel, my view was from directly beneath him. When he squatted, his penis dangled against his leg, and I found myself turning my head right and left to keep it from hitting me in the eye. He saw this as uncontrollable twitching and thought I was convulsing.

"Oh my God, are you having a seizure?" he cried just before Marley came on the scene.

"I'm fine," I said, trying to sit up. However, my head was spinning. I thought it was from hitting the wall, but it could've been from the shock of seeing my friend's penis. It was thin and freakishly long.

"Baby, go put some clothes on," Marley said. Cole was completely oblivious about his scanty blue towel, but she was not. She clearly wanted to keep his python under wraps, but it was too late. I'd seen it, and it was going to be on my mind for at least a week.

Cole glanced at me to assure himself that I was

okay and then went to the bedroom. Marley sat with me until Cole returned. I made up a lie about going to the kitchen for water, and after a few minutes everyone was back in bed. However, I was awake the rest of the night.

Early the next morning, I called Satchel to tell her what had happened, but she wasn't home. I guessed she had stayed with her friend last night, too. It seemed everyone was getting lucky but me, the virgin widow. When Satchel called back, I grilled her about her new love interest. She withheld all information, which meant she saw potential. I told her about listening to Cole and Marley, but I left out the size part. I normally told Satchel everything, but something about that didn't seem right.

I went to the hotel and went over payroll with Warren. He explained how everything worked as he officially took over Adrian's job as executive manager. It was amazing how much it took to operate this hotel. One week's payroll was over fifty thousand dollars. We had downsized as much as we could, and we still had to hire a night manager. I suggested we train Ndeeyah for the job, but she didn't want to be away from her son at night, so we offered the position to another front-desk manager, who gladly took it. We just filled his spot with another front-desk person and shifted the schedules so that there would be no gaps.

At Ciel that evening we were busy. There was an exotic automobile convention in town, and these car owners were some heavy drinkers. We were packed to capacity the entire evening. Thankfully, there was no downtime to experience any more awkward moments with Cole. Yet every time I looked in his direction, he was glancing at me, so I made sure I didn't stand next to him most of that night. He'd become a distraction, for I couldn't get the size of his penis off my mind, and I wanted to share the information with someone, but I couldn't. Mei would be tickled pink to know that Cole was sporting a long male organ, and I would have loved to be the one to share this naughty tidbit, because I never had any dirty details to tell.

I looked at Mei, who was at the end of the bar, making a martini. I then glanced back at Cole. What the hell? I decided to do it. Just then Keith Carson stepped to me. He leaned over the bar and wiped a tiny piece of lint from my face. Somehow, he always found a way to touch me. It had bothered me at first, but I was used to it by now. If he didn't do it right away, I would wait and see how long it would take him. He always touched me within the first five minutes. He did the same to Mei.

"Scotch and water?" I asked.

"You know it," he replied.

I poured him a glass and slid it across the bar. "I'll start your tab."

I then began my trek toward Mei before I lost nerve. However, Keith wanted to talk. Not really being in the mood, I was about to blow him off, until he mentioned Satchel's name.

"Why do you care about Satchel's favorite place to travel?" I asked.

"Because I want to take her somewhere nice. But I want to make sure she likes the place. You know how your sister can get."

"I do, but how do you know?"

He gave me a smug look.

"You're Mr. Potential?" I asked.

"What does that mean?" he asked.

"It means I'm going to kick Satchel's ass."

Keith slid his empty glass to me and motioned for another. I hadn't trusted him before I knew Satchel was seeing him; now I definitely didn't. Carl had said he was shady, and I knew I should have mentioned that to Satchel. Now I had no choice. I poured his drink, and this time I gave him a little more Scotch. The more he drank, the more he talked, and I wanted to hear it all. By his third glass, I had the full details. He and Satchel had been going out for a few months. She had insisted that they take it slow, but he admitted that he really was digging her. They hadn't had an out-of-town tryst, but he wanted to take her somewhere. If she went, this meant the relationship was a big deal for her. Satchel didn't leave town with a man unless she was falling hard. She had trust issues, and she swore that foreign soil was a dangerous playground. It got the woman wrapped up in scenery, and eventually, she swept the details under the rug. I suggested the Cook Islands, a place she had always wanted to go. But he said that was too expensive; he wanted something a little closer than Polynesia. So I recommended Kona, Hawaii.

He said, "Your taste is expensive."

To this I replied, "No, I like hiking in Scottsdale,

Arizona. But you're not dating me. You are dating my posh sister, who desires finer things."

The bar was packed the remainder of the night, and I never got the chance to talk to Mei about Cole. However, as soon as I got home, I called Satchel. I didn't let on that I knew about her and Keith, because I wanted to see how long she was going to drag this thing out. I did, however, mention seeing Keith to see if she was going to say something, but I got nothing. With long-pole Cole still on my mind, I decided to stay in my room. After I got off the phone with Satchel, I took my shower and went to bed.

Two more days passed, and I hadn't heard a word from Jonah. I called him, but, of course, he didn't answer or return my call. Satchel was supposed to go before the judge as Shanice's lawyer next week. But if I didn't talk to Jonah before then, I was going to be pissed if she represented Shanice for naught. I got out the calendar and marked the countdown to the hotel's auction. I had opened the letter three days ago, but I had let the mail sit on the desk for four days before opening it. I hadn't paid attention to the date, but I thought it said August 20. Thirty days from that date would be September 18, unless they meant thirty business days. Either way I had less than a month to get that money, and I was nowhere close to accumulating it. If I didn't hear from Jonah in the next couple of days, I would have to go see Shanice again.

* * *

I continued to call Jonah over the weekend; however, I still could not reach him. It was too late for Satchel to go back on her word, and she and Shanice were to appear in court on Tuesday. I was starting to believe Shanice had set me up.

It was rare that Mei, Cole, and I all had the same day off. We went to the park together that Sunday, chilled, and drank wine. It cleared my mind, which was necessary. I didn't think about Shanice, the hotel, or Carl. I relaxed on a blanket and got red wine tipsy. It was a wonderful day. But, in less than twenty-four hours, it would be Monday, and my issues would start all over again.

Before I could get into the office on Monday morning, Warren met me in the hallway with another letter, stating our property taxes were due. I invited him into the office and told him about the auction letter. He knew we were in a financial bind, but he had had no idea how bad it was. We both agreed that there was no reason to pay these taxes if the hotel might be auctioned off next month. Whoever acquired the hotel would also incur its tax debt. This reminded me to call Jonah again. This time he picked up, and he agreed to meet me on Tuesday, after Shanice's arraignment. He said that he was going to visit Shanice today to get the details of our arrangement, which made me more nervous. It clearly felt like a setup, but I would have to wait until Tuesday to find out.

I was busy with paperwork the remainder of the day. Warren went over everyone's title and got ready for job evaluations. I had reviewed Adrian's lease on the house, but I decided to have my own drawn up. I was charging him eight hundred dollars per month for the house, with an option to buy the property from me in six months. He sent Ndeeyah in to sign the lease. I felt sorry for her, because she really looked clueless as to what was going on. And, though I still needed Adrian's signature, I also needed hers, and Satchel would have been proud. I looked into her big, sad eyes and made her sign. She felt it was fair, and though she admitted it would be difficult to sacrifice that amount monthly, she said they would make it happen.

I checked with the realtor, who informed me that five people had come to view Carl's house that weekend, and that two of them had seemed very interested. She agreed to follow up with me after they were preapproved. However, she gave me the number of Normandy Collins, one of the interested home seekers. He had a few questions for the owner. I called him within the hour and left him a message, looked at the clock, and saw it was time for my second job.

In a month's time, I had gone from one easy, breezy job, and little to no debt, to working two jobs and a shitload of debt. I could not believe this was happening to me.

Tuesday morning, after Shanice's arraignment, during which she pleaded not guilty to murder, I spoke with Jonah. Apparently, nature was dealing out several decks of bad hands. It seemed that the Franklin family had control of Shanice's assets. The only money Shanice had was the amount in her personal checking and savings accounts, which was not much more than I already had. After Carl's murder, the family had decided not to deal with Shanice any longer. She'd been in minor trouble with the law once and had a previous drug habit. They were done dealing with her. Shanice had enough money to pay for her legal counsel, and that was about it. Jonah was still riding the fence. He didn't want to bail on his baby sister, but he wasn't about to risk getting his family ties snipped by lending me the money himself. After I told Satchel, she had only one thing to say.

"You should have gotten the scoop before you asked me to represent her. I'm in it now for better or for worse. I've given her my word, and I'm not bailing. Plus, I believe her."

I was pissed, but I was more shocked over the fact that Shanice was still pleading not guilty. I asked Satchel about her case one more time. She looked me square in the eyes and made me swear not to say a word. I did as I was told, and then she spoke.

"Shanice got the gun, initially containing wax bullets, from Adrian. Adrian switched them to the bullets that killed Carl."

With this, Satchel waltzed away, but before she got out of sight, she glanced over her shoulder and said, "I never liked that bastard, and now he's going down."

Satchel winked and walked out.

Chapter 6

Booty Call 101

1 ounce Black Haus blackberry schnapps
1 ounce DeKuyper Peachtree schnapps
1 ounce Bacardi Limón rum
2 ounces sweet and sour mix
1–2 ounces cranberry juice

Stir all the ingredients together in a highball glass filled with ice cubes, and serve.

Once word officially spread about Satchel representing Shanice Franklin, the press went berserk. They waited for Satchel outside her office and at the courthouse. Finally, she had to issue a press release to the local stations. She did it the Friday before the trial was to start. I loved the way my sister acted under pressure. I wished I had some of her skills. As soon as I got in front of large groups of people, sweat built on the bridge of my nose, my palms got clammy, and then my armpits moistened. It never failed. But Satchel lived for the limelight. Though she didn't like the press for its vicious habit of rewording the truth, she loved attention.

I wanted to attend the press conference outside city hall, but I couldn't bear the media talking to me, so I hid out in the one of the hotel rooms and watched my sister go to work. Satchel and her assistant counsel, both in black suits, stood behind the podium, smiled politely, and put on the most confident of demeanors. Satchel gave her spiel about the justice system and being innocent before proven guilty. Then she reiterated that Shanice had entered a not-guilty plea, that this case was hopefully going to be tried swiftly, and that her client would seek a fair trial. She took one question from a reporter, one whom she had planted in the audience. This way she seemed to be fair to the media but would not be caught off guard by a crazy reporter. He asked his question, for which she already had a prepared answer, and then she responded to it, placed on her shades, nodded, and said, "No further questions."

It was a great performance, as usual. I should have taken notes, for when I left my room and headed down to the bar, I was bombarded by three news media people. They swarmed around me so quickly, my head was spinning. Questions were coming right and left. I simply covered my ears and rushed to the back kitchen of Ciel. I watched through the oval window as they lingered in the bar. Suddenly, the door flung open and hit me in the nose. I didn't hit the floor, because Mei caught me and prevented me from falling, but I was stunned.

"What are you doing? I could have broken your nose," said Mei.

Whispering, I kept peeping through the window. "I'm hiding from those damn reporters. I don't want to talk about the case."

Mei, being only five feet tall, was unable to peep out of the kitchen-door window, so she swung the door open and stuck her whole head out. Then, just as obvious, she popped back in.

"I will go say something to them," she declared.

Before I could stop her, I saw her tiny body sidle up to reporter number one. I didn't know what she was saying, but her right hand was on her hip, and her left was pointing and thrashing around. She was so petite, her little frame was never a threat to anyone, but that mouth of hers was atrocious. After a few seconds, the three reporters gathered their things and left the bar. Mei soon came back into the kitchen and told me the coast was clear.

"My hero," I said, grabbing her arm and walking back into the bar.

I poured drinks with joy for another hour. I noticed an older, distinguished gentleman at the end of the bar. He was smoking a very large, strong-smelling cigar. I hated cigar smoke, but this was not why I noticed him. It was because every time I glanced down at the end of the bar, he was peering at me. I walked over to Mei, who was serving him, and asked her what his deal was. She said he had asked if I was Isabelle, but that he had sworn he wasn't a reporter. I heard him ask for bourbon neat three consecutive times. This was a very distinguished drink for the illustrious mystery man. With his order in his hand and his pinkie purposely set apart from his other fingers, he sauntered down six seats and placed his body in front of me. His walk was very erect but not rigid. He had a swagger, one of confidence. He wasted no time before he introduced himself.

"Hi, I'm Normandy, Normandy Collins. You can call me Norman."

"What if I want to call you Collins?" I asked.

He took a sip and gave me a leer. He was sleazy. I could tell by his squinted eyes. "For you, Collins is fine," he responded.

"Are you the Collins I called today?"

"In the flesh," he replied, with a sneer and a snicker.

We proceeded to talk about the house, which he was looking at for his daughter and soon-to-be son-in-law. She wanted a big family and thought the house was perfect. He said it was going to be the perfect wedding gift for them. I told him how I wished I had a father like him, and that I wouldn't be in half the mess I was in now if I did.

He leaned over the bar and whispered, "If you had a man like me, maybe you wouldn't be in that mess, either."

I knew he was sleazy. I tended to a few other customers and then went back to speak to Collins. He was rather charming and sort of handsome if you were into the father-figure type of guy. Mei thought he was extremely sexy; she kept swishing her way down to my section just to check on him. However, before the night was over, Collins had offered to take me to dinner and to discuss how he could help me with any and everything in my life. He drank two more bourbons, neat, of course, and slid his business card across the table to me. As I reached for the card, he held on to it until I made eye contact with him. He took his fat little thumb and circled the fleshy area between my thumb and index finger. He said no words, but his stare penetrated through my soul. It was eerie. Upon releasing the card, he tapped the number and nodded.

I felt the need to respond. "I will call you, Collins."

He left a hundred-dollar bill underneath his empty glass and walked away. Before he could get out of the bar, Mei rushed over to me as I was gathering the money.

"Who was that? He talked to you a long time. What did he want?" she asked. Just then she noticed the money. "Is that a bill?"

"Yes, Mei. His drinks came to twenty-five. I'll get your part of the tip."

"Fuck the tip. Who was he, and is he looking for a cute Asian girl to give him oral pleasure?" she said, with an accent, just before taking a traditional bow.

"Your parents would be so proud," I joked.

"No, seriously. He was very sexy, like Ed Bradley."

"Please. Ed Bradley was sexy fine. He could've easily gotten the booty, God rest his soul. Collins is nothing like Ed Bradley. More like Ed Asner."

"Well, he can 'Ed' my 'Asner' all day."

I gave Mei one of those puzzled, "why is this person my friend?" looks and tended to my next customer.

The bar was not so busy that night, so I actually
got home before one in the morning. My back
was a little sore, so I decided to take a warm bath.
I drew the water, lit my candles, and settled in the
tub. I was in for about six minutes when Cole
knocked on my door.

"Can I use your toothpaste?" he called from
the outside.

I pulled the shower curtain forward to cover my
body and told him to come in. He quickly apologized for interrupting my peaceful evening, yet he
lingered in the bathroom and wanted to talk. First,
it was about the hotel, then it was about him going
back to school, and lastly, it was about women. I
didn't know how he made the transition, but
before long I was sitting in lukewarm water, giving
him girlfriend advice. This was not the evening
I had planned. I pulled the shower curtain back to
expose my face and talked to Cole as he sat on the
closed toilet. Finally, I thought, *What the hell? Since
he is in here, he should scrub my back.* I asked, and, of
course, he obliged.

Cole reached in the water, wet his hands, and
lathered up the bath sponge. He began scrubbing
my back, and it was wonderfully sensual. I covered
my chest and leaned forward in the water to keep
from exposing my breasts. Cole moved to my
shoulders and my neck, scrubbing in a circular
motion. But then I had to stop him. He was care-
fully feeling his way around my body, and I knew
my breasts were next. I took the sponge and
thanked him for the rubdown. He continued to
sit on the toilet and talk. Just his being in the bathroom was giving me jitters. Cole had never seen

me naked, yet I was so comfortable with him there. So comfy that he had to go.

"You have to leave now," I told him.

He nodded. Just before leaving the bathroom, he whispered, "You have smooth skin." I sunk down in the water and tried to enjoy the rest of the fleeting bubbles. I sat in the water for another ten minutes, then went to bed.

Early the next morning, I called Collins. We spoke briefly, and then he asked me to dinner tomorrow evening. I was hoping we could take care of all our business during daylight hours, but he wasn't that type of man. He was the "wine and dine" type, which meant he had to have at least three unnecessary meetings to get to the official one. Even though it was all a part of the game that I hated to play, the next night I was at home, getting dressed to go out on my non-date with Collins. I had seven garments picked out and lying on my bed, and I couldn't decide what to wear. I commandeered Cole to help. I modeled each outfit, complete with shoes. Two were too sexy, two were too corporate, and one was not fitting properly. That left two to choose from, one being a little black dress, of course, and the other being a colorful knee-length skirt with a white, V-necked, fitted T-shirt. We chose the second outfit. The black dress always worked, but it showed little personality, and if I wanted Collins to buy that house, he needed to see my character.

I arrived at the restaurant ten minutes early and waited for him in the lobby. Although this was not a date, it was nice to be eating out at an exquisite restaurant. Collins arrived right on time and greeted me with a kiss on the top of my hand. I looked at him very closely; he was definitely no Ed Bradley but did have nice bone structure. He had probably been a looker back in the day. But I lived in the present day, and now he was simply an old, horny man. As soon as we sat, he ordered a bottle of Shiraz. He picked a great brand and a perfect year. I complimented him on his choice, and he invited me to visit his wine cellar, assuring me I would be impressed.

"I'm sure I would," I responded softly, but in a very nondescript tone.

We drank and talked nonstop until dinner arrived. Collins was a very interesting man. He had served his country in the Vietman War, had married twice, and had three children. He'd been single now for six years and loved being a fifty-six-year-old bachelor. He was an Ivy League educator and had sued his prominent university for the unfair treatment and firing of several African American staff members, including himself, and had won. He had taken that money and invested in the right companies and was now a millionaire. Once dinner came, the conversation slowed a little, and he wanted me to talk about my situation. He admitted that he'd done some research on me and had heard about the drama that I was going through. He wanted me to tell my side, which I did very expressively after three glasses of red wine.

I didn't leak all the information about the hotel, but I did admit that I was looking for a potential investor to assist with some of the financial burden. I thought I had spoken too much, but when he gladly agreed to support my cause, I figured I had said just enough. We finished dinner, and while I was perusing the dessert menu, I noticed him ogling me. I smiled, and he smiled back, but then he continued to look. The waiter came to the table, and I ordered key lime pie. Once the waiter left, I asked Collins about his offer to help. He gave a simple response.

"You have something I want."

"You want the hotel?" I asked.

He shook his head and gave a hearty, short laugh before answering. "There are plenty of hotels around, but full-grown virgins, that's another story."

My endearing smile turned daunting as I let out a few nervous chuckles. But then I realized he was probably joking, and my chuckles turned to big rolls of laughter. He laughed along for a few seconds, then stopped and leered at me from across the table. I felt like prey. His hand grazed the top of my arm.

"You're not joking, are you?" I asked.

"That depends."

"You want *me?*" I whimpered.

He gave a growl and laugh, and it made the hairs on my arms stand straight up. Finally, the sleaziness had been confirmed. I knew it. He then proposed exactly what he was thinking.

"I've never been with a virgin. I was a little older when I got married, and I always wondered what it would be like to be a woman's first." I was so shocked, my mouth dried out from being stuck wide open. Nevertheless, he continued. "Let me have one evening with you. For that, I will be very grateful and will help you out with your hotel and take that house off your hands."

I was so shocked that my appetite disappeared. I asked the server to wrap up my dessert, and I quickly ended the dinner. When we walked to our cars, Collins took me by the hand and apologized in advance if his offer had offended me.

"Well, it did," I responded.

"Again, I didn't mean to. I've learned that in life, if you don't ask for what you want, you'll never get it."

"I see."

"I don't expect you to answer right away, but do think about it."

Collins kissed my hand, and I got into my car and drove off. The first few minutes of my ride, I was still in disbelief. However, once I got home, I was steaming mad. Luckily, Mei and Cole were at the house, and I was able to vent some of the steam. I stomped in, ranting and raving over the situation. Neither Cole nor Mei was shocked, as I had suspected. Mei was enthused. She wanted to know if she could take my place. Cole agreed it was very offensive but said that he wasn't surprised.

"Men with money think they can do and say anything," said Cole.

"You got an indecent proposal. I think it's hot," added Mei.

I listened to the voices of my two misguided friends, but I still felt offended. Later that evening, I told Satchel, and she agreed that it was highly offensive, but that women often gave it up for much less. I couldn't believe everyone's nonchalant attitude about the situation. Not that I was expecting Satchel to sue, but I had hoped that she would at least offer to curse him out. This got me to thinking. Why would I keep suffering through this financial ordeal when I could just sleep with him and it would all be over? I continued to ponder this through the night, until my phone began ringing early the next morning.

Before I could say hello, Mei blurted out, "So you gonna do old man Ed, or what?"

"I don't know."

"Well, that's a better response than last night. I tell you what. You woo him into bed, turn off the lights, and then I will come from the closet and change places with you." I could only laugh at my kooky friend's attempt to help. Sadly, she was very serious. "He won't know the difference."

"You're barely five feet."

"Honey, it's all the same size lying down."

"Good-bye, Mei." I hung up the phone and stared at the ceiling. Of course, she called right back, but I didn't answer. I gathered my thoughts, walked into the kitchen, and ran smack into Marley, in a tiny silk robe, drinking a cup of coffee. She spoke and I spoke, and then on my way out of the kitchen, she mentioned my dilemma.

"I think you should sleep with him," she said in between sips. "Obtém esse dinheiro."

My Portuguese was rusty, but I believed she said, "Get that money." I gave her a bewildered look, rushed to Cole's door, knocked, went in before he answered, and shut the door behind me. Immediately, I laid into him.

"How dare you share my business with your chipper-ass, coffee-drinking, Portuguese-speaking girlfriend. And why is she up all early drinking java in the center of the kitchen, wearing some little-ass geisha robe?"

Cole sat on the edge of the bed and listened to all my fussing before saying a word. "Marley normally gives good advice, and I thought she would tell you not to sleep with him."

"But she didn't. She said I should sleep with him."

"I know." Just then Marley walked into the room.

"You talking about me?" she asked, still sipping from the edge of my favorite mug.

"Yes, I was just telling her that I thought you would tell her not to sleep with Collins," replied Cole.

"Why would I do that?" asked Marley. "Women are always compromising themselves and getting nothing out of it. If this man is going to get her out of financial debt and solve her problems, just for one night, hell yeah, she should do it."

"I think it's degrading," said Cole.

"No more than what men do to women all the time," Marley argued.

Next thing I knew, they were in a full-blown debate. I stood there for the first two rounds, until Marley said, "Maybe you don't want her to sleep with Collins, because *you* want to sleep with her." She looked at me to respond, and I flew from the room. When I got in the hall, I heard her continuing.

"Is that what the problem is? You want the virgin pussy? Do you?"

"Why is my virginity becoming such a big issue?" I said aloud.

I began thinking that women must hold it in

higher regard than they cared to admit. Maybe they were jealous of the fact that I'd saved myself. Perhaps in some way they coveted my pureness, because it was something they'd lost a while ago and were never going to get back.

Although I was quite curious as to what Cole's answer would be, I closed my door before he spoke and turned on my music to drown their noise. By the time I was ready to leave the house, Marley was gone. I tiptoed into the kitchen and was almost in the clear when Cole came rushing up behind me. In an awkward moment, we gazed at each other. Finally, Cole spoke.

"Sorry about this morning."

Trying to make light of it, I replied, "Yeah, tell Marley the Spike Lee mug is my favorite. She can drink from one of the others."

Cole didn't say anything; nor did he laugh. I didn't know what to say, so I waved and turned to walk out. However, just before I closed the front door, he declared, "Maybe I do want to sleep with you. Not 'cause of the virgin thing. Just 'cause it's you."

I kept walking. I didn't have time to address his comment; nor did I know how. It was best if he just assumed I didn't hear him.

By the time I got to the hotel, I had convinced myself that I wasn't going to sleep with Collins. However, once I opened my office door and saw the bills mounting on my desk, I quickly went back to contemplating the situation. I received a call from the hotel's bank representative, and she confirmed that the official date on which the hotel would be repossessed by the national credit institution was twenty-one days from today. That wasn't business days, but total days. So, September 16 was the final date, not the eighteenth, like I had expected. I could give up now, or I could drop my cotton whites for old man Collins. I picked up the phone and dialed my indecent proposer. I wasn't going to sleep with him, but I was going to make him think I would entertain the idea if he agreed to invest in the hotel and keep my staff on. He was elated and wanted to waste no time. He scheduled our rendezvous for tomorrow evening. I gave him a very soft okay and hung up the phone. Immediately I regretted my decision. I knew I had no plans to sleep with him, and now I was simply playing games to get the money. I felt like a gold digger. I called Satchel and gave her the news. She was so engrossed in Shanice's case that she only gave me three words of advice.

"Wear black panties."

"I'm not sleeping with him," I declared.

"Just in case," she said before hanging up.

Next, I told Mei, who then wanted to go lingerie shopping. Again, I informed her it was only a supposed sex date. I would try to woo him into thinking he'd eventually get it, but not until we closed the deal. Mei said he wouldn't go for it, but I had to try. I decided that I wasn't going overboard with this complicated booty call, in which no one would get booty. But my friends were psyched.

That evening, Mei, Satchel, my cousin Karen, and another friend, Ryan, came over to give their sisterly advice. Mei even brought a chart with big red letters placed on it. They spelled *Booty Call 101*. I couldn't believe it. I was extremely embarrassed. I knew they meant well, but I didn't want to discuss how I needed to conduct myself during what might be my first sexual experience. No one believed that I was not going to sleep with him. They insisted that once things started rolling, I would probably go through with it, considering what was on the table. Satchel, of course, had drawn up a quick contract, which I refused to even display. But here I was, going over positions, distraction techniques, and ways to simply get up and leave once the deed was done.

"I'm not kissing him," I told them.

"What if he wants you to go down on him?" asked Satchel.

"What? Hell no. We didn't discuss that," I said.

"Well, you should have," said Mei. "He's gonna want head. All men want head."

"He said he wanted to be with a virgin. My mouth is not pure and untouched," I argued.

"You're not getting this money," Mei insisted.

Satchel laid down the plan. "You're best bet is this. Tell him that this is business, and let him know what you are willing and not willing to do up front."

"Pray it doesn't take a long time to come," added Karen.

Before this booty powwow, I hadn't been at all nervous. Now, they had me thinking about dozens of disastrous situations. I kept insisting that I wasn't going to sleep with Colllins, but they kept telling me I should be prepared for any and everything.

"At least try to have an orgasm," said Mei.

"No, don't have one. It's best," said Satchel.

"Let him do it from behind. That's very impersonal, the best way to keep it business," added Ryan.

"You don't want it to be so businesslike, 'cause you'll feel like a prostitute," said my cousin Karen.

"I AM NOT SLEEPING WITH HIM!" I yelled.

Mei rushed over to comfort me as Satchel looked on. She rubbed my shoulders and whispered, "He's not going to look at you like a prostitute. He thinks you're special."

"Yeah, Carl thought I was special, too. Look where that got me," I muttered.

Finally, I got a hint of reassurance from Satchel. She sat on the other side of me and placed her hands in mine. "I know you're not going to have sex with this strange man, but I needed to do all of that just to show you how stupid this whole thing is," she said endearingly. Then she sat there and contradicted herself. "But if you do, no one is going to look at you any differently. In fact, if people knew, they would look at you as a shrewd business-woman. Lots of powerful women go through lots of men to get to the top. You have to go through only one dick. Consider yourself lucky."

After Satchel's unsupportive, compassionate words, the booty-call crew left me to deal with my whoring demons. In God's eyes, this couldn't be right, even if I did do it for a good cause. I was just going to pray that this whole thing would be over soon and I could go back to my normal life.

Behind bars, Shanice wanted the same thing. The trial date was set, and she and Satchel were rapidly preparing. Shanice, who was normally laid back, now feared that she might spend a lifetime in jail, or worse, get the death penalty. She began spilling the beans. Apparently, Shanice and Adrian had had a deal, and she'd got the gun from him. She'd told Adrian she wanted to shoot blanks into Carl's crotch area on the night of his bachelor party. Shanice had even planted a reporter at the party to take pictures. Once the story came out, Carl would be forced to admit he had been having an affair. Shanice swore that she had never meant to kill him. She'd practiced with the wax bullets that she got from Adrian and had the receipt for the new ones she'd purchased. She said that Adrian preferred Carl dead but would settle for his embarrassment. She also admitted that Adrian wasn't going to go along with it at first, but after Carl fired him, he felt it was just.

Shanice even gave Satchel a bit of information that hit home. She informed her that Carl had hired Keith Carson to trail Adrian and look into his dealings, but that once Keith hadn't come up with anything, Carl suspected Adrian had paid Keith off as well. Since no one knew that she and Keith were dating, Satchel had to play it cool, but inside she was boiling over the fact that Keith had not given her the information first. Shanice also said that Adrian must have changed the wax bullets to real ones so that he could take over the hotel and sell it. He stood to gain the most from Carl's death. He had even said on numerous occasions that he hoped he outlived his brother so that he could sell the real estate and make a fortune. Right now, this was all conjecture, but Satchel was determined to prove it. The first person she had to speak to was her man, fine-ass Keith.

* * *

The next day, while Satchel was interrogating Keith, I was getting ready for my night with Normandy Collins. I was wearing a tangerine dress with pearl accessories, and Satchel would have been upset to know that I was wearing my favorite white cotton panties underneath. Thankfully, Cole was at work. Therefore, I didn't have to hear his comments about going out with Collins. I didn't get to talk to Satchel before I left to meet Collins, but it was probably best. I was nervous enough.

I walked into the Georgian Terrace and took two deep breaths. I had suggested we have our booty tryst at a hotel. This way we were closer to an even playing ground. We had plans to eat out on the patio of the hotel's restaurant, but I wasn't hungry. Truthfully, I didn't want to be there. Immediately after dinner, Collins wanted to go upstairs to the room he had reserved. I knew at that moment, he was serious and that there was no wooing him into helping me on the premise of getting some later. We got up to the room, and he tried to set the mood with music from one of the television music channels. He put on easy listening jazz. This was not going to get me excited. Then, suddenly, I realized that I might not get excited at all. I was as dry as a July noon in Phoenix; this might be a problem. Maybe I could say I had a problem. Then I remembered the paperwork. I pulled the legal forms from my purse.

"You have to sign these first," I said. "It doesn't mention anything about sex, but it says you agree to give a certain dollar amount, which will be used toward the Shelby, in legal terms, of course."

I knew this would buy me some time. He wasn't going to sign a document without his lawyer looking at it. He tried to push the paperwork aside and kiss me, and that was when I started feeling sick.

"I have to go to the restroom. Look over these," I said, pointing to the forms. I got to the restroom and paced rapidly, trying to figure out how I was going to get out of this situation.

"I could simply tell him I changed my mind, but that I really would like him to consider investing," I whispered. I could've just pretended to be distraught and simply run out. Then, to keep up the charade, I flushed the empty toilet and walked out. Collins was standing in the center of the room, buck naked. He was in amazingly good shape for a man in his fifties. But then I saw his testicles, and my Lord . . . they were the size of plums, two very low-hanging plums.

"I signed your paperwork. Now come here," he growled. I was scared out of my mind as he launched his body in my direction. He backed me up against the door and tried to kiss me. I knew I was in over my head.

"Let me see the papers," I shouted, but Collins wasn't moving. "And, and . . . you don't even have a condom on." I was desperately looking for things to say, anything to make him turn so that I could flee.

He sucked his teeth and said, "Baby doll . . ." His starting a sentence with that, I already knew it was going to be some bullshit. "You can't expect me to layer up. You are a virgin. I have to *feel* you, understand?"

I wasn't about to let his nasty thing inside of

me *with* protection, but without it, well, he had to be out of his senile old mind. I pounded his chest and ducked underneath his arm, which was pressed against the wall just at my shoulder.

"Why did you think I would let you have unprotected sex with me? Are you crazy!"

"I'm clean. I've got the paperwork to prove it."

I grabbed my purse and headed for the door. As I was leaving, he called out, "I thought you wanted my help. Who do you think you are?"

I spun around, clutched my pearls, and left him with these distinct words.

"I'm a virgin, for God's sake."

That was that. I needed a new plan. By the time I got home, I found the entire situation hilarious. As soon as I walked in the door, I told Cole everything. He only shook his head and said that I wasn't supposed to get the money that way, and it was all for the best. I guess, but hours ago, it had seemed like such an easy solution. But who knew what ties could have come with that. He could have expected me to sleep with him in order to continue soliciting help, and I could see how it could have ended in a big, fat mess. I didn't share the story with the rest of the gang until the next day, and even Mei was disgusted. But if it looked like a duck and walked like a duck . . . I should have known better.

Satchel was in full trial mode. She had her researchers going nearly twenty-four hours a day. She had inspected the bullet residue from Carl's clothing. Turned out, there was some wax residue among the bullet fragments. This could be a good thing for Shanice. If Satchel could prove that her intention had been to hurt, and not kill, she could get less time. But Satchel needed to prove that Adrian had purchased the real bullets and had given Shanice the gun. Unfortunately, the gun used was registered to Carl, and both Shanice and Adrian had had access to it. It was going to be difficult to prove he had more of a motive than she did. She'd been angry that Carl wasn't marrying her, and she was the shooter, but then again if Satchel could prove Adrian had been stealing money from Carl and had just gotten fired, this would also give him a motive.

Only a few people at the hotel knew Adrian had been fired, and we couldn't count on Ndeeyah testifying against her husband, so Keith's testimony was definitely going to be needed. Keith gave Satchel all the information he had gathered for Carl, but none of it was proof of stealing. We didn't realize at the time that Keith was going to be working with the state to prove Shanice's guilt. However, one bit of information Keith had obtained would probably be of use. Adrian had a different mom from Carl. Adrian's mother and Carl's father had had an affair while he was married, and this tryst had produced Adrian. Their father, Walter, had promised to leave his wife and marry Adrian's mother but never did. Adrian's mother had gone into a depression and taken her life when Adrian was four, and Adrian had then gone to live with Carl's family. Carl was just eighteen months old at the time. Carl had never mentioned it; we didn't even know if he'd known. Yet, this did say a lot about Adrian's repulsion for Carl, his dad, and the dream of owning a hotel. In fact, it said a great deal about Adrian's personality. He probably blamed his father for his mom's death. This trial was going to be a doozy.

Chapter 7

Virgin Whore

1/2 ounce vodka
juice of 1/2 lime
1 ounce Kool-Aid Lime mix
1/2 ounce cranberry juice
2 drops red food coloring
2 drops blue food coloring
1/2 ounce apple juice
1/2 ounce tequila

Mix the vodka, lime juice, Kool-Aid, cranberry juice, and food coloring in a shot glass. Slowly add the apple juice around the side, add tequila, and serve.

By now the entire virgin thing had gotten way out of control. I was no longer known as Izzy the bartender. I was known as Izzy the virgin. I even got an invite to speak at some virgin women's group. I didn't want to go, but I agreed to go because I didn't want them to think I was ashamed, but at the same time I no longer wanted to be affiliated with that word. My period was in full throttle that day, and it was difficult for me to experience new things when my period was on. Satchel agreed to go with me. I think she was simply fascinated that there were others out there like me. She'd always thought my cause of saving it for marriage was odd. Mei was off work that Tuesday and said that she wanted to go for support. But I believed it was because she wanted to be like a vampire waiting to contaminate a room filled with fresh blood.

At 8:00 p.m. sharp, Mei, Satchel, and I walked into October, a happening little coffee spot downtown. In the corner of the room, I noticed a small gathering of women. Most of them looked to be in their twenties, but I spotted a few older ones in the bunch. Mei, Satchel and I didn't wander into the group at first; we remained by the coffee bar and watched a few other women mingle into the corner.

"Talk about your homely-looking females," I whispered to Satchel.

She didn't respond. Thus we continued to look. Between the long skirts, the thick eyebrows, and the tousled, thrown-together ponytails, these women could all be candidates for makeover Mondays on Oxygen.

"They look like worn-down housewives, each with three children," Mei whispered.

"Let's go over there," I replied.

We walked over and sat down. Moments later, I realized one thing. These women were pathetic. They were either bitter, extremely insecure, or had some sort of physical dysfunction. The two that seemed normal and somewhat cute suffered from some sex phobia that I'd never heard of. I sat and listened to some of the women's virgin hardships until it was time to speak.

I was introduced to the club, and I stood up to say a few words on behalf of the proud virgins. But as I stood before the women, all I could think was, *I hope I am not at all like these women.* Luckily, they didn't want me to say much, but instead to answer questions. This I could do. Plus, this would spark conversation, and soon they would be talking among themselves and I could slip out the back. My first question was a breeze. How do you ease your way into telling a man that you aren't going to have sex? I gave my top five:

1. I'm just not ready for anything serious. Half of the time this works, but the other half, the guy will just offer a purely sexual relationship.
2. I decided to get back with my ex-boyfriend, and he's very jealous, so you really shouldn't call, either. This works because most men don't care to get into altercations over potential cootchie, but if he still wants to call, you can always throw in the appendix to this excuse, which is, by the way, he just got out of jail.
3. I realized that I'm really attracted to women, so this isn't going to work for me. Now, most men will ask to join in that experience, but you just have to tell them that the girlfriend is really not into that, and it will totally turn her off.

4. I had a family emergency, and I've decided to go home for a while. This works for most men, who don't want to get attached too soon, which is just what a family emergency does. But just in case you get that extremely caring man, you just have to tell him your family is ready for you to be married and it would be too much pressure.

5. I don't want to go to hell by having sex before marriage. This always works, especially if you say it with a crazed gleam in your eye.

As planned, this sparked conversation, and before long Satchel, Mei, and I were on our way across town. The meeting and the women occupied my mind the remainder of the night.

While Mei and I were watching our third consecutive *Law & Order* episode, I clicked off the television, turned to her, and spoke.

"Am I a loser?"

"What?" Mei quickly asked.

"Those women were a mess. Am I a mess? I always thought I was sexy and cute, but now I don't know. They looked like losers," I whined.

"No, baby, you are not," she answered while consoling me with a soft leg rub.

"It's not like I couldn't get a man. I just decided to wait. In fact, I could have any man I want if I put my mind to it," I said.

"Of course you can," she responded.

"That sounded condescending."

"No, you had a man, a very handsome, eagerly sought-after man," she said.

"Maybe I should just do it and get it over with.

I mean, I was waiting for the perfect husband, who turned out to be a cheating husband, and it just doesn't seem as important anymore."

"I think it's very important," Mei said. She knew by my expression, I seriously doubted her comment. "Just because I choose to have sex doesn't mean I don't value your decision. I respect you so much for waiting. Other people do, too, even if they joke to you about it. They're just jealous."

"That's what I think," I said, with a bit of perkiness.

We sat watching television for a while longer, as I continued thinking about my situation. I truly wished my virginity held its same value, but in some way Carl had tainted it. Yes, he had married me, but not because I was a virgin. He'd loved Shanice, too, in his own way, and she was far from pure. I suddenly questioned if I'd been saving it because of how I felt about myself or because of how I wanted my future man to feel about me.

"It doesn't really matter to men if you're a virgin or not, does it?" I asked Mei.

"I'm sure it means something to them, but how much, I don't know."

I pondered "to fuck or not to fuck" for the next few hours, and my head began to throb. Finally, I turned to Mei and declared, "Fine, I'm going to do it, and not for money. I'm just gonna find a man I really think is fine and get this virgin monkey off my back."

Mei rushed from the room, and grabbed a notebook and a pen. She returned, scribbling names in the notebook. "Oooh, you should do it with Paula's son." She was way too excited about this decision.

Paula, the redheaded bartender that managed Ciel, had a son named Vic, who'd had a crush on me for years.

"Vic is too young and goofy," I replied.

"Young and goofy is good. You don't want anyone too advanced. Vic looks like he might have a nice-size one."

"What? How could you possibly know about his penis size?" I asked.

"I don't know for sure, but I'm very good at guessing. It's a thing I do," Mei replied.

"A thing you do? You guess penis sizes for fun?"

"It's not like I follow up to see if I'm right. Well, not anymore, anyway. I just do it for my friends. When I meet their prospective dates, I give them a length/width guesstimate, and nine times out of ten, I'm right."

"I've heard women at the bar ask you to size up this guy and that guy. I didn't know they meant literally," I said. "You've never shared this with me."

"You don't have sex. It was pointless to share my gift with you. But, since we are talking about it now, here you go."

As if she'd been waiting for years to hand down this secret memo, Mei gave me a list of names, with size increments beside each. I glanced down the list of our mutual friends and possible firsts. Cole's name was on the list. I pointed to it and raised my brows.

"Cole certainly has a long one. I don't know how fat it is, though," Mei hinted.

"You know this for a fact, or is this some sort of prediction?" I asked.

"I've never seen it, but here is part of my theory. Now, take notes, for I've never shared this with anyone."

Mei positioned herself as though she was passing on her great-great-grandmother's ancient Chinese secret. I listened with intensity. She was right about Cole, so I figured maybe this friend of mine did have some sort of divine gift. God did give us different things for a reason. But this talent God himself was going to have to explain to me in some sort of dream. Mei maintained her position and began her explanation.

"Cole is cute, but not fine. There is no way he would approach women as boldly as he does if he didn't have an incredible package to back it up with. Size affects a man's personality." Taking mental notes, I nodded as she continued. "I'm not saying it determines the man that he will become, but if a guy knows he lacks in other areas, looks, social skills, etc., a big dick will certainly give him that boost he needs to succeed. Now, if they are tiny, they normally overcompensate in certain areas, knowledge, finances, material things, etc. I'm convinced that most men in lower-class society are the ones that really put it down. It's the rich, upper-class men that are hanging short and could care less about pleasing their women. They don't have to. They have money and power. When men lack money and power, they usually rely on their dick skills."

I stared at Mei in sheer disbelief, wondering if this was the most ignorant thing I'd ever heard or if it was sheer brilliance. I had no idea.

She continued. "I've tested my theory, trust me. The prisons are probably filled with long-dong men that had no true goals in life except to excel in the bedroom."

Now I knew that was ignorant. I didn't say anything, but I did give her a very disbelieving look.

Mei shrugged her shoulders and tossed her hands frivolously in the air. "I don't know a lot of things, but trust me, I'm very knowledgeable in the penis territory." She paused for a moment and looked at the list. "Oooh, maybe you should do him," she said, pointing to number five on her "men to do" list.

"I could go out with him. I've always thought he was attractive. Is he single?" I asked, not as enthused as Mei would have me be.

"Yes, and he's not too big and not too little. I think he'll be just right."

"Okay, Goldicocks. Let's call him."

We went over the list one by one and ended up with three possibles. It was a good start, or at least a good distraction from my current financial chaos.

Cole got off of work and came home just at the end of our conversation. Thank God. I didn't want him to even know I was considering having sex. Ever since our kiss, things had been awkward between us, and I didn't want him offering his services. However, he did spy his name on the piece of paper. He questioned us about the list of names, but Mei and I both answered only with a crafty smile. Cole nuked the quesadillas he'd brought home from the bar ,and we sat on the couch and scoffed down the reheated meal. I looked at the list again as Mei and Cole watched television. Here we were, the three amigos, now renamed Mama Bear, Papa Bear, and Goldicocks. I chuckled to myself.

I knew how this would look, but honestly I didn't care. My husband was deceased, and there was nothing I could do about it. I loved him, but he would want me to move on. Though this had all started as fun, I had made up my mind I was truly going to finally do it. I could already feel the difference. I felt sexier. The next day, men were flirting with me more than normal, and I got a few numbers within the first hour of being at Ciel. I told Mei, and she responded crazily, as usual.

"You have the scent."

I gave her a puzzled look.

"The I'm fucking scent. Men can smell it from yards away."

I inconspicuously sniffed my arms and hands. Again, I didn't know if this was ignorance or brilliance, but I just went with it, smiled, and kept making drinks. If anything, I was using this as a distraction to keep my stress down. In less than a month, I could lose a legacy. I didn't want this to happen, but the way things were looking, it was now a possibility that I had to accept.

While I was making a second Long Island for some extremely pale woman dressed in all black, a man with a familiar face walked up to me and spoke.

"You Isabelle?"

"Who are you?" I asked, thinking he was a reporter.

"I'm Ron Young," he said proudly. "I know your mother."

I didn't put two and two together immediately, but I did remember my mom having a friend named Ron. He'd eaten with us one Thanksgiving, when he'd got stranded in Virginia.

"Yes, I do remember. What can I do for you?"

"I talked to your mom the other day, and she told me to come by and check on you. I'm in town on business."

"I just talked to my mom. I told her I was okay," I replied.

"Yeah, well, she said for me to lay eyes on you, just to be sure. I decided to come here and see you while I wait on my son."

He ogled me up and down and gave me a shifty grin. I didn't think that was what my mom had been thinking when she told him to lay eyes on me. I prayed this was not another Normandy Collins episode, 'cause I didn't have the energy to dis another old man. I fixed him a Jack and Coke, and he sat down quietly at the end of the bar. Moments later, my dream man walked in and greeted Mr. Ron. It was Ron Young, the baseball player. I finally put it all together. I remembered my mom wanting to introduce me to his son, but she had said he played basketball, a sport notorious for its unfaithful husbands. I'd had no interest in that. Of course, now I recognized the irony in that theory. However, my mom had had the sports confused. His son was the reason I and a half dozen women I knew bought season tickets to the Braves games. Before I could get my thoughts together, Mei swooshed up beside me.

"Did you see who just walked in the bar?" she asked.

"I saw, I saw. I know his dad."

She flipped. "This is it. This is who you're supposed to do it with."

I looked down the bar, with doubt.

"You wanted it to be a crush, and what better crush than Ron Young?" said Mei. "Plus, you know his dad. This is fate."

I wished it were fate. But I was sure God was not lining up this situation just so I could fornicate. The two men walked over to a table near the back. Moments later two more men sat down at the table. I went to the back and called Satchel on the phone. I gave her the news about Ron. She gave me advice about my approach.

"Make nice with the father, and then he'll want his son to go out with you, because all men want their son to settle down with a nice girl. What can be nicer than a virgin?"

She rushed from the phone to continue working. I walked back to the front and stood by Mei.

"Okay, Goldi. What do you think?" I asked.

She looked at Ron and contemplated the matter while wiggling her nose like Samantha in *Bewitched*. Finally, she responded. "Six to seven inches, nice girth." I nodded in approval and made my way back to my end of the bar.

I grabbed another round of drinks and took them to the table. I purposely stood by Ron Sr. and stirred up idle chitchat. He introduced me to his son, and it seemed that the plan was working. I didn't want to seem to eager, so I gave the girly eyes and told them I'd be back to check on them. I normally stayed behind the bar, for we had servers for the tables, but this was special. I had to pay off the server in that section, but it was going to be worth it. When they were about to leave, I came around from behind the bar and said my good-byes. This was when Ron Sr. swaggered over, placed his hand on my shoulder, and spoke.

"So, my son is speaking at a leadership conference this Friday at the Westin. If you're not busy, you should attend. He's very talented, if I must say so myself."

Ron Jr. took my hand and also gave me a formal invite. Satchel had been right; I was in there. I agreed to go to the conference, and they left.

Cole had been eyeing me the entire night. It was like he knew what I was up to but didn't have the nerve to say anything about it. All I could do was giggle when we locked eyes. I really wished Mei hadn't said anything about his penis size. It just brought the whole imagery back.

"What can I get you?" I asked the gentleman next to Cole's customer.

"A shot of Absolut," he replied.

"I gotcha," I said, reaching for the bottle of vodka.

Minutes before closing, Ron Sr. popped back into Ciel. He strolled over to the bar and tapped the granite.

"Ron. You're back. Did you leave something?" I asked, not caring about his answer.

"I sure did," he said, with a curious smile.

I stared at his interesting expression and then asked, "What?"

"Your phone number," he answered.

Nervously, I tap the bar with my nails. Glancing over at Mei, I tried to get her attention, but she was wrapped up with a customer, and Cole was in the back, cleaning. The other two bartenders were working. No one was there to witness this heinous act of pimpery.

"Excuse me? My phone number?" I asked.

As Ron Sr.'s hand softly grazed my lower arm, I could feel my dinner rumbling in my belly. "Isabelle. I think you and I should have dinner."

"Do you now?" I asked. "Well, I'm going to have to get back with you on that."

"I'll just leave you with this." He handed me his business card. "Call me."

Ron Sr. gave the infamous cheesy wink with a nod and exited. As soon as he left, I rushed over to Mei and handed her the card.

"He wants us to have dinner," I griped.

Mei let out a huge laugh. "I warned you. You've got the scent. You really have to be careful now. If you don't use it wisely, you're going to be picking up all kinds of strays."

"I don't want the scent. I just want to get laid," I whined.

"The scent is nothing to fear. It's like skunk spray. You have to know how to aim and how to use it. Skunks use it as a defense mechanism. During mating season, female skunks spray those that they do not want to mate with."

"Okay, what about the male skunks?"

"Male skunks spray any and everyone, much like human males. But you're a female. You have to hone your spray. If not, you'll pick up grizzlies, like ol' Ron and Normandy."

"Grizzlies?" I queried.

"They call the old women cougars, and I call the old men grizzlies . . . as in grizzly bears." Mei picked up Ron Sr.'s card again and laughed.

I thought about all the unwanted male attention that I had received that day. It made sense. I had always loved Mei's use of analogies; this was one I could really appreciate. As I walked across the closed bar, I continued to whisper one phrase. "Hone my spray. Hone my spray. Hone my spray."

The next couple of days zipped by, and not much changed with the hotel business. Unfortunately, I was getting closer to the repossession date. Yet all could think about was sleeping with Ron Young. This was just the distraction Izzy the bartender needed, but Izzy the business executive did not.

Satchel was more obsessed with the case. After getting the information from Keith, she spoke with Adrian. However, Adrian insisted that he had had nothing to do with Shanice and her antics. He finally admitted that she had told him about the joke, and that he'd gone to warn Carl the morning he was fired. He'd been so angry, he didn't tell Carl, and part of him had wanted Shanice to embarrass Carl, but that was all. Adrian pointed the finger back at Shanice and said that she had used real bullets, with plans to set him up all along. He also threw another iron in the fire. The same day he'd been fired, he'd met with Keith and, over drinks, told him that Carl was going to his superiors about the bribe. He said Keith had been irate. Adrian, in his drunken anger, had also mentioned Shanice's poor taste of a joke. Adrian suggested that Keith could have changed the bullets. Satchel's case was blown wide open. She now had three suspects to look into, and one of them was her boyfriend. With this new information, Satchel asked for a continuance, and thankfully it was granted. She was swamped with work, but now she was even more convinced that Shanice's story was true. Her client was a scorned lover who was guilty only of a bad joke and informing the wrong people of her playful intentions.

The continuance gave Satchel a little more time to plan her case as well as tend to her sisterly duties. She came over that Friday and had me try on my entire wardrobe to pick out the exact dress I would wear to the leadership conference later that afternoon. She wasn't 100 percent sold on the Ron Jr. thing, but she was ready for me to stop yapping about having sex with him. We finally decided on a mustard yellow spaghetti-strap dress with an empire waist. She said it clung to my hips perfectly and swished when I walked. Apparently, swishing was in. Ron Jr. was five feet ten, and I was five feet six. Therefore, I wore short heels. Furthermore, we found out that the event benefited a kids' athletic summer camp, and so I was also prepared to make a donation and volunteer my services. All this seemed to be a lot just to have sex. However, Mei assured me that it wasn't regular sex. It was celebrity sex, and women went far beyond these minute details to score with professional athletes. I was in the major baseball sex league now. Satchel was unable to attend the conference, but my old trusty Mei wouldn't have missed it for the world.

Once we arrived at the hotel and checked in for the speaking event, I found out there were dozens of women there waiting to see the baseball player and a few of his ESPN compadres. In total there were four professional athletes speaking. Warrick Dunn, of the Falcons, was speaking on community-service involvement for African Americans. Royal Ivey, of the Hawks, was talking on mentoring. Jim Slater, of the Thrashers, was speaking about political involvement. Lastly, Ron Young was talking about leadership responsibilities. However, with the number women in attendance, one would've thought that this was a conference on how to get a free lifetime supply of designer shoes. We walked in and headed to the front.

Mei vigilantly scanned the room, picking out my competition. This was like some sort of flea market, only we were the merchandise. With the variety of women there, these men could have their choice wares from any part of the world. The European goods were up front on the right. The African merchandise was along the left aisle, directly in front of the Latin commodities. The Asian stock was positioned in the right back section. Of course, there was a variety of other international wares sprinkled throughout the market.

"I don't want to meet him anymore," I whined as Mei shoved me to the front.

"Hush. We are here now," she whispered forcefully. "Plus, you are nothing like any of these women. They just want these men for their money. You want Ron for his dick. Stay focused."

Once we got to the front, we saw the African

section was packed. Therefore, we positioned ourselves in the center of the Europeans and took a seat.

Fifteen minutes into the event, I was already bored out of my mind. I started looking at the scalps of the women, trying to guess whose hair was real and whose was not. I couldn't help but doze. After the first hour, it was time for a break. And during the break, Ron Jr. approached us. It felt great that we were the only goods getting personal with the prospective buyers. My heart started beating fast as he approached. He had on a slate gray suit, a light gray shirt, and a pale yellow tie. *My God, he looks so good,* I thought. Suddenly, I was nervous, as though I'd never talked to a man before. It was so easy when I was serving drinks, but in the outside world, I didn't know how to break into normal conversation.

Mei excused herself to give us a moment of privacy. Just then, one of Mei's sisters, from the Asian stock section, walked up and stepped in between us. As if I weren't there, she turned her back to me and began talking to him. No excuse me, no nothing; she just started yapping. This I could not have. I politely tapped her on the shoulder and cleared my throat. She turned, gave me the once-over, and continued to speak as though I was Casper the Friendly Ghost. I'd heard the phrase "You snooze, you lose," but this was not the time or place for that. Therefore, the next time, I didn't tap her. I simply stepped to the side and took Ron Jr. by his arm and ask if he wanted to continue our conversation on the other side of the room. He obliged. Thus, we floated away, arm in arm, leaving her flabbergasted. This immediately gave Ron and me something to chat about.

"I can't believe she simply walked up and interrupted us," I said.

"Yeah, these women are very bold these days. I appreciate you handling that, though."

Inside I was boiling over with joy, because the whole situation could have turned ugly had he ignored me and continued to listen to her. It was a gutsy move that paid off. Thankfully, that little maneuver jarred my flirting Cliff Notes, and I started in with his giving nature. Satchel had said this was a good way to break the ice.

"So, how long have you had your charity, and what made you do a camp?" I asked.

He leaned against the wall and brushed his hand across his beard as he began to speak. His eyes lit up when he talked about the camp's successes and the mentors that came year after year to help. Of course, I volunteered. We got so caught up in talking about that, we never got into anything personal. I realized that the conference was about to start back up, and I had to make my move.

"Would you like to have coffee sometime?" I asked.

It seemed like he was taking twenty minutes to give me an answer. I didn't know if I should retract my statement. Mei was a few feet away, and I knew that once she returned, it was a wrap.

Finally, he answered. "I'm not a big coffee drinker." He looked up and saw another one of the speakers attempting to get his attention. "I need to get going," he said as Mei walked up.

My heart was beating extremely fast, and I could feel a little sweat near the nape of my neck. As we were parting, Ron Jr. leaned in and brushed a piece of lint from my shoulder. He whispered to me, "I do, however, like sake. Maybe we can go out for Asian?"

I nodded as though I was an out-of-control bobblehead doll and then finally spoke. "That would be nice."

"Let me get your number. I'll call you this week," he said just before walking away. I was so excited that I almost peed on myself.

The rest of the day, I yapped about my baseball player. However, after hours of gabbing, Mei knew exactly how to shut me up.

"So are you going to give him some the first night, or are you going to wait to see if you get a second date?"

Just when I was having fun fantasizing about him taking me into his sculpted arms, she had to ruin it by bringing up the particulars.

"I don't know," I answered. "I think I should wait at least until date three."

"What if he asks you out but once? Then what?"

I'd never thought about that. Now I was nervous all over again.

Mei continued. "I have to admit, I really didn't think this would be so easy—"

"It just shows you what you can do when you put your mind to it," I interrupted.

"Well, like I said before, you are in another league now. You have to deal with this professional athlete and his groupies. Are you sure you want to do this?"

"I was sure before you started talking," I responded.

"Well, play it by ear. But whatever you do, don't kiss him. It's too personal," Mei said.

"But all I do is kiss. I'm a good kisser," I admitted.

"That's before you decided to have sex. The combination is a double whammy. You cannot fall for this guy. Your mission is to get in and get out. Remember that."

Ron Jr. called me the next day, and we made plans to get together Tuesday night. He picked me up in his Mercedes CLK350 Coupe. Although I had no plans to sleep with him tonight, I did have on a colored thong. The entire time we were eating, I was sliding my butt around on the seat just to keep it from cutting my cootchie in half. I never wore thongs, because I never wore clothing that clung tightly. Maybe I was a bit of a tomboy, but I already missed my cotton undies. Anyway, our conversation flowed from one subject to another, and I couldn't keep my eyes off the adorable cleft in his chin. It was amazing how the mind worked. I'd been on plenty of dates and never had pulsating, tingling sensations in my underwear before. Now that I'd made up my mind to respond to his flirting, my body was also reacting.

We had two bottles of warm sake, and all seemed to be going well. I was sure he was going to ask me out again. He had to, because I didn't want to do it tonight. While we were sharing a piece of tiramisu, Ron reached across the table and placed his hand across my arm. I gave a bashful smile, but inside I was shouting across the restaurant, "Ron Young Jr. is enjoying me!" What was it about athletes? They were normal, just like everyone else, yet they seemed so much larger than life. But I couldn't get caught up. I had to get in and get out. We finished dinner, and while we were waiting for the valet to bring the car around, Ron reached for my hand and gave me the interlocking fingers grasp. This was a definite second-date sign.

"Where are we going next?" he asked.

Now normally, I would be ready to go home, as to not deal with any sexual situations. However, I wanted to go back to his place. I told him my wish, and without a second thought, he began driving home. His humor was very sarcastic, much like mine, and we had a lot in common. All I kept thinking was, *I must not kiss him.* Fortunately, he brought up his father, which got my mind off kissing.

"My dad said he asked you to dinner."

"What did you say?"

"I told him you weren't into sugar daddies."

"No, you didn't," I responded, with a little giggle.

"He'll be okay."

I kept looking at his lips. "Mei doesn't know everything," I whispered very softly.

We pulled into the garage of his humungous brick home, and as the garage door was closing, Ron reached across the seat and pulled my face toward his. He was going in for a kiss. Suddenly I was scared. What if this was the double whammy? I turned away.

"We should go inside," I said, snubbing the potential lip-lock.

Quickly, he rushed inside the house. Next thing I knew, he had me pinned against the wall and was thrusting his pelvis against mine. I didn't know what had happened. One minute we were talking, and the next we were grinding.

"I have to go. I want to go home," I said.

"Did I do something wrong?" he asked.

I took a breath and spoke. "I can't do this."

He pulled back and walked into the powder room. Again, I stood in a room, wondering what in the hell was wrong with me. It was apparent my virginity was not about a man's image of me, but my self-image. This made me feel great, and yet, I wondered if I was crazy to be turning down Ron Jr. He was gorgeous. I stood there, frustrated, waiting for his return. When he came back, he placed his hand over my head and spoke.

"You ready to go?"

I thought he was upset with me, and I was not sure what to say. Though I was ready, I wanted to secure my second date.

"I don't want you to be upset with me. I just don't want to move too fast, and I want you to respect me."

I couldn't believe I was resorting to my old lines. This was not how this was supposed to be going down. We should have been rolling around in his five-hundred-thread-count sheets, and I should not have been feeling bad about it. But I did. Old habits died hard.

Twenty-three minutes later, I was on the phone, explaining the situation to my sister. She said I was putting too much pressure on myself by aiming so high on the sex scale. She told me to forget about having sex and concentrate on saving the hotel, and then she had to go. The weekend passed, and as expected, I did not hear from Ron. I guessed he was only after one thing. Ironically, I was, too, but I just couldn't do it. I wanted a second chance. But I refused to call him, at least for now.

Monday night at work, I was positioned behind the bar and was pouring drinks with an attitude. My tips were horrible. And I wasn't any closer to coming up with the money to save the hotel. However, just before close, Ron Jr. and another gentleman strutted into Ciel and took a seat at the bar. We made eye contact, and Ron walked over to me and immediately spoke.

"Why haven't you called me?"

"Why haven't you called me?" I countered.

We stood there silently. Just then Cole walked over to us. He needed me to sign for my credit-card tips. I introduced the two of them, and then Cole left.

"I thought we were having a great time, but after I didn't hear from you, I assumed you were upset that I didn't want to have sex. Is that the case?" I asked, very proud of my mature comment.

"Not at all. I'm an athlete. If I want ass, I can get it all day long. I didn't call, because I assumed you were upset with me."

I waited a few seconds to take in his answer,

and then I replied. "Well, I'm not upset, so if you want to go out again, that would be nice."

He nodded, with a smile. Man, I had almost forgotten how gorgeous he was when he smiled. "So I will call you," he said.

"We'll see," I said smugly.

Just then a young beauty rushed over to the bar, poked me in the chest, and slapped Ron in the face. She silenced everyone in the bar as they awaited her next move.

"I'm so sick of you and your whores," she yelled at Ron as she gawked at me. "I've been following you. I know you're fucking her."

I quickly defended myself. "No, no. I'm the virgin," I whispered loudly, as if my name were Mary Magdelene.

"Virgins don't fuck my husband," she yelled.

From my peripheral vision, I could see cell phones snapping pictures of the episode. I was going to be front-page news once again. Ron tried to subdue her, but she was feisty. She fought him off until security ushered her out of the building. She didn't go down without a fight, though. We could hear her yells echoing through the hotel lobby. Ron Jr. immediately left after she was escorted out, and I spent the next thirty minutes in the back kitchen. I tried to clean up while I was in there, but I slowly began to break down.

"Not again," I said to myself. "Why do I keep crying?" I slowly slid down the wall and crashed onto a step stool. "I can't save this hotel. I officially give up."

As I had suspected, the next morning there was a blurb on page two in the local tabloid paper about me and the woman who had claimed, very loudly, that I had slept with her husband. Now my virginity and my loyalty to my deceased husband were being questioned. *Is this virgin a whore?* This was the question on people's minds. After looking at my behavior, I wondered this myself.

Chapter 8

Borrowed Time

1 1/2 ounces Canadian whiskey
1/2 ounce ruby port
1 egg yolk
1 tsp grenadine syrup

Combine the Canadian whiskey, port, egg yolk, and grenadine in a cocktail shaker half filled with ice cubes. Shake well, strain into a cocktail glass, and serve.

Satchel still had no solid evidence that Adrian was responsible for Carl's death. She had proof that Shanice had bought wax bullets, which matched the residue on Carl's clothing, but of course, the prosecution would argue that she had used them to create an illusion of innocence, and that she had put the real bullets in the chamber as well. Carl had been shot twice. The first bullet had been wax, the second had been real, and there had been a real bullet in the chamber. Satchel was also going to use the fact that Shanice didn't run once she shot Carl, because she was convinced that she hadn't harmed him. However, the prosecution could combat that with the fact that she again wanted to create an illusion of innocence. Furthermore, the prosecution could argue that not everyone ran from murder, and that the defendant didn't look sorrowful.

Shanice had given Satchel everything, but it wasn't enough. The evidence against her didn't look good. We now had proof that each deposit Adrian had made from the Shelby was short; this was proof he'd been taking money off the top. Plus, one of the bank accountants had agreed to testify that Carl had asked to be made aware of any deposits and withdrawals Adrian made from accounts associated with the Shelby. Keith had also agreed to testify that he had told Carl about the evidence. Keith still hadn't admitted to the bribery, and since it was his word against Adrian's, this would be damn near impossible to prove. Keith had supplied pictures showing that Shanice and Adrian had had several meetings. He'd suggested to Satchel that Adrian and Shanice had been in on it together. Yet, Adrian continued to swear his innocence.

Again, Adrian admitted that he had known about Shanice's plan, but that he hadn't thought she was serious at first. It wasn't until he'd realized that Carl had truly ended things with her that he'd started to believe she might go through with it. Adrian had also said it wasn't the first time Shanice had talked about killing Carl. Shanice had had access to Carl's revolver, and Carl had taken her to the shooting range on several occasions. Adrian said that she'd been completely jealous about my relationship with Carl, and that she'd been determined that if she couldn't have him, no one would. Adrian again placed the blame on Shanice or Keith. "I believe Shanice wanted my brother dead." There was such detestation in his stare.

That night Satchel had a long talk with Shanice. The prosecution wanted to bargain. If Shanice would change her plea from not guilty to guilty, they would change her charges from premeditated murder to accidental homicide. Satchel told her to take the plea. Normally, my sister didn't bargain, but with all the evidence pointing against Shanice, she really didn't have a choice. Her client was going down for murder; all Satchel could do now was hope for a lighter sentence. Shanice refused to agree. She didn't change her story. She admitted to buying the wax bullets and said that she and Adrian had loaded them in the gun. She gave a very tearful explanation of what had been going on in her mind that evening. She swore that she'd never meant to kill Carl, and that she'd even done research on wax bullets and knew that they wouldn't hurt him. She only wanted to cause a scene and have it reported, and then Carl would have to tell me about the affair. Satchel asked her a series of questions to prepare her for the trial.

"Why didn't you just go to Ms. Trotter and tell her about your affair?"

"I wanted *him* to tell her. I wanted him to admit what he'd been doing." Shanice broke down. "I loved him," she said over and over. "If I'd told her, he would have denied it."

Shanice admitted that several of Carl's friends had known about their affair, but that Carl had gone out of his way to make sure I never knew. He wasn't going to let his precious Izzy's opinion of him be ruined. Though money was the strongest motive for murder, Shanice had been scorned, and this was the second strongest. Sure, Shanice gained revenge from Carl's murder, but Adrian thought he'd gain a hotel, which he assumed was worth a million or more. This was the stronger motive, especially given Adrian's constant gambling debts. Satchel would have to get a subpoena to talk with Adrian's associate Jones. First, she decided to speak with Ndeeyah. Maybe she could give an account of Carl and Adrian's relationship. If Satchel could prove it was rocky, this would be a start. Adrian had gone out of town, and Ndeeyah didn't want to come to Satchel's office, so she asked Satchel if could she meet her at the house. Satchel agreed.

Oren greeted Satchel at the door and escorted her to the kitchen, where Ndeeyah was setting the table.

"Dinner is just about ready. Oren, pour our guest some lemonade." Satchel hadn't realized she was having dinner. She only wanted to ask a few questions, but she admitted the food smelled so good that she had to have a taste.

"I hope you like spicy curry," Ndeeyah said.

"My mom makes really hot food, but it's good," Oren added. He was so polite and adorable, odd looks aside.

* * *

During dinner Ndeeyah mentioned that she'd spoken with her mom and that her father still wanted her to come back home and marry a guy named Olumuah, whose family owned several trade warehouses in the Mobasi region. But, she said that she loved Adrian and that her life back home would be one of servitude to a man she didn't know. Ndeeyah then spoke about Adrian's temper but said that he truly loved Carl.

"My husband has made some mistakes, and he's lost money, but he always looked at Carl as his brother. There was never any hatred."

Ndeeyah didn't know about Adrian's gambling debt or him stealing money. Adrian had told her he'd been fired because Carl wanted to bring in an executive with more experience. If Ndeeyah had any damaging information, she was not going to share it. Satchel thanked her for the meal and went home to prepare for the trial, which was to start in two weeks.

Satchel ended things with Keith because she had to consider him a suspect. She never admitted to me that he was the one she'd been seeing, but suddenly she wasn't dating anyone. I could tell that she was really into the mystery man, so I didn't have the heart to tease her about him. I'd always felt Keith was shady. I didn't know the level of his involvement in Carl's murder, but I was praying Satchel was willing to bring him down if necessary.

* * *

Early Saturday morning, Mei and I went to yoga class. We normally took this class every Saturday, but I hadn't been since Carl's death. I was attempting to get back into my routine. We were thirty minutes into class, and I was just feeling comfortable in my Downward-Facing Dog, when I heard Mei hissing from the next mat over. I opened my eyes, and hers were blinking uncontrollably.

"We need to talk," she whispered loudly.

I gave a perplexed look and then closed my eyes again. However, she kept making hissing noises to get my attention. Finally, I stopped concentrating on my pose and tried to read her lips. I couldn't make out a single word.

"Just wait," I whispered.

We finished our class, and before I could roll up my mat, Mei was rushing me from the room. We hopped in her car, but she didn't speak immediately.

"All of this rushing, and you have nothing to say?" I asked her.

"I have to show you something," she said.

We went to the bookstore just down the street. Mei hurried to the history section and perused the shelves. I simply tagged along behind her. Finally, she found what she was looking for. She pulled the book out and flipped through the index. She handed the book to me, turned to page twenty-three.

"Read this," she stated, pointing to the second paragraph. I glanced at the cover and then back at the appointed paragraph and began to read aloud.

'If a man seduces a virgin who is not pledged to be married and sleeps with her, he must pay the bride-price, and she shall be his wife. If her father absolutely refuses to give her to him, he must still pay the bride-price for virgins.' I gave Mei a confused look and kept reading. "Most people would recognize the moral difference in paying two hundred dollars for a cutting-edge sex toy and buying a kidnapped girl's virginity in Thailand on a sex tour for nearly the same price. Most is not all. Roughly twenty-five to thirty American travel agencies offer 'sex tours' primarily to Thailand, South America, and the Philippines, where the tourist is guided through brothels, massage parlors, clubs, and other venues for the intent of having sex with prostitutes. What the agencies do not say is that many of the sex workers have venereal diseases, like AIDS, and that many of the promised virgins are actually kidnapped minors, sometimes as young as eight years old."

I now gave her a more confused look than before. We headed outside.

"I have something to tell you," Mei finally admitted as we walked toward her car. "There's this Web site, and men go on and bid money for virgins."

"What?" I shrieked.

"I know it sounds crazy, but it's true. I have family members that have done this. I mean, they pay lots of money, rich men with nothing better to do. People like Collins."

I gave her a blank stare, because I was afraid of where she might be going with this. "I'm not doing whatever it is you're suggesting. I've already made peace with selling the hotel."

"Why are you giving up?" she asked.

"Why are you trying to be my pimp?"

Mei and I stared at each other across the top of her Mini Cooper. After a few seconds of staring, she opened the car door. "I wasn't going to say anything until—"

"What did you do?" I asked her.

"I put you on there," Mei murmured.

I was enraged. Once we reached my house, I stormed around the other side of the car as Mei backed away from me.

Mei rolled down her window. "Your bid is up to fifteen thousand dollars," she called. I stopped dead in my tracks. Mei pulled out a printout. "I know you need a lot more, but that's a lot of money. It could climb higher."

I took the printout and read it in disbelief. I was on some secret virgin sex site similar to any other auctioning Web site.

"I can't talk to you right now," I said to Mei as I walked to my car. Mei watched me closely, all the while apologizing.

"I was only trying to help," she pleaded. But I didn't want to hear it. I felt violated. I slammed the car door to block her apologies and sped off.

Before the evening was over, Satchel came into the bar. She ordered a drink before she could sit. I knew it had been a rough week, because Satchel wasn't that big of a drinker. In fact, she only drank under stress, and as she was sipping her Long Island, I could see the bags under her eyes. I came from around the bar and placed my arms around my sister.

"You are doing an amazing job," I said just before kissing her cheek.

Satchel took another sip and said, "How are you holding up?"

I nodded and placed my head on her shoulder.

"How many more days?" she asked.

I held up two full hands and then five fingers and sighed heavily. Satchel rubbed my shoulder.

"Nine until the trial," she said.

"I contacted two different investment groups, but it's hard to push a hotel with debt. One of the guys said he was interested in putting a group of different investors together, but once they did their research and found out about the lien against the property, they decided to wait until it was seized. Everyone knows they can get a better deal at the auction than to help me up front."

"You did the best you could," Satchel said.

"Did I? I'm not sure," I replied.

I felt Carl had entrusted me with something and I'd failed. Of course, he hadn't realized that he was going to get killed before he had taken care of the debt, but there had to be more to this. The trial hadn't started, so Izzy wasn't at liberty to give too many details, but I tried to piece together the ones I did know about. Shanice did admit to slashing Carl's tires on the Jaguar, the Jag she'd purchased. It was a birthday gift, which was why we couldn't find a record of Carl paying for it. Apparently, she'd given him many gifts over the years. His home was damn near a museum of all her offerings.

It still didn't add up. Why would Shanice so whimsically tell Adrian about her plan if she wanted to set him up? This would give him time to plan an alibi and/or tell someone about the plan. She knew he wanted Carl's money; if she had intended to set him up, she would have planned better, leaving a trail pointing right to him. Plus, the bachelor-party attendees had said that the shooter almost went into shock when she witnessed the blood. Satchel was convinced that Shanice hadn't known about the bullets, and since I couldn't save the hotel, I was now committed to helping her find evidence. Though she had law associates looking through Carl's things, I could also go back to the house and search for clues. I made plans to go to Carl's house the next day.

Sunday morning, Cole and I got up and went to church. Between yoga, work, and church, life was starting to feel normal. Therefore, to top things off, I decided to have a soul food Sunday dinner. Carl and I would do this every Sunday. I'd loved cooking for him. Since I was going to his house, anyway, to search for clues, I could also cook there. All of my good pots and pans were at his house. I called Satchel and told her to meet me at Carl's house. I sent Cole to the store with a grocery list, and I began preparing my last meal at 4429 Caslin Road.

It was weird being back in Carl's house. Yes, I'd

been there right after Carl's death and a few times with the realtor, but now I was being active in the house, doing something I'd done only with Carl. I felt as though I was doing something wrong. I sat on the granite slab in the center of the kitchen and stared at the silver fridge.

Suddenly, my phone rang. The house was so quiet, the ring startled me as it echoed from the high, arched ceilings. I ran to my purse and answered, but the caller had nothing to say. I said hello several times, but there was only silence on the other end. I returned the call, but it went to a generic voice mail. I stood in the center of the open living room and viewed its perimeter. I swore I could still feel Carl's spirit. I walked outside and sat on the porch until Cole came back. Satchel was only a few blocks away. Once she arrived at the house, I went back inside and prepared my Sunday soul-food meal. I was still upset with Mei, so I hadn't invited her. Plus, I didn't want her mentioning any of the Internet stuff to anyone. We ended up spending several hours at the house. I had forgotten how cozy it was. There was no way I could keep it, but it was certainly a warm, beautiful house.

That evening, after Cole and Satchel went home, I went upstairs to Carl's office and grabbed that tackle box with the pictures and mementos. I searched every crevice of the office, pulling out old folders, bank statements, tax returns, and anything that looked like it had some value. I hadn't informed Satchel about my plan; I was simply hoping I could find something that would help. Carl hadn't been the most organized, but he did have all of his financial items in one place. I figured that would be a good place to start. I went through all of his items, and in the process, I came across an envelope with ten deposit-slip receipts. The account number on the receipts didn't match any of Carl's accounts, but the receipts were from the same bank. I made plans to visit the bank Monday morning in hopes that Carl's banker would give me some information about the account.

Close to 1:00 a.m. that same night, Mei gave me a call. At first she was acting strange on the phone, and I was about to hang up, but then she finally got to her reason for calling.

"You're up to twenty-two thousand dollars," she said quickly and hung up.

I sat up in bed. "Twenty-two thousand dollars?" I said aloud. I glanced at my cell phone and called Mei back. She answered anxiously.

"This is a lot of money, Izzy."

"Then why don't you do it?" I asked.

"I'm not a virgin. They have a doctor, and they make the girls get tested to see if their hymen is broken."

"That's dumb. Your hymen can get broken doing a bunch of stuff."

"Well, I don't know how they tell, but trust me, my gap is so big, Old Navy thinks I'm their competition."

"And you say that proudly?" I said, with cynicism.

In the course of our conversation, Mei convinced me that I should just keep my listing up for a week and see what happened.

"I'm not sleeping with some weird guy who's bidding for me on an online auction Web site. It's insulting," I said.

"And yet flattering at the same time?" Mei asked.

I said nothing. Mei said she was leaving it up until Friday, and then I could decide what I wanted to do. I already knew. A part of me didn't want her to keep me on that site, because I was afraid of what I might do if the bidding got up to six figures. *Could my virginity be worth that much?* I wondered. I fell back onto the pillow and closed my eyes. I couldn't believe what I was considering. I couldn't believe that people actually bid money to sleep with virgins. After chewing this over a little more, I finally fell asleep.

Monday morning I went to Carl's bank. There were a couple of bank assistants willing to help me, but I needed to wait for Mr. Locksdale, Carl's personal banker. Mr. Locksdale was an older gentleman who had worked with Carl since the opening of the Shelby. He was kind but very serious about his job, and he didn't bend the rules at all. I walked into his glass office and showed him the bank receipts.

"These are deposit-slip receipts, and I need to know the owner of this account," I said.

Mr. Locksdale looked at the receipts and typed something into his computer. "This account is closed," he said.

"Was it Carl's?" I asked.

Mr. Locksdale shook his head.

"Can you tell me who the account belonged to?" I queried.

Mr. Locksdale shook his head again and slid the receipts back to me.

"Please," I begged him.

"I am not authorized to give that information, unless there is a warrant for it."

I would have to call Satchel and give her the information, and then she'd have to ask her friend who had arrested Shanice to get a warrant, and that probably wouldn't happen. As far as the police were concerned, Carl's murder was an open-and-shut case. They had the murderer, the weapon, and a room filled with witnesses. Dejected, I left the bank, but as I was driving down the street, I thought I would try another approach. I went to another bank branch and tried to make a deposit into that same account. I filled out a deposit slip, filled in a fake name, and walked up to the teller.

"I would like to make a deposit," I said as I gave the young woman a fifty-dollar bill. She tapped a few numbers and told me the account was closed.

I looked completely surprised. I launched into my story. "But this is my brother's account. He asked me to put this money in here. Did I write it correctly?" I pulled out the latest receipt and placed it on the counter. "Here's his last receipt."

She looked at the receipt and back at the computer. "The last name on this account is Carson," she said.

"Oh, I must have pulled the wrong receipt," I said. "This account is Keith Carson's?"

"Yes," she responded.

"Oh, that's my assistant. Let me call my brother and confirm his account number. Thanks." I left the bank.

I sat in the car and counted the receipts and added the deposit amounts. The oldest receipt was from June of last year, and the last one was from two weeks before Carl's death. The amounts varied, but they totaled $17,860.00. I immediately called Satchel as I headed to her office. Once I reached her office, she looked at the receipts.

"This can't prove anything," she said.

"But why was Carl giving Keith that kind of money?"

"You said he hired Keith to follow Adrian. I'm sure these are payments."

"But Carl also said that was last spring, and that Keith didn't find anything. These payments don't start until summer and keep going until last month. It doesn't make sense."

"I agree, but we don't have any proof. I will ask Keith about this, but you didn't get the information legally. Plus, Keith could say Carl was paying him for numerous things. It would be hard to prove otherwise."

"You just don't want to admit Keith is guilty," I shouted.

"Hold up!" Satchel rose from her desk. "Are you saying I'm not doing my job?"

I quieted down, for my sister had a temper, and I didn't want to get her rolling.

"I'm in this mess because of you, but now that

I'm defending Shanice, I will look into every aspect of this case. But if I say it's hard to prove, then it's just that!"

"Okay," I murmured.

Satchel moved toward her bookshelf and removed a couple of pamphlets from the second shelf. She handed them to me. "Since you want to play lawyer, you need to brush up on your technique." She sat down and kept working.

"I didn't mean to upset you. I'm only trying to help."

"I know," Satchel said without looking up.

I stood by her desk a few more seconds but then left the office. I called Satchel once I got to the hotel, but she didn't answer, so I left her alone the remainder of the day. This was certainly one of her most difficult cases, and I knew my sister was a professional. If she believed Shanice, she was doing everything possible to strengthen her case. I knew these receipts were linked to something dirty, so I was going to do more snooping to find out.

When I got to the Shelby, I called Warren into the office. I questioned him about Carl hiring Keith, and he said that he didn't remember when Carl first hired Keith, but he recalled Carl saying he didn't believe that Keith was bringing him accurate information, so he was not dealing with him anymore. Warren said that Carl had stopped working with Keith around May of last year, around Memorial Day weekend. I didn't mention the deposit-slip receipts to Warren, but this whole matter was definitely looking seedier, especially when Warren confessed that Carl had mentioned he was being blackmailed.

"One day he just let it slip out, but he didn't say who and what for," Warren said.

I felt these deposits had something to do with that, but I couldn't say anything else to Satchel or mention it to Keith. I had to dig further into this information.

I didn't have much work to do that day, so I left the Shelby around three o'clock, went to Carl's house, and sifted through the remainder of Carl's things. I didn't glean anything from his things, but I separated his bills, the house particulars, and hotel business and placed everything in folders.

Later that evening, I had to speak to a group of young women about abstaining. I had quickly become "the virgin about town," and people were contacting the hotel about speaking engagements. This was hilarious because before this incident, I had tried to speak to young groups about abstaining, and I had had a hard time organizing events. Now they were coming to me. Why did I have to go through a tragedy for people to recognize that I had something to offer? Owing to this misfortune, I was being depicted as this extraordinary virgin who had triumphed through all the odds. Hell, being a virgin alone should have catapulted me to the status of a conqueror. People had no idea how hard it was to live in this sex-craved society and still save it. Though plausible, it was damn near impossible. This was how I started my talk. I tried to make my lectures conversational. I never wanted young women to think I was preaching to them. I only wanted to let them see that saving it was an option, and that one could still be cool and be a virgin.

There were close to twenty young women at the community center. Some were virgins; some weren't. The talk was very casual, just as I liked it. They asked questions, I asked questions, and a few girls admitted that they'd had sex but wanted to wait before doing it again. I always gave an analogy that a friend told me once. She'd said, "Just because you get in a car accident and nick your car doesn't mean you have to total it." This would always stimulate dialogue; that day was no different.

I forgot to turn off my phone, and right before I was to answer a question asked by one of the counselors at the center, it vibrated. I ignored it at first and answered the question. It vibrated once again, so thinking it might be Satchel, I checked the text. *Your cootchie is up to $32,370.*

"Oh shit!" I said aloud. The young women looked at me with gaping eyes. "I'm sorry." I was so stunned, I couldn't continue the talk. I opened the floor for dialogue and stepped away from the platform area. I was wearing a blanket of hypocrisy, and it was covering me from head to toe. Here I was, talking to young women about saving their virginity and at the same considering doing it with some stranger who could pay for me via the Internet. I couldn't get out of there fast enough. I said my good-byes and thanked the counselors for inviting me. I rushed to the car and called Mei.

"You are lying!" I said to her.

"No, I'm not, and it's just Monday. Maybe they found out you were linked to the murder case. That could make you more valuable."

"You mean my picture is up there?" I yelled.

"Yeah, I had to put your picture up there."

I hung up instantly.

"Dammit!" I was furious, but I couldn't get that figure off my mind. How often did one get over thirty thousand dollars for sleeping with someone one time? I wondered if my cootchie could actually save the Shelby, and what would happen if someone got wind of this story. I could just imagine those headlines.

Chapter 9

Brazilian Bitch

1 ounce Amaretto almond liqueur
1 ounce vodka
4–5 ounces cranberry juice
1 splash Coca-Cola

Combine the ingredients in the order listed in a highball glass, add the Coca-Cola on top, and serve.

Mei and I decided that since my bid kept climbing, we had to keep my listing up just to see how high it went. It made me feel like a prostitute, but I couldn't help but wonder. People could judge and say what they must, but I swore if others were put in my position, they would be on their backs faster than FloJo in the 1988 Olympics. It was now Thursday, four days before the hotel repossession and one day before my virgin bidding closed. Surprisingly, I wasn't stressed or upset. I still wanted to save the hotel, but the bidding hadn't gone high enough yet, and I had no serious investors. The thought of taking the money from my cootchie and investing it in resort property was running through my mind. It was a win-win situation.

I decided to take a day off from the hotel business and only go to work that night at Ciel. Mei came by and picked me so that we could spend the afternoon together. I thought Mei and I were going out to eat. However, she surprised me when she pulled up to her spa.

I looked down at my nails and said, "I could use a manicure. This was a great idea."

Mei said nothing as I followed her into the posh salon. Mei told the receptionist that we were here to see Ming Cho, and we sat and waited. A minute later, I was called to the back, and Mei mentioned it was her treat, so I figured I might as well get a "mani-pedi" combination. However, when I got to the white, sterilized room, there was no manicure table or bottles of polish. There was only a counter with jars of paraffin and a table.

"Remove your bottoms. I be right back," said the petite woman, with a thick accent. She handed me a disposable G-string.

I lightly grabbed her wrist and asked, "What's this? I thought I was getting a manicure."

She giggled and replied, "No, no, this room for wax. Remove your bottoms. I be right back." She walked out.

"Wax?" I said as I stood alone in the center of the room. I'd never had a wax before, and I wasn't sure I was prepared to have one today. I was going to kill Mei. She was always getting me into freaking predicaments.

Just then Ming walked back in and stared at me.

She said, "Remove pants and underwear! Busy schedule today!" She shut the door once more.

I looked at the wax again and then slowly removed my pants. I felt my pubic area. It was hairy, not out-of-control, jungle-bush hairy, but hairy enough to take more than a couple strips of wax. I was getting scared, yet I removed my panties and got on the table and covered myself with the sheet. Just then there was a light tap on the door, and then Mei walked in.

"Don't be mad," she said quickly as I peered angrily at her. "I heard you were being resistant, but you'll love it. It will be like brand new."

Still covered, I sat up and retorted, "My cootchie is brand new on the inside. I don't need outside re-decoration. That's for women like you who have worn their insides out."

"Sticks and stones," she replied just before closing the door.

Seconds later Ming came in the room and checked the temperature of the wax. I kept leaning up to see what she was doing, but it was only making me more frightened.

"This is my first time," I said nervously.

Ming giggled and replied, "It's okay. I do lots of virgins."

I could only wonder if the supposed online auction sponsor would say the same thing. Ming walked over to the table and removed the sheet. She didn't even look at my area. She pulled my leg to the side and applied the wax between my legs. She put a strip on the wax and told me to take a deep breath. I did. She then said, "Let it out," and when I did, she snatched the strip off.

"Oh shit!" I yelled. Ming snickered and applied more wax. "Hold up. Hold up," I said.

"It better if I keep going," she said, applying on the next strip. "Deep breath."

I took in a breath and tried my best to prepare for the next round of stinging pain. It didn't work. This strip of wax was worse than the first. Nine hairy strips later, I was as bald as I'd been at birth. Ming patted my shoulder and continued to snicker as I lay there in tears. This was not at all amusing. My once-covered area now had a pink hue. Ming wiped it down with aloe, but the cool breeze was no comfort. I continued to lie on the table after she left. I managed to get myself together and meet Mei in the lobby. I immediately put my hands around her throat and playfully shook her body. She played along, although part of me was not joking.

"Don't you feel free?" she asked.

I didn't respond. I only put on my shades and walked out of the salon. Mei tagged along behind me. For this agonizing pain, she would have to pay for lunch as well. Therefore, we went to a great Cuban spot in Midtown and feasted.

Though the initial pain had left, my pubic area still hurt when I walked. Mei suggested I numb the pain with marijuana. We all had that one friend who constantly suggested bad ideas, and this was my one. My jeans were rubbing against the skin, and therefore, I was trying to walk without the fabric touching my skin, and I looked like I had a stick up my butt. So I changed clothing before work, opting for a black skirt tonight instead of pants. After I changed, the pain started again. I wasn't a smoker, but Cole surely was, so I grabbed a little weed from his room before I left for work. I had no plans to smoke, but if the pain got unbearable, hell, I would have to light up to make it through the night.

I arrived at work close to thirty minutes early. It was packed, and we were swamped. Cole was out of town, and Paula had called in sick. Therefore, I went to work immediately, and I didn't have a break until three hours later. The tips were flowing in, but for some reason, I didn't care. I felt like my money issues were soon to be over. Yes, my credit would be ruined, and I would no longer have the hotel, but my vagina was up to forty-two thousand dollars, and I was considering just doing it. Once the hotel was repossessed, Ciel would be closed, so I would need either a job or a wad of money. I walked over to Mei and asked her about the Web site again.

"Who's on this site again? What if my family sees me on there?" I asked.

"Mostly eccentric millionaires, foreigners," Mei replied.

"Are you sure?"

"Trust me. It's a very secret society. You have to have all kinds of codes just to find the site."

I didn't have time to discuss it further, because I had a drink in one hand and another to make, and before I realized it, we had one more hour before closing. While I was in the middle of making a cosmopolitan, Marley and another woman walked in. I smiled at Marley as she walked toward the bar. With the cosmo in my hand, I walked to the edge of the bar and greeted Marley. I could smell the alcohol on her breath as she said my name loudly.

"You've been . . ." I couldn't even get the sentence out of my mouth before Marley raised her hand and slapped me across my face. The contact was so hard, the drink spilled, and her nails grazed my face and broke the skin. Marley then let out a sharp half laugh, half smirk. Her girlfriend followed the slap with an accusatory remark.

"Man-stealing bitch," she growled.

Normally, I am the peaceful, turn-the-other-cheek type of woman. I actually hated fighting. However, something came over me, and I immediately retaliated. I dropped the glass I was holding and slapped her back. Marley then kneed me in the pubic area, and after that, it was on. Our fight turned into a full-out brawl. Mei, who'd been in the kitchen, came running from the back and jumped in. Marley was swearing in Portuguese, her friend was swearing in Spanish, Mei was swearing in Chinese, and I was using plain ol' hood cursing. It was an international brawl fest.

Next thing I knew, an off-duty cop was breaking in between the swinging arms, tousled hair, and exposed boobs. In the mayhem, Marley had managed to rip my shirt. The off-duty cop radioed to another cop, and within seconds another officer was rushing into the bar. They had all of us up against the bar. This was the second time in a month that I'd been accused of stealing someone's man. I couldn't believe it. I looked down at my ripped shirt and exposed demi-cup tan bra, and I noticed the tiny plastic baggie sticking slightly out of my bra. It was the weed I'd taken from Cole's room. I'd stuck it in my bra because my skirt had no pockets. The off-duty cop told us to keep our hands behind our back as we faced the bar, so I tried to push the baggie farther down into my bra cup with my chin, but I was unsuccessful. I attempted to push it down quickly with my hand, but when I moved my hand, the other officer noticed and then turned my body around.

"What happened?" asked officer number two.

I snarled at Marley and responded, "That Brazilian kneed me in my Brazilian, and I defended myself." I tried covering the baggie by placing my arm across my chest and pretending to scratch my cheek, but it didn't work.

"What's that?" officer number two said, nodding to the weed.

I didn't bother answering. He called the off-duty cop over, and the off-duty cop asked me to remove the baggie from my bra. I did. He took the baggie and sniffed it. Without any questions, he told officer number two to take me to the police car. I looked at Mei, who shouted, "I will call Satchel."

The off-duty cop kept the other women there and took their names as I was hauled off downtown for possession. I didn't know how much marijuana I had, but obviously, it was enough to be taken in. When I got to the jail, they immediately took my belongings, which amounted to only to my cell, and fingerprinted me. Satchel had already received a call from Mei, but it didn't matter, for she was out of town for the day. Satchel promised to get me out by morning.

"Morning?" I asked Mei. Mei said that was the best Satchel could do and told me to keep calm until then.

I sat in the square room behind bars with eight

other people. The woman next to me looked like a prostitute, plastic hooker boots and all. I felt like I was in a movie. Therefore, I delivered the classic movie line.

"What are you in here for?" I asked.

She looked me up and down, smirked, and turned away. I did the same to her, turning and then scooting a few inches to the left. This was going to be a long night. I prayed Satchel could come through before the morning. Within the next hour, three people left and two more came in. One of them was definitely a streetwalker, and wouldn't you know it, she plopped down right beside me. It was like God was trying to show me how I would end up if I didn't watch it.

Unlike the first woman of the night, this one was very chatty. She glanced at me and said, "What's your deal?" Finally, I had someone to do my movie scene with, and so it began.

"I was in a bar brawl," I said, proudly showing my tattered shirt. "And you?"

"Pandering," she replied. I gave her a puzzled look, and she quickly added, "Hookin'."

I nodded as if I were surprised. I started wondering how much she made in one night. I wanted to ask, but I thought it would be rude. I was sure she'd never made forty grand, so it didn't matter. That night I discovered the difference between a hooker and a high-priced call girl. Both were illegal in the eyes of the law, but a hooker would have to do years of leg spreading to afford the property I could purchase after one evening. If only she'd saved herself like me, her shoes wouldn't be plastic. They'd be Prada. I was having insane thoughts, but it helped pass the hours, which actually came to eight before I made bail.

I walked down the corridor and went into the office to collect my cell phone. I signed the paperwork and walked into the lobby, where I saw Keith Carson leaning against the wall. Assuming Satchel had called him, I thanked him immediately, and we walked out. I didn't want to be seen with Keith, considering he was going to have to testify, but I wanted to bleed him for information, so I agreed to go with him to IHOP when he asked. Over blueberry pancakes, we chatted about my fight with Marley and my relationship with Carl.

"I used to think sistas had attitude and temper, but they don't have shit on girls from South America. You're lucky she didn't cut you," Keith said.

My response didn't match his comment. "Did you know about Shanice?"

Keith didn't want to answer me, so he played coy and kept talking about Brazil. I finally slammed my fork down and demanded he answer.

"I knew Carl was trying to end it with her. But she had something on him," he said. He refused to go into any details. "Several people could have benefited from Carl's death. Your sister isn't looking in the right places."

He was being cryptic, and suddenly, all my reservations about him came back. "You ready to go?" I said, finishing my last bite.

Keith walked me to my car, said good-bye, and walked across the street. As he was stepping onto the sidewalk, a truck came speeding by. I noticed it wasn't slowing down, so I called Keith's name, and when he turned, the truck brushed against his side, knocking him to the ground. A few on-lookers and I rushed to his side. We attempted to identify the truck as it sped down the street. It was an old red and white pickup. Some thought it was a Chevy; others, a Ford. Keith stood up and dusted himself off. Luckily, he was only stunned and not physically hurt. When he looked at me, I saw the fear in his eyes. That attempt to run him over had been no mistake. He knew it and so did I.

"Maybe there are people who could benefit from your death, too," I said to him.

Keith was silent.

"You okay?" I asked him.

Keith nodded and looked in the direction of the pickup truck, which was no longer in sight.

"We should call the police," an onlooker said.

"I am the police," Keith responded.

Keith walked back to his car. I followed him, all the while talking. "Keith, if you know some-thing, you should tell Satchel."

Keith still said nothing. I desperately wanted to ask him about the deposit-slip receipts, but I knew not to.

Finally, he said, "Isabelle, I have to phone this in. I'm okay. You can go now." Keith got in his car and radioed into the station. I couldn't hear what he was saying because he had closed the car door, but I saw that he wasn't going to say any-thing else to me, so I looked right, left, and right again before crossing the street. I got in my vehi-cle and went home.

Once home, I quickly jumped in the shower and then went to bed. I slept until seven that evening, woke up, ate a snack, got back in the bed, and watched television. Close to ten that night, I heard a faint knock at my front door. I called Mei on her cell, thinking it might be her coming to check on me, but it wasn't. She was at work. So we stayed on the phone while I peered through the peephole. It was Keith.

"What the hell is he doing here?" I whispered to Mei.

"Open the door and see," she said.

"Hold on, Keith," I said while still on the phone with Mei. I hung up, got my keys, and opened the door. "What's up?" I asked, keeping him at bay.

"I was just checking on you," he answered as he was about to step over the threshold.

"You can't come in," I announced. "How do you know where I live?"

"I'm a detective," he smirked.

"So you've been following me?"

"No, I've been over here before with Satchel. I just stayed in the car when she had to come in and get something."

Keith leaned in and softly touched my face, inspecting the scratches I received during the brawl.

"You should put something on those," he advised. You wouldn't want to leave a mark on that soft skin of yours."

"Somebody tried to run you over this morning, and you're here to check on me? I don't buy it," I said.

Just then Mei called me back.

"Yes, Mei," I answered.

"What did he want?" she asked as Keith was taking a step into the house.

With my right hand, I resisted his forward

movement; with my left, I held my phone. "I'll call you back." I then turned my attention back to Keith. "I'm fine. You can go home," I told him.

He leaned against the open door and stared at me.

"What do you want, Carson?" I said.

"Your sister broke up with me," he said.

I shrugged my shoulders and replied, "That's Satchel. One minute she loves you, and the next . . . Hell, you have no idea what happened."

He continued to stare. "She thinks I might be a suspect. What do you think?"

"This is so inappropriate," I told him. "You have to go."

"I didn't kill your husband."

"Tell that to the jury," I said before pushing him out the door. I locked the door and peered through the peephole to make sure he was leaving. I didn't get Keith, and I was too worn out to try to figure out what was on his mind. I was glad that Satchel had ended it with him. I had to call and inform her of this unexpected visit. She didn't answer, but first thing that Saturday morning, she called me.

Before I could say hello, she was screaming on the other end. "If you call me to help you, let me know if you don't need me any longer."

Still dazed from my slumber, I had no idea what Satchel was talking about. But after she explained herself, I realized that she'd called one of her assistants to bail me out, but I'd already been released by the time she got there. Neither of us had any idea how Keith had known I was locked up. When I told her about his late-night visit, it only infuriated her more. Shanice's trial was starting in three days, and it needed her full concentration, but Satchel swore she would get to the bottom of this.

By the time I walked into the hotel, the Keith situation was giving me a headache. This was compounded by constant questions about the fight at Ciel. Thankfully, no members of the media were around, but my coworkers were just as bad. I couldn't take two steps without someone asking about Cole and me. Amazingly, Cole hadn't called, and he wasn't answering his cell phone. I assumed Marley hadn't spoken with him, either. But since everyone at the hotel knew about the brawl, it wouldn't be long before he did. This place was a big gossip factory.

Warren mentioned that Ndeeyah hadn't shown up for work that day. This was completely out of character for Ndeeyah, who only called in when her son was sick. To not show up without calling was something she'd never done. Warren said she wasn't answering the phone, and the front desk was short. He was filling in until her substitute showed up. I tried her phone as well, but my calls went unanswered. I looked at Adrian as a loose cannon, and I wondered what he'd done to his family, so I went by the house about an hour later. I knocked on the front door, but no one answered, so I walked around the back and peered in the kitchen window, but it was dark. When I walked back to the side, there was a gentleman in the front yard. I called out, he quickly walked up to me, and I questioned him.

"You're Carl's wife," he said, with a grin. "Nice to finally meet you. I'm Jones."

"Hi," I said, with little enthusiasm. "No one's home."

"I know. Adrian asked me to grab a few things from the house."

"Where is he?"

Jones shrugged his shoulders and headed to the front door.

"This is my property. You can't walk in there."

With an obvious scowl, Jones turned around and pointed at the house. "This is yours?" he asked.

"Yes, it belonged to my husband, and now it belongs to me."

"But I have keys," he said, dangling them in the air.

"It's still my place, and why are you going inside?"

Jones approached me, with a slick grin. "I was told to grab something, but if it's your place, I guess that would be trespassing, so I'll leave."

Jones walked back to the street, and as I followed him, I saw a red and white pickup truck parked diagonally.

"Is that your truck?" I asked quickly.

"Nope," he retorted. "It's Adrian's. He left it at my place."

"When?" I asked, but Jones didn't answer.

Jones hopped in the pickup and drove off. I knew Satchel was going to be upset with me for going over to Adrian's house alone, but I had too much information to keep quiet. I hopped in my car and called her on the way back to Ciel. She wasn't as angry as I thought she would be. She took all the information down and told me she'd call me back later tonight. This entire case was becoming a big riddle.

I went back to the office, and there was a huge line at the front desk. Although Ndeeyah's stand-in was there, Warren was still working. I rushed to him to find out the cause of the backup. He said the computer system was down, and they couldn't tell which rooms were available or clean. There was a hair convention in town starting that Thursday, and many of the attendees were staying with us. These were the early comers. I walked down the line, apologizing to people and offering coupons for free drinks at Ciel. Warren gave me a confused look.

"What are you doing?" he whispered.

"Trying to appease the guests."

"But we don't own Ciel. They pay us rent to have the bar here. We can't take money from them."

"Soon we won't own anything, so does it really matter?"

Warren was more confused than before, and I realized I'd just let the cat out of the bag. He didn't know about the looming repossession, so I told him we needed to talk today before he left. It was only fair to let him know what was really going on. I went back to the office and checked my messages, but there was only one, and it was menacing.

"You and your sister better stop digging into my business, and tell her boyfriend to stop following me, or else." He didn't leave a name, but it was Adrian's voice. Once more, I called Satchel. However, she referred me to her assistant. She was prepping Shanice for trial and didn't have time to take in any more information. I told her assistant the time the message came in, and she recorded what he'd said. As soon as we hung up, Warren knocked on my door. He'd spoken with the computer techs, and the system would be running shortly. I nodded nonchalantly. He noticed my disturbed demeanor and, of course, asked about the source, but I didn't want to mention Adrian, so we spoke candidly about the bank repossession.

"How are you going to tell everyone?" he asked. I shrugged my shoulders and gave him a blank look. We both pondered that for a while, and then he said, "You could just be honest and say Carl left you with debt and you had no choice."

I'd thought of that, but I would rather people think I'd succumbed to pressure than know Carl had been in over his head. People had already been left with the memory that he was a liar and a cheat; there was no need to add this to his legacy. I still couldn't explain why I was being so loyal to my cheating, lying husband. True, I'd been completely in love with him, but it was more than that. I'd respected Carl, and I refused to believe that he'd been a horrible man. Maybe I was totally blind and naive, but all of my experiences with him had been respectable and caring. And so many people respected what he'd done for the community and how much he'd achieved. I just didn't want the hotel's potential failure to defame his name. Even if he'd been involved in something shady, we'd had enough black men taken down by the media. I refused for Carl to be one of them.

When I got to Ciel, I immediately went to speak

with Paula about what had happened two nights before. I told her it wasn't my fault, but she didn't care. She had the nerve to say she was going to write me up, but she didn't. Not that I cared either way, and I immediately went to work. A gun convention was in town, and most of the men were hunters, and hunters sure knew how to drink, and they liked easy drinks that didn't require lots of mixing and shaking. I knew I would make great tips tonight. I remembered that when the convention came to town last year, I made over a thousand in one weekend.

An hour into the night, the place was packed with beer-bellied sportsman, and the cash was flowing in. A tall gentleman with a very light blond beard walked up to me and smiled.

"You remember me?" he said.

I didn't recall his name, but his face looked familiar. "Should I?" I asked.

"I remember you," he said, smiling before removing his hat.

Suddenly, it came back to me. This was one of the hunters I'd met last year. He and I had got into a long debate about killing animals for sport. We'd agreed to disagree, but he'd ended up tipping me close to two hundred before the weekend was done. "Yes, I remember. You're the elk hunter."

"That's right, honey. Now give me a whiskey on the rocks."

I made his drink, and he sat down, but before we could strike up a conversation, in walked fine-ass Keith, who was not looking so fine these days. He came right up to me and tapped my arm.

"Here I am, trying to do you a favor, and you turn on me," Keith growled.

"How did you know I was in jail?" I asked.

"Oh, you're too pretty to be in jail," interrupted the elk hunter, whom I ignored.

Keith then responded. "I came to the bar, and Mei told me what happened. I went to the jail to see if I could help, because I knew Satchel was out of town. I posted your bail on my own."

I looked at him and then walked away to make another drink. Things got so busy, I never made it back to continue my conversation with Keith. Not that I wanted to. But when I saw him making nice with the elk hunter, I cut in.

"Keith, go home. You're getting drunk," I scolded.

"Then maybe I should stay here tonight," said Keith.

"Hell yeah!" replied his drunk companion. "Stay here with us. You stay, too, pretty lady." The elk hunter was getting a little too cozy. "Hey, you remember those things I gave you last year?"

"No, I have to go," I said.

"What things?" Keith asked. But before the elk hunter could continue, I pulled out Keith's chair and pulled him from the table.

"You need to stop following Adrian," I said.

"I'm not," Keith claimed.

Paula quickly called me back to the bar, and I went back to work before I could continue, but I gave Keith the eye to let him know I wasn't done talking. Keith lingered for a while, said a few things to the elk hunter, and then left. Since most of the hunters were staying in the hotel, they closed the place down. A few minutes before close, the elk hunter came back down to the bar.

This time he formally introduced himself, as if we hadn't ever spoken.

"My name is Hank. I live in Nebraska."

"Yes, Hank, we've met."

"I know we have, you pretty little thing. Where's that man?"

"What man?"

"The one with the bald head. Looked like Michael Jordan."

I began to laugh. White people thought every dark-skinned, bald-headed man in America looked like Michael Jordan. Light-skinned ones looked like Charles Barkley. It was hilarious.

"He left. Why?"

"He wanted me to show him something, but I guess I might see him tomorrow night."

"I hope not," I whispered under my breath.

Hank staggered back upstairs, and we closed another night. Mei and I walked to the garage together, and we finally got to talk. It had been so busy, we hadn't said four words to each other all night. I told her that I still hadn't heard from Cole, and she mentioned that I should press charges against Marley. She also revealed that my cootchie bid had closed out at $44,800. I was so stunned, I nearly tripped over my own feet. Then, unexpectedly, my phone rang.

"Who's calling you this time of night?" asked Mei.

"Probably Satchel," I replied.

I looked at the caller ID but didn't recognize the number.

"I'm not answering," I said, tossing the phone back in my purse. "You know who's been acting very creepy is fine-ass Keith Carson."

"He has been coming around more. What's that about?" Mei asked.

"Why did you tell him I got arrested?" I asked.

"I didn't," she said.

I gave her a confused look before responding. "But he said he came by the bar the other night, after the fight, and that you told him I was taken downtown. That's how he knew I was in jail."

"Before tonight, I hadn't seen Keith since last weekend."

"You sure?" I asked.

Mei nodded, gave me a hug, and got in her car. I sat in mine for a few minutes before pulling off. I was officially creeped out. How had Keith known I was in jail? When I was a few miles from home, my phone rang again. It was the same number, but this time I answered. It was Cole.

"Are you okay? I heard about what happened," he said.

"Why is your girlfriend crazy? She can't come to the house anymore."

"Marley and I broke up the day I went out of town. I couldn't be with her anymore."

"Why?" I asked, but he didn't respond. Honestly, I was glad he didn't. Any answer he gave would have been too much for me to digest at that moment. The hotel was going into foreclosure at the end of next week. I was going to have to appear in court on possession charges, Keith Carson was stalking me, and I had a forty-four-thousand-dollar date waiting to de-virginize me. It was just too much.

"We should talk when I get home tomorrow," said Cole.

"Cole, not now. I'm dealing with a lot."

"I'm here if you need me," he stated.

"I know. Get home safe." I quickly hung up the phone and drove home.

By the time, I walked in the door of my home, I could barely breathe. I felt like everything was closing in on me. My breaths became short, and I suddenly felt sick. I rushed to the toilet, but I couldn't vomit. Yet I felt as though food was stuck in my esophagus. I slumped over the toilet and eventually made my way to the tiled floor. I stripped down to my underwear. With my clammy face against the cool tiles, I lay on my bathroom floor, wearing only my white cotton panties and black dress socks. Finally, my pubic area had stopped hurting, and I remembered that being my last thought of the night. Then, with one hand still draped around the base of the toilet and one hand placed atop my hairless cootchie, I fell asleep.

Chapter 10

Deep Dark Secret

1 1/2 ounces dark rum
1/2 ounce anejo rum
1/2 ounce Kahlua coffee liqueur
1/2 ounce heavy cream

In a shaker half-filled with ice cubes, combine all of the ingredients. Shake well. Strain into a cocktail glass.

I felt one hiccup away from vomiting all that Sunday before Monday's foreclosure. I moped around the house until it was time for me to go to Ciel. However, when it was time for me to go, I couldn't get dressed. Though I had done nothing all day, I had no energy. I really wanted to make that money, but the desire to lounge was much more overwhelming than the desire to make money. Therefore, I called Paula and told her I wasn't coming in. Though I pretended not to care, the notion of actually losing the hotel was affecting me more than I'd thought. I did have a few interested investors, but I wasn't prepared with fancy presentations, and I felt like I'd gone about this whole thing wrong. This line of questioning made me wonder if I honestly wanted to save the hotel. Maybe I was looking for a cop-out. The notion of keeping the dream alive sounded good, but I didn't like long days or stress, which was why I had chosen the life of a bartender. I didn't have to wake before 1:00 p.m., and I made money by socializing with people. Funny, prostitutes probably said the same thing, which brought me to the other pain in my side. My bid had closed, and now I had to deal with the bidder, who was supposed to contact me any day now. It had seemed like such a game at first, but it was real, and I had to deal with the consequences.

I hadn't finished going through all of Carl's paperwork and the trial was beginning tomorrow, so I decided to go through his cell phone. I was going to call the people on the contact list and inform them of his death, just in case they didn't know. I made it through thirty-five numbers before quitting. Most of them had heard, but a few were shocked. I didn't ask people about their involvement with him. First, I didn't want to get into long-drawn-out conversations. Secondly, there were enough bones running around, and there was no room for any more skeletons. I briefly spoke with Satchel, who had spoken to Jones and to Keith by then. There was a subpoena out for Keith and Adrian to appear in court, and she needed to know Adrian's whereabouts. Jones said Adrian had left town because people were after him about money owed. Apparently, the insurance company hadn't paid up yet. Because this was a murder trial, and Adrian was affiliated with the main suspect, the insurance company wouldn't pay until the trial was over. Jones said he honestly didn't know where Adrian and Ndeeyah had fled to but that he would let Satchel know if he was contacted.

After I got off the phone with Satchel, I glanced at the time and saw that it was after nine o'clock. The urge to go to work hit me; therefore, I took an Alka-Seltzer, got dressed, and drove to Ciel. It was a reoccurrence of the night before. The bar was packed wall to wall with men of the wild. There were so many hunters there, the bar smelled like raw meat. I didn't see Paula when I first walked in, so I immediately jumped behind the bar, washed my hands, and began serving. Mei rushed by, grabbing lemons, and patted my bum.

"Some guy was looking for you," she said.

I acknowledged her while mixing a green appletini and kept working. As usual, the hours passed like minutes. I looked around for Hank, but he was nowhere in sight tonight. I assumed he went home. I did, however, see Keith lingering for a few minutes, but before we could make eye contact, he was gone. His behavior was becoming very odd. If Satchel had any notion of taking him back, she needed to forget about it. I started a conversation with the female convention attendee who was drinking that green appletini. Her name was Maria Sue. She was a former beauty queen, and during her reign, she'd realized she was in love with her runner-up. After several unsuccessful advances, she was exposed and dethroned. She sued the pageant for discrimination and won. With the money, she moved back home and expanded her daddy's gun shop in St. Louis. She now had the largest gun shop in the city. She was extremely feminine, and judging by her looks, one would never guess that she had this history. In a nutshell, this was why I loved bartending. Other than being a therapist, no job gave the 411 on average Joes like bartending.

Since the night was winding down, we were able to have some conversation. I shared a bit of my story, and she shared more of hers. I asked her how she could hunt animals for sport and if killing ever bothered her. She confessed that it used to but that she hunted only quail. She admitted that she'd gone deer hunting a few times but could never kill Bambi. We laughed as she broke down the rules of quail hunting. She could kill quail only between November 10 and December 20, but she could hunt them year-round, but not to kill. She explained the difference between a centerfire rifle, used to hunt big game, and a rimfire rifle, normally used for small game. Maria Sue worked best with a pump-action shotgun. That was what her daddy had trained her on. She was truly a country girl who loved her hunting. She said that when she first went elk hunting, she would use pellets, but after going on several elk hunting excursions, she learned that most of the time the elk were so injured by the pellets that they ended up dying or so weak that they were quickly killed by predators. Therefore, until she gave up elk hunting altogether, she went for the kill. She went in her purse and started pulling out ammunition. She had blanks, pellets, rubber bullets, hollow points, boat tails, jacketed bullets, and more.

I was so enthralled by the bullets, I stopped

making drinks. Maria Sue could tell by my expression that something had changed. I had started thinking about Carl, and my had mood sobered. I told her what happened to him. She expressed her condolences but then said something very interesting.

"Wax bullets are used for target practice. They shouldn't have killed him."

"Yeah, the real bullets after the wax ones killed him," I answered.

Maria Sue gave her condolences once more, and I wrapped up our conversation. We closed the bar that night at 1:00 a.m., and by 1:45 Mei and I were walking to our cars. All Mei wanted to talk about was when I was going to make plans to meet the winning bidder. Now that the excitement had climaxed, I was having serious regrets.

"Can I renege?" I asked.

Mei made a face and replied, "It's frowned upon."

"By who?" I asked. "If it's such a secret society, how are they going to frown upon me? How do you know about this again?"

"My cousin did it. And, there are several people I know back home that told her about it. They will call you and set everything up. Then your sponsor will fly here to meet you. The money is placed on hold in an account and is transferred the next day."

This whole thing sounded extremely ridiculous.

"How do you know so much about this?"

"Stop asking so many questions," Mei said. "If you don't do it, then I guess you just don't get the money, that's all.

"How can you talk about this so easily?" I asked.

Mei shrugged her shoulders, and we continued to walk to our cars. I felt like there was more to this story than she was letting on.

"Mei, why don't you come clean."

She turned around and yelled, "I know the woman who started the site. Okay! My grandma's friend's husband started this business. He was really into ancient cultures and believed that sleeping with virgins would add extra years to your life. That turned into a cult of men who wanted to sleep with virgins, and then when he died, his business was so lucrative, his wife kept it up."

I stood in the empty parking garage in silence as Mei continued.

"I was hoping I wouldn't have to explain, but my cousin runs the business with her."

My silence was coupled with an openmouthed stare. Finally, I spoke. "So you're from a family of pimps." Mei became upset.

"You don't understand. Women in my culture rarely get to run successful businesses or companies that they can call their own. When my grandma's friend took over her husband's business, his brothers tried their best to take it over. My cousin helped her save it. They are like what you would consider Mafia princesses. It may sound crazy to you, but them running this business is a big thing. I never thought about getting involved until you needed this money. I really thought I was helping."

"So now you want to be junior Mafia?" I laughed. "Why didn't you just tell me?"

"Because I knew you wouldn't understand. As long as you thought this secret man society was running it, everything was cool. But now you're laughing. Fine. Fuck it!"

Mei stormed away. I walked behind her and tried to make amends. "I'm sorry. It just sounded better as some secret society. It's different knowing my friend is trying to pimp me," I said.

Mei whipped around and let me have it. "I am the first generation to even be able to go to school. My family was *really* poor, beyond your knowledge. When my father died, my cousin fed her family and our family off this business. Hell, you had an opportunity to run this hotel and turn it into something, and you squandered it. You will not stand here and judge me when I have the opportunity to keep further generations eating." Mei stormed off once more. Again, I rushed behind her.

"So you'll make money off this, too?"

"Yeah. So what?"

"I'm not judging you, but shit, Mei, you're trying to eat off my cootchie. You should have at least told me. You're a Chinese pimp," I said. "You're a chimp."

"Your mamma's a chimp," Mei retorted.

Forgetting for a second that Mei was Chinese, I almost slapped her across the parking garage. I had to tell her.

"You can never mention primates and black people in the same sentence. That will automatically qualify you for a beat down." Mei didn't understand, but she saw I was serious, so she stopped smiling and nodded okay.

Suddenly, we both stopped in our tracks as we approached my car. Marley was parked next to me. She was outside the car, leaning against the driver's door. I looked around the empty garage

and called out, "Maria Sue! I need you." Hell, elk
had to run twice as fast as any other animal. One
shot could surely take ol' Marley down.

Mei gave a confused look, which I simply dis-
regarded, and then Marley spoke.

"We need to talk. I feel bad."

Mei yelled out, "Look here, bitch. If you start
up tonight, you will get your ass kicked. I'm not
in the mood."

Marley started approaching us. "I don't want
to start anything. I want to apologize."

Mei and I stood still and listened. Though
Marley wanted to talk to me alone, I didn't feel
comfortable. The entire situation felt like a setup.
I told Mei to stay as Marley began explaining.

"I was drunk the other night, and I'm sorry
you got arrested."

Marley started crying, and Mei started up.

"Boo hoo, bitch, boo hoo. Because of you, she
has to go to court for possession."

"I didn't know she had weed on her," Marley
answered. "I didn't think you smoked," she said,
turning to me.

"Long story," I replied.

Marley continued. "I was only supposed to
start something with you and then press charges
when you retaliated and then drop them."

"What do you mean, you were supposed to?"
I quizzed.

Marley grew quiet, but Mei and I forced her to
speak. "Keith paid me to pick a fight with you,"
she confessed.

"What?" I said.

"I've known Keith for a few years, and we talk,"
Marley explained. "I was complaining about Cole

and telling him about us breaking up. Keith told me that you and Cole were messing around and that I should get back at you. He said that if I started a fight and had you arrested, it would be funny. We were hanging out, drinking, and he convinced me to do it. It was supposed to be a joke. But the weed—"

"That shit is not funny. I may have to do time," I yelled.

"Girl, it was weed, not coke," Mei countered. "But that's not the point. Why would you do that, Marley?"

Marley shrugged her shoulders and said she'd been hurt, and that she hadn't been thinking straight. However, she had spoken with Cole, and she believed that he hadn't cheated on her. "Izzy, I know you wouldn't do something like that. Again, I'm sorry." Marley turned and walked away, leaving Mei and me baffled. Before Marley could get to her car, I called out to her.

"How do you know Keith?"

Marley turned and replied, "He's the cop that solved my cousin's murder. After that, we just became friends." Marley got in her Miata and drove off. Mei and I stared at each other.

"Why in the hell would Keith do that?" I said to her.

She shrugged her shoulders and responded, "Are you going to sleep with the winning bidder or what?"

I had to get away from Mei immediately, but I didn't want to go home and face Cole. Therefore, I drove around the city for an hour.

"I have to get more friends," I said, pulling into my parking lot. I braced myself for a conversation; however, when I walked in, Cole was asleep on the couch. I watched him sleep for a couple of seconds. Something told me to keep walking, but I didn't. I knew I watched him too long, and before I could leave the room, he opened his eyes and reached for my hand. I cuddled up beside him and placed my head on his shoulder. Cole caressed my arm. We didn't say anything to each other that evening, and eventually, he fell back asleep. I left him on the couch and went to bed.

Early Tuesday morning, before the trial started, I called Satchel. I told her all about Keith, and she was beyond livid, but opening statements were today, so she couldn't talk to him about it. She needed time to get her game plan together. She told me not to say anything to Keith. I promised, hung up, and got ready to meet her at the courthouse. I didn't want to be there for the trial, but Satchel had insisted that the widow had to be there. It would look terrible if I didn't show up. Of course, it was already confusing that Satchel's firm was handling the case, but I had to support my sister. She'd prepped me on everything, from how to dress to where to rest my gaze. She warned me not to look at the jury, because they'd be eyeing me for looks of remorse or revenge.

On my way to court, I received a call from a woman, who informed me that my bidder had made contact and wanted to meet me this Friday.

I was going to receive an e-mail with instructions to go to the doctor on Wednesday, where I would get an exam. A follow-up e-mail would have all the banking information and instructions on where we were to meet. I still couldn't believe this was actually happening.

I arrived in court and sat in the back, on the defendant's side. As the widow of the deceased, I was doing a rare thing; I should have been on the state's side, as they were the plaintiff. But since my sister was defending Shanice, we didn't want the jury to think we were divided in our opinion. By now, I was fully convinced that Adrian had exchanged the bullets. I was only hoping Satchel could work miracles. Each lawyer gave an opening statement. But immediately after the trial started, the state claimed that they had new evidence to bring forth, and Satchel asked for a twenty-four-hour continuance to review the new evidence. The judge allowed it, and the court adjourned. I quickly left before Satchel rapped with Shanice. I put on my shades, breezed past reporters, and made it to the Shelby in twenty minutes.

As I walked in, I couldn't believe that it was all soon to be over. I stood in the center of the lobby and looked around. Could this be the end of the Shelby legacy? Had I squandered my opportunity to save this hotel, like Mei said? I glanced at the granite floor. The centerpiece was etched with the hotel's logo, which was the original sketch made by Carl's dad. Something I would have never known had I not rambled through Carl's safe. I had lost focus of what was important. Now the hotel was almost gone, and I was probably going to be out of a job. Sure, I could bartend anywhere, but I loved Ciel. Just then Satchel's distinctive ring came blaring through my purse. Quickly, I picked up as I walked toward the office suites.

"Where are you?" she asked.

"At the hotel."

"I'm on the way." Satchel hung up, leaving me wondering her about urgent tone.

Exactly thirty minutes later, Satchel was storming into my office. She threw a folder on my desk, which contained a letter.

"Why didn't you tell me you had wax bullets in your possession?"

I was dumbfounded. "What?"

"Some hunter named Hank gave you wax bullets last year," she yelled.

"I forgot."

"You forgot! How could you forget? This whole case has been about wax bullets versus real bullets. How could you forget you had been in possession of wax bullets!"

"I don't know," I told her.

"Well, you better come up with something, because you are going to be called to the stand."

"What? Why is this happening?"

"It's happening because Keith Carson found out about your wax bullets, and he works for the state. He thinks you and Shanice were in this together, and now that's what they are planning to prove. They also motioned that I be thrown out as lead counsel because with you now as a possible accessory, it's a definite conflict of interest."

The room began to spin as Satchel walked over to the window and gazed out at the city. After a few seconds of silence, she turned around and shouted, "I can't believe you forgot!"

"I'm sorry," I whined. "I only had them a couple of days, and then I cleaned out my purse, and—"

"And what?"

"I don't remember what I did with them. I think I gave them to Carl, or I might have thrown them out."

Satchel opened the folder and pulled out a blue bullet. "Did they look like this?"

I took the bullet and inspected it. "I think so."

My sister's tone turned more grave. "Isabelle, this is the same type and color wax found on Carl's body."

"How did Keith know about any of this?"

"Your ol' buddy Hank told him. When I took Shanice's case, Keith got suspicions about you. He's been following you since. He needed your fingerprints to match against the gun but didn't have a warrant or any substantial evidence to get them. When you got arrested, they just took your fingerprints. Luckily, your prints didn't match any in Shanice's room or on the gun, but then, when Keith secured this letter from Hank, along with more bullets, it was enough."

I looked at the letter Hank had written and read it.

Hope you made good use of the bullets I gave you last year. Here's a few more. Thanks for the pretty smile and the good alcohol. Happy elk hunting. Hank

I looked up at Satchel, who had a distinct look of fear in her eyes. Her expression frightened me. I hadn't seen fear in Satchel since we were kids and she was about to get a spanking. "But I didn't do anything. I didn't even know about Shanice," I told her.

"I pray you can convince twelve of your peers. Robert, assistant counsel, is going to call you in a few. He's taking my place. You have to start prepping your cross-examination with him. They're not calling you tomorrow, but they will call you the next day. Adrian is back in town, and he's taking the stand tomorrow. Do not have any more contact with Adrian or Keith. This is serious, Isabelle. I can only help you so much."

"But—"

"No buts. And, you still cannot mention that you went to Shanice and asked for money. Luckily, we have witnesses that saw her ask me for my card the morning of your wedding. She called me on her own, and after hearing her side, I decided to take the case. I have to go."

Satchel exited briskly. My heart began racing. I didn't know who was guilty, but I knew it wasn't me. Suddenly, I started thinking maybe Shanice had set this whole thing up, and that she and Keith were in on it together. Perhaps, Shanice, Keith, and Adrian were all in on it.

Satchel's office was now in complete chaos. They had everything set up to blame Adrian, but now that I was on the chopping block, they had to prove my innocence before pointing the guilty finger at him. Moments after Satchel left, my cell phone rang. I didn't recognize the out-of-state number but assumed it was the cell of one of Satchel's law assistants. However, it was an old friend of Carl's. He'd gotten my message about Carl's death and was stunned. He'd been out of the country and hadn't heard from Carl in a couple months, but he'd assumed Carol was busy with the new marriage. He knew all about me and said Carl had talked to him at length about us. He was a friend of Carl's dad and said he'd known Carl all his life. He seemed distraught over his death. After he got my call, he decided to come to town, and he wanted to meet me. He said he'd be here all week, and so I promised to call him back, but I couldn't say when. Of course, he was staying at the Shelby.

Robert called me an hour later, and I went to Satchel's office and was there until midnight. We went back and forth with possible questions and how I should answer. I recounted my story over and over. But even as I heard it, I knew how crazy it sounded. My husband had had a lover for four years, whom I hadn't known about. His lover, who knew about me, had shot him in the groin with wax bullets that I had once had in my possession. Now my sister was trying to get her off. It sounded just as the state was claiming: Shanice and I had been in it together. Now, if Satchel's legal team pursued the argument that someone else had changed the bullets, all the fingers would point at me, and the state would argue that I had acted on my own after I'd found out about the affair. I was up shit's creek if Satchel's legal team couldn't prove that I had known nothing about Shanice. Adrian, who had once been public enemy number one, could be my savior. He knew that I had had no idea about Shanice. Question was, would he tell the truth?

Chapter 11

Trial of the Century

1/2 ounce Jagermeister herbal liqueur
1/2 ounce Goldschlager cinnamon schnapps
1/4 ounce grenadine syrup

Layer the ingredients in a shot glass, and serve.

Last week Warren and I had drawn up a letter providing information about the hotel changing owners. I still didn't want to alarm everyone that the hotel would be closing, but we'd decided that if nothing came through by Monday, we would give everyone letters. Unfortunately, there was no money to give anyone severance, and now I felt like the horrible businesswoman. To make matters worse, I couldn't give the Shelby any attention; my life was on trial, and if I didn't get out of this hot water, the hotel would not matter.

I was so nervous by the time I arrived in court that I was sick. Literally. I had to rush to the bathroom as soon as I entered the building. I had a headache, diarrhea, and cold sweats. Although, I wasn't on trial today, my reputation was. The defense called Warren to the stand first. He testified about the hotel's debt, and the fact that Carl had often paid Adrian's gambling debts, and if Adrian's debts weren't paid, people often looked to Carl to pay them. This conclusion to be drawn was that other people, including Adrian, could have benefited from Carl's death. Of course, the state cross-examined and asked questions about Shanice and Carl's affair. Warren admitted that it had been torrid and that Carl had wanted to end it before he got married. The state also asked if people had known about the affair. Warren said a few people had known, but then threw in that I absolutely had not known. I could feel the jury looking at me, but the prepping about where I would rest my gaze didn't matter anymore. I was in a trance. My mind was unreadable.

Adrian took the stand right after Warren. Satchel had no solid evidence that Adrian was responsible for Carl's death. She had proof that Shanice had bought wax bullets, but of course, the state's attorneys argued that she had purchased them to establish her innocence. Satchel's legal team tried to use the fact that Shanice hadn't run once she shot Carl, because she was convinced that she had not harmed him. However, the state combated that with the fact she could have used this to prove her innocence as well. Satchel had no solid proof that Adrian had been stealing and that Keith had been hired to follow him. But again Keith said that no such evidence had been found, and Satchel still couldn't prove that Carl hadn't known about those bank accounts.

After Adrian was sworn in, Robert, now head counsel, began his questioning. Adrian admitted to the gambling and debt but said that Carl had always helped him and that he had had no reason to harm his brother. Adrian also admitted that he had known about Shanice, that she had come to him with her plan, that he hadn't thought she was serious, but that he had mentioned it to Keith just in case.

Obviously, this was the first time the state heard that Keith had known about Shanice's plan. They called for a conference at the judge's table. After a few minutes, the questioning of Adrian continued. If Adrian came clean about the bribes, Keith could be a possible suspect. I saw Satchel furiously writing notes and passing them to Robert and the other counsel at the table. Robert asked Adrian why he hadn't told his brother about Shanice's plan. He admitted that he'd tried but that his brother hadn't wanted to hear it.

"What is your definition of *tried?*" asked Robert.

"I told him that Shanice was crazy and that she was not going to let him marry Isabelle without a fight. When I was about to tell him the details, he fired me," said Adrian.

"For what?" asked Robert.

"He thought I was stealing money, but the truth is—"

"That's all," interrupted Robert.

In the cross-examination, the state's attorneys put all their energy into proving that Shanice had wanted Carl dead and that she had had the opportunity and the perfect motive. They asked Adrian if Shanice had ever mentioned killing Carl.

"A few times, but she was joking," Adrian said.

Shanice went ballistic. She was almost thrown out of court. The judge warned her that if she made one more outburst, she would be in contempt. Adrian said that Shanice had been completely jealous about my relationship with Carl, and that she had been determined that if she couldn't have him, no one would.

"Do you believe Shanice Franklin went to that room with the intention to kill your brother, Carlton Trace?" one of the state's lawyers asked.

Robert quickly objected on the grounds of speculation. However, it was overruled. Adrian answered.

"I believe Shanice wanted my brother dead." There was such detestation in his stare.

Shanice lost it. She jumped up again, yelling obscenities at Adrian and swearing he'd been in on it. She said he'd given her the gun, and that he was always talking about getting rid of Carl. The guards hastily escorted her from the courtroom. Satchel quietly bowed her head. Once things simmered down, my name came into play. The state asked Adrian if he'd ever seen me in the vicinity of Carl while Carl was with Shanice. Adrian admitted that Carl had been very covert when it came to his affair. He also said that he'd been with Jones the entire day of the shooting. However, he also threw in a bit of information that no one knew about except Shanice and Carl.

"Carl told me that Shanice rear-ended him once while Isabelle was in the car. She threatened to expose him then if he didn't end it with Isabelle."

My mouth dropped open, and my mind went back to the accident that day. I couldn't believe I'd been that close to finding out. I knew Carl's behavior had seemed odd. Why didn't I question it?

"Is there a possibility that Isabelle Trotter, the wife of the deceased, knew about Shanice Franklin?" asked one of the state's attorneys.

Robert objected again on speculation. This time it was sustained. So, the state rephrased the question.

"Did Carl ever mention that he suspected Isabelle knew about his lover?"

Adrian looked at me. I had no idea what he was about to say. He paused, took a couple of deep breaths. His ten-second break in testimony seemed to last an hour. Finally, he spoke.

"According to Carl, Isabelle was completely clueless."

He made me sound like a complete idiot, yet that one statement might have saved my life.

Robert countered with one last question. "At the time of Carl's death, weren't you under the impression that the Shelby Hotel and Carl's insurance money would go to you?"

"I was."

"No further questions," said Robert.

That was the end of the day one.

Satchel was furious that Shanice had never mentioned the Jag incident and that she'd showed her temper in court. Shanice was supposed to testify, but after this flare-up, I wasn't sure what Satchel was going to do. She could single-handedly lose this case with her testimony.

It was 5:00 p.m., but I had to go to the Shelby and deal with the dozens of questions about the closing. Warren had scheduled a meeting for seven that evening, and everyone who could was to attend. But as soon as I stepped into the building, three people simultaneously came rushing up to me. They were all speaking so fast, I could hardly hear what they were saying. Warren was handing me a letter, a front-desk clerk was saying there were people in my office, and another front-desk clerk was making me aware that Mei was also looking for me. I rushed through the hail of questions and made it to my office. I opened the door and quickly shut it behind me. I locked the door and took the phone off the hook. There was no severance; there was nothing. I was about to put one hundred people out of work. I couldn't stop the tears from falling. Just then Warren knocked on my door.

"Not right now," I called out. He insisted it was important and wouldn't leave. I opened the door, and Warren stood there with a handsome man who looked to be in his early sixties. He introduced himself as Peyton Jones Jr. He was Carl's visiting friend. This man had to be at least twenty-five years Carl's senior, but once he explained the relationship, it made sense. Peyton had been Walter's best friend; therefore, he was like an uncle to Carl and Adrian. When Carl's father died, he became a surrogate. He and Carl had talked about everything a father and son would discuss. I told Peyton I didn't have time to chat, for I had a meeting that I had to prep for, but he wanted to let me know how much Carl had loved me. Carl had sent Peyton a few e-mails about our relationship, and Peyton revealed that when Carl had referred to me, he'd said, "God has delivered me an angel in the form of a bartender."

Normally, a sentimental statement like that would have made me cry, but my romantic senses were long gone. It was great to know Carl had loved me, but the mess he'd left me with had overruled his admiration.

"It was nice meeting you, and thanks for the e-mails," I said, trying to get rid of the old man. However, he wasn't so quick to go. He walked around the office, looking at pictures and awards.

"Did you know this hotel was Walter's idea?" he asked.

"Yes, I found sketches Walter did."

"Did you know Adrian and Carl were half brothers?"

"Yes, I did."

"Seems you know much. Walter was a brilliant entrepreneur but a bad husband. He had many affairs up until his death. Marge threatened to leave but never did. Carl and Adrian both knew, but Carl idolized his father." Peyton continued to stroll around the office. "Affairs aside, he could do no wrong in that boy's eyes. I'm not justifying any of Carl's behavior, but maybe that gives you some understanding."

I nodded quietly. This was great information, but this conversation was happening all at the wrong time. "I know Carl loved me, in his own way," I told him.

"Do you know his son?"

"Huh?"

"Oh, I guess he didn't tell you that."

Here was another damn skeleton; this hotel had officially become a cemetery. Warren popped his head in the door. "Everyone is starting to gather downstairs," he said.

"I'll let you go," said Peyton.

"Can we meet tonight at Ciel? It's the bar down-stairs," I said.

"I'm in room six sixteen. Call me," said Peyton. He nodded to Warren and walked out.

"You okay?" Warren said, noticing my thunder-struck expression.

I simply shook my head, grabbed a folder from my desk, and moved like a zombie down the hall.

As expected, the staff wasn't pleased when I told them about the hotel closing and the lack of severance. People ranted about it being poor business ethics, and many said Carl would have never treated his employees like this. Many called me names and said that I should go back to making drinks and leave the hotel business for the professionals. Warren became irate; he got to the podium and spoke his piece. Against my better judgment, he told them that I was in the position that I was in because of Carl, that it wasn't my fault, and that I'd done everything I could to keep this from happening. The staff didn't care. Again, I apologized and then left the conference room. I was sad that it was coming to this, but I still had two very important pending issues: my day in court and this supposed son.

After the meeting, I probably should have left the building, but I hadn't spoken to Peyton yet. Therefore, I called his room and told him to meet me at Ciel. I figured we could go some-where and have a late snack.

I walked down to Ciel and spoke to Mei, who seemed to have an attitude. I assumed it had everything to do with the fact that I hadn't given her an exact answer about the winning bidder. I walked up and gave her a bear hug from behind.

"You don't have to do it. I don't even know how you're still holding up with the trial and everything," Mei whispered.

"Mei, I'm sorry. I can't even think about it right now. But, after the trial, I mean . . . Shit, I'm really going to need that money."

I couldn't believe my own words. So much had changed within the last months. I'd changed. I realized that those who played fair in life and lived by the rules finished last. I was tired of finishing last. Maybe if I hadn't been a virgin, Carl wouldn't have kept cheating. Maybe if I did this stupid auction thing, it would put me ahead of the game this time. Surprisingly, it was no longer about the virginity; it was now about the *come up*. Like I said, I'd changed, and being a virgin didn't seem precious anymore. Though I wasn't working, I walked behind the bar and poured myself a Coke while I waited for Peyton. I hadn't called and told Satchel about Carl's child because I honestly felt like Peyton had made a mistake.

It took Peyton twenty minutes to get to the bar, but once he came down, we quickly exited and went to a quiet café around the corner. I chose not to waste time. Right after Peyton ordered a plate of hummus, I started in.

"You said Carl had a son. Please explain," I asked.

"Not much to explain. He met a woman some years ago, and they had a child."

"Where is he? Where is she? How come he never said anything?" I was oozing with questions.

"I'm really not sure where they live."

"Carl never mentioned having a son."

"He never mentioned having a girlfriend, either," Peyton replied.

"Good point," I retorted.

"If anything ever happened to Carl, he wanted to make sure his son was taken care of. Carl took an additional insurance policy out on himself and made me the beneficiary. That money was to go to his son."

"How much was the policy?"

"Five hundred thousand dollars."

I was silenced. I didn't know if Peyton knew about all the trouble the hotel was in, but he was about to find out. I gave him the details about everything, from Adrian's gambling to the bank lien on the property. Peyton had had no idea about Carl's debt. He said Carl wouldn't have told him. "He told me things were smooth sailing."

"Yeah, smooth sailing down the river." I became quiet as I finished my food. Peyton knew what I was thinking.

"I have a few investments here and there, but I'm not a rich man. I would love to help you, but I made a promise. I can't give you this money."

"I know," I murmured. "So you're just going to hand over five hundred thousand dollars to some stranger?" I asked.

"No, the money goes into an escrow account, and the son gets it when he's eighteen. But I have to contact his mom to let him know."

That was a lot of money, and normally, it would have made the mother a suspect in a murder case, but since she couldn't touch the money, I guessed there had been no reason for her to hurt Carl.

"Do you have her phone number?"

"No, they shared a PO box. I will just mail all the bank information there."

"So was he in his son's life at all?"

"I don't think so."

That seemed so unlike Carl. He'd told me he loved children and that he wanted to have at least three. It didn't make sense.

"I want to meet him."

"Now, don't go stirring things up. If Carl had wanted you to know he had a son, he'd have told you. My instructions were clear, and they didn't involve you. I'm sorry."

The server left the ticket on the table; Peyton pulled out his wallet and paid. It was quiet as we rode back to the hotel. Before we parted, I asked Peyton one more question.

"Why didn't Carl leave the hotel to his son?"

"Because he left it to his wife, with whom he was supposed to bear other children. He and the woman did not have a good relationship. Leave it alone." Peyton gave me an assertive nod and walked across the lobby to the elevators.

I immediately called Satchel, who was with Shanice, preparing her for court. I quickly gave her the information about Carl's son, but she didn't have time to digest it. She did agree to ask Shanice if she knew anything about it and told me to make sure I was ready for court in the morning. Therefore, I went home and went over my notes for court. I pulled out my notepad, and reviewed the possible state questions and my responses. I was extremely nervous, although I hadn't done anything wrong. Thankfully, Cole was still at Ciel. We hadn't seen each other much lately, which was good. Things were still a little awkward between us, and every time we were alone, he wanted to talk about it. He looked at me differently now, and I didn't know why it was affecting me, since it never had before, but it had to be something about that kiss. Either way, I wasn't ready to deal with Cole.

I took my shower, and while I was drying off, Satchel called. She said Shanice didn't know anything about Carl's son and doubted very seriously that he had one. I found it hard to believe that Peyton would create an imaginary son. But five hundred thousand was a lot of money, and maybe Peyton was supposed to do something else with it and was using the son as an excuse to keep it for himself. He had appeared out of nowhere. Where had he been all the time Carl was alive? He had added more extraneous pieces to this wicked little puzzle.

The next morning I arrived at the courthouse at eight o'clock; the hearing began at nine. I spent that extra hour in a back room with Satchel and Robert, doing one last review. Satchel could tell my mind wasn't on the trial, and she continually snapped her fingers in my face to bring me back to the situation at hand.

"You have to be alert, Izzy. They are going to make you look guilty," she said.

"I know. I know," I bellowed.

We wrapped at 8:40 and were in the court-room at ten minutes before nine. I was a nervous wreck. I was the first person to be called up. I stood there with my right hand on the Bible and repeated what the bailiff said. By now I was tense. I had a pain shooting down my back and a pulsating headache. Robert walked up and handed me a glass of water before starting. I had to state my name, my connection to the deceased, and particulars of our relationship. I told them how long Carl and I had dated, when we got engaged, and when we got married.

"Mrs. Trace, it's been said that your husband had a mistress the entire time he knew you. Were you not aware of this?" asked Robert.

"Of course not," I responded as planned. "If I had known about a mistress, I would never have married Carl."

"Did you trust your husband?" Robert quizzed.

"Yes. He never gave me any reason not to trust him."

I was then asked about Carl, my taking over the Shelby, and what I stood to gain from his death. I mentioned that I hadn't known that Carl was leaving me the Shelby until after his death, and I had thought Adrian would get the hotel. I hadn't known of any insurance policies listing me as the beneficiary, and the only thing I'd been aware that I would receive was his home. This took away any motive I might have had for killing Carl, but there was still this lingering notion that I had known about Shanice and had killed Carl out of revenge, and it was the state's turn to make this assumption more of a reality. The prosecutor stood, then paced back and forth in front of me a few times before speaking.

"You're telling this court that you dated Carlton

Trace for nineteen months, worked closely with him at the Shelby, and never heard about his affair with Shanice Franklin."

"That is correct."

"I find that hard to believe when we have witnesses that will testify that Shanice was in and out of the bar in which you work on several occasions."

Robert objected on the premise that these witnesses had not testified. It was sustained. The DA continued.

"Shanice was in Carl's home, in his car, and stayed at the Shelby, according to her recorded statement. You never saw her?"

"If I did see her, I was unaware of who she was, and I just became aware of an incident in which I did come face-to-face with her. It was during a car accident. However, I thought she was a stranger."

"Where were you the night of the shooting?"

"I was at my home, waiting for Carl."

"Were you there alone?"

"Yes," I stated.

"However, Shanice Franklin claims that she loaded the gun that morning and left it in a room at the Shelby all day. She returned to the hotel that evening, which would have given you ample time to go to the hotel room, change the bullets in the gun, and go home without anyone noticing."

"Objection, leading the witness," Robert shouted.

"Sustained," said the judge.

"Where were you after you and Carl left the courthouse the morning of the shooting?" asked the DA.

"I went to Ciel for a celebration, then went out

to eat with my friends while Carl took care of hotel business," I replied.

Just then the DA switched tactics. "Were you in possession of the same type of wax bullets that were used to kill Carlton Trace?"

"I was," I answered, with a staid tone. From the neck up, I was calm and collected, but below that bench, my legs were quivering.

"Why did you have these bullets? Are you a hunter?"

I explained why I had had the bullets, bringing in Hank and our elk-hunting conversation. I stated that I had given the bullets to Carl and didn't think about them anymore. I also put in that I'd forgotten about the bullets until the hunting convention this past weekend, when Hank dropped by Ciel. Of course, the prosecutor stated that it was hard to swallow that I had had wax bullets in my possession and that the accused murderer had used that type of bullet to shoot my husband. I followed his statement with, "I gave the bullets to Carl, and Shanice could have very well gotten them from his house."

However, the DA threw in a question that I hadn't planned. "Do you believe that Shanice Franklin intended to kill your husband?"

I glanced at Satchel, who refused to give me eye contact. I was on my own to answer a question about which I was undecided. "I believe that Shanice orchestrated a very poor joke to expose my husband. I believe the joke spiraled out of control."

I could see the corners of Satchel's mouth turn upward slightly. I'd answered the question well.

"Now, knowing about his infidelity, do you believe your husband deserved to die?"

"Absolutely not."

The DA finished his accusations, and Robert stood and asked me my last question. "Isabelle Trace, did you have anything to do with the murder of your husband, Carl Trace?"

"No, I did not."

That was it. I was asked to step down. Judging by Satchel's expression, it had gone perfectly. There was a slim chance that they could link me to Carl's murder, but it was slim enough that my anxious energy dissipated. During the remainder of the day, two more witnesses testified, including the psychiatric doctor that had interviewed Shanice right after she was booked. He stated that Shanice seemed to have been in her right mind and well aware of what she had was doing when she shot Carl. He maintained that she had sincerely thought the bullets were wax and that they wouldn't harm Carl. Though intent held some weight, Shanice was still the person behind the gun.

On the fourth day, Shanice took the stand. She didn't change her story. She admitted to buying the wax bullets and said that she and Adrian had loaded them in the gun. She gave a very tearful explanation of what had been going on in her mind that evening. She swore that she'd never meant to kill Carl, and that she'd even done research on wax bullets and knew that they wouldn't hurt him. She only wanted to cause a scene and have it reported. Then Carl would have to admit to me that he'd been having an affair. The defense questioned her.

"Why didn't you just go to Ms. Trotter and tell her about your affair?"

"I wanted *him* to tell her. I wanted him to admit what he'd been doing." Shanice broke down. "I loved him," she said over and over. "If I'd told Isabelle, Carl would have denied it."

She admitted that only a couple of people had known about their affair, and that Carl had gone out of his way to make sure I never knew. She confessed that her first conversation with me had taken place after she'd shot Carl. This made me look great, but it didn't help her at all.

That night Satchel had a long talk with Shanice about her plea. If Shanice would change her plea from not guilty to guilty, the prosecutor would agree to change her charges from premeditated murder to accidental homicide. Satchel told her to take the plea. Normally, my sister never bargained, but with all the evidence pointing to Shanice, she really didn't have a choice. Her client was going down for murder; all she could do now was hope for a lighter sentence. Shanice refused to agree. She felt that pleading guilty would send the message that she had meant without a doubt to kill Carl. She wanted to maintain her innocence to the end. We would have to wait to see what the jury decided.

I was three days from the hotel's repossession, and unfortunately, I'd had only two offers for Carl's home, and neither had gone through. It just wasn't a great market for high-end homes at the time. Mei suggested I just move into Carl's home, but it still gave me the chills. Plus, if I was to ever start over, I would feel weird living my life with another man in that house. I went to the hotel and started packing up Carl's office. Warren had started packing two days before, and his office was just about clean. I couldn't believe it was ending like this. I hoped that someone would buy the property and keep it as a hotel; at least this way the beauty of the building wouldn't go to waste. Either way, it was depressing.

I went to Ciel to talk to Mei and ran into Peyton while he was checking out. There was still something very peculiar related to him. I couldn't help but wonder why there was nothing about him in any of Carl's personal items, no pictures, no memories, nothing. I walked up to him and said my good-byes. He apologized for everything and promised to see what he could do about the hotel. I told him thanks, but I really thought it was too late. He winked and said, "It's never too late."

I waited with him outside until his taxi arrived. Peyton gave me all his information and told me to call if I ever needed to talk. He never explained why he had come to town, and I didn't buy his story that he had just shown up to say his good-byes. Carl was already gone. Who was he saying good-bye to?

That evening I perused the phone book and jotted down the name of every place in the city that had PO boxes. There was a total of thirty-two. I was going to call each and every one to see if I could find any boxes belonging to Carl. I pulled out Carl's folder of bills once more, and with Cole's help, I went through invoices and receipts dating back twelve months. Cole stumbled upon a receipt from Mail Boxes Etc. for $122.00.

That was where I would start my search. I'd found over sixty keys, on eight key rings, in Carl's house. There were ten keys that looked like they belonged to a PO box. It was worth a try.

Therefore, the next morning I went to the Mail Boxes Etc. located in Midtown and asked the woman behind the counter to research the account of Carl Trace. I was in luck. Carl had leased a PO box from them twelve months ago, and the bill was actually due. She said that his name was the only one on the box, but two keys had been issued. I told her I was Carl's widow and asked if anyone else had dropped by to inquire about the box. She had no idea.

"People come and go. They don't check with us," she responded.

I understood. I checked the box, but there was nothing in it. However, as luck would have it, when I was sitting in the parking lot, making a few phone calls, I saw Adrian. He was walking into Mail Boxes Etc. I got out of my car and peered from behind a car closer to the store's window. I saw him go in the vicinity of Carl's box, but I couldn't tell if it was the same one. It was too much of a coincidence. I was convinced that Adrian, and possibly Peyton, had something to do with the insurance policy involving Carl's supposed son. I walked from behind the car and ran into Adrian as though by chance. We spoke, but I could tell he wasn't pleased to see me. He seemed jittery.

"Hey, Adrian. What are you doing on this side of town?" I asked.

"Picking up some mail," he said as he continued to walk.

"Me, too. Carl has a PO box here."

"Okay," Adrian said, as though he had nothing to do with that. He didn't have any mail in his hand. He only slowed his stride but never came to a full halt. I watched him get in his car and leave. I was so deep in thought, that my cell phone ring startled me. It was someone from the virgin bidder Web site. I made up an excuse for why I couldn't talk and asked them to call back.

I had to call Satchel and tell her about the PO box and Adrian. I figured I needed to tell her about the virgin Web site as well. I could tell she was still distracted about the case, because the final day of the trial was that coming Monday, and she felt that Adrian was guilty, but she couldn't prove a thing. Just as we were about to hang up, I mentioned the online auction.

"So, there's this thing . . . more like a society. It's a society that has a thing for virgins." Satchel was silent. "It's a group of men that bid money to have sex with virgins," I said rapidly. She remained silent. "They bid on me, and my price got up to forty-four thousand." Satchel then cracked up laughing.

"Okay, you wanted me to laugh, and you finally did it." Satchel chuckled a few more times and tried to hang up.

"I'm serious, Chully. I have a doctor's appointment tomorrow to have everything checked out. I think I'm going through with it."

Satchel didn't believe me, and there was no way to prove it to her except to show her my bank account balance in a few weeks. Satchel kept trying to say something, but it was like she didn't know how to form the right words. It took nearly five minutes for her to speak.

"You know that's prostitution, right?"

"The correct term is pandering," I countered.

"Correct this! I'm not representing your ass if you get caught."

"Yes, you will," I murmured.

Satchel was quiet another couple of minutes and finally ended the conversation with, "You're full of shit."

That was it. She hung up. It was a hard pill to swallow. If I weren't going through it, I wouldn't have believed it, either. But I knew my sister well. She just needed time to digest the information; she was going to call me back within the next twenty-four hours and would let me know just how she felt about the situation.

I went back to the house to prepare for my day. We were still cleaning things up at the hotel but were no longer taking reservations, so the staff had been cut down tremendously. Many of them didn't return the day after the meeting. I couldn't blame them.

It was still very early, so I was quiet so as not to wake Cole, who hadn't gotten in until almost three the night before. However, while I was gathering my things to work at Ciel that evening, Cole walked into my room. He sat on my bed and stared as I was placing my hair in a ponytail. Then, out of nowhere, he told he loved me, but that he didn't want to pressure me. I attempted to act as though it were no big deal and asked when he had made this discovery, and he said it was long ago. He had just assumed we were meant to be friends.

"But one night I saw how you looked at me, and I then I knew," he said.

"Knew what?" I said.

"I knew I had a chance," he said. "You gave me what all guys look for, the go-ahead glance."

"I didn't. . . ."

"Yes, you did. It was when we were on your supposed honeymoon."

"I was vulnerable," I admitted.

Cole looked at me with doubt, and I gazed at him.

"You're doing it again."

I quickly closed my eyes and shook my head. We laughed, and he moved closer. I could feel that he wanted to kiss, so I turned my head away from his.

Cole asked, "Are you going to do the virgin bid thing?"

"How did you know about that?"

"You and Mei don't keep secrets well."

"Did you tell anyone?"

"No. Why would I do that?"

I shrugged my shoulders but didn't give him an answer. Cole caressed my shoulders, got up, and walked away.

Had I given him the go-ahead glance? I was still unsure how I felt about Cole, but for some reason, I knocked on his bedroom door before I left. I walked in his room and got in bed beside him. I snuggled up close, and it was the most comfortable feeling I'd felt since before Carl's death. Problem was, I didn't know if I was cozying up to Cole for him or for the sake of nestling. We didn't say anything to each other, and I stayed there only for ten minutes, but I knew

I'd opened the gate. I needed my friend, and I prayed I wasn't adding confusion to this already perplexing situation.

By Saturday morning the Shelby was near empty. There were no padlocks on the door, but I had officially received the certified letter. It was a wrap. I'd never felt so defeated in my life. We had Ciel's closing that Saturday night, for I knew by Monday the hotel would be locked up. I'd contacted the owners of Ciel and advised them of the situation, and they actually came to the bar that Saturday. The owners were two men, one white, one African American. Of course, the hotel's repossession broke their lease agreement, but thankfully, there was a clause in their lease that dealt with a situation just like this. According to the lease, I was to inform them thirty days before closing, but I had only given them an eighteen-day notice. Fortunately, they empathized with my situation and sent me a formal letter stating that they'd been informed of the hotel's repossession and that no legal charges would be brought against the owner of the Shelby for the short notice. One of the gentlemen had known Carl well and said that he wished Carl had reached out to him for assistance. He loved the hotel and would have done what he could to invest in the property. I wished I'd known. Fortunately, these guys were opening another Ciel in Buckhead. They'd recently acquired a building, and I spoke to them at length about managing the bar. It wouldn't be open for months, but they wanted to discuss the matter in more detail next week.

Ciel didn't close that night until 4:00 a.m. We went out with a bang. I made $262.00 in tips. Mei made over three hundred dollars. I normally made more than her, but I hadn't gotten my bartending mojo back since Carl's death. I was thankful, however, because come next week I wasn't sure what I was going to do. Of course, the virgin bidder was still lingering like a bad hangover, and I had a few more days before the deal was off. It was a lot of money to think about, and it wasn't a decision I could come to grips with easily.

All day Sunday I slept. Neither Cole nor I stirred until after 3 p.m. Even when I did awaken, I never got dressed. I threw on my sweats, ate some food, and watched television the remainder of the day. It felt odd not having to go to work. Next week I was going to have to start looking. Tuesday I had a meeting with Satchel's financial advisor. He was going to talk to me about how this bank repossession would affect my credit and what I could do to leverage Carl's home since it hadn't sold.

That Monday morning Shanice's trial began its last day. The lawyers for both sides were prepared with closing statements, and now that Shanice, under the strict advisement from her attorney, had reluctantly changed her plea to guilty, Satchel's closing statement made Shanice look like a weak victim that was pushed to the edge. The district attorney made her look like a vindictive woman who had refused to let anyone steal her man. I believed she was both. I looked at the faces of the jurors. I wasn't sure what they were going to believe, but as they left the court-room in single file, I was praying that they wouldn't think she should die. They deliberated for three hours on Monday. I knew this wouldn't be a quick decision. There were only five women on the jury, but I bet they were heavily weighing both options. Most every woman had her heart broken and probably felt like killing while going through the pain. Shanice had acted on that pain and had taken a life. Be it accidental or not, she killed my husband, and these twelve people would decide her fate. The jurors had kept look-ing at me during the closing statements, as though they wanted me to give them an answer. But I wouldn't even look in that direction. I'd sat in the back of the courtroom and shifted my focus from the Constitution behind the judge to the Bill of Rights on the left wall.

When the jurors did not reach a verdict on Monday, the judge ordered them to reconvene on Tuesday. I left and went home. I had a mes-sage from Normandy Collins. I called him back immediately. I wasn't going to sleep with him, but I thought he might have had a change of heart and had decided to assist. I was wrong. He wanted to inform me that he was going to buy the property, and that he would keep it as a hotel. His nephew would come in and manage it, but he wanted me to manage Ciel. He wanted to show me that he was a fair man, but a businessman nonetheless. This was good news. Maybe Warren could go back to being the night manager and I would get the opportunity to run the bar. On

Tuesday morning, I rushed off to the courthouse. By the time I got there, the jury was filing in. The small brown courtroom had an eerie calm that morning. As soon as I sat down in the back row, an old woman patted me on my back and smiled. "I'm sure you feel good about today," she told me.

I was glad the trial was coming to an end, but that was not what she meant. We lived in an eye for an eye society. I was supposed to be happy that the woman who had killed Carl was about to be punished by twelve strangers. But I wasn't happy, because Shanice wasn't a stranger to me. I understood. I saw the pain in her eyes. Whether it was regret or sorrow, it was still an ache brought on by the man we had both loved. It just didn't seem right. But I couldn't explain this to the old woman, so I simply smiled back and nodded politely. I took off my shades. I had gotten flack for sitting in the back the whole trial, and today would be no different. I was supposed to sit in the front and face the murderer, sneer at the decision, and then burst into tears either over the justice or injustice inherent in the verdict. I wasn't in the mood to pretend. Satchel caught my eye and gave me a half smile, half frown. I knew she was glad this day had come. I mouthed *I love you.* She winked, and we waited for the judge to enter. About six minutes later, the lead juror passed the little white note to the judge. She began to read.

"On the count of murder in the first degree, the jury finds the defendant not guilty." Sighs ran through the room, and the juror continued. "On the count of second-degree murder with a deadly weapon, the jury finds the defendant guilty." Bigger sighs and gasps breezed through the benches. This was a class one felony. Going from first-degree murder to second may have saved Shanice from the death penalty, but it was bound to translate into a hefty sentence. Shanice lowered her head, Satchel tensed her lips, and I closed my eyes and took several deep breaths. The judge finished reading and said that everyone would reconvene in an hour for Shanice's sentencing.

I rushed outside to avoid the crowd leaving the courtroom. I quickly threw on my shades and walked across the street to grab a cup of coffee. I got on my phone and talked to my mom almost the entire hour. I didn't even feel like talking on the phone, but I knew this would keep people from approaching. It worked; several people passed by and eyed me, but none of them stopped.

An hour and sixteen minutes later, Judge Thomas Young was announcing Shanice's fate.

"On the count of second-degree murder with a deadly weapon, I sentence Shanice Franklin to ten years in the federal penitentiary. On the count of aggravated assault with a deadly weapon, I sentence Shanice to an additional five years in the federal penitentiary. These sentences are to run concurrent, with the chance of parole after seven served years. Ms. Franklin, do you understand the sentencing I've just read to you?"

Shanice whispered a soft "I do." Judge Young then adjourned the court, tapped his gavel, and went to the back. The bailiff escorted Shanice out of the courtroom. I saw her making eye contact with someone as she was leaving. I looked in that direction and saw her brother, Jonah, who was walking up to Satchel. I remained against the back wall, with my shades on, as people filed out. This was it. It had been much more expeditious than I'd thought it would be. I heard about people staying in jail for months before ever getting a trial. But in less than two months, Shanice had had her trial and been convicted. Jonah walked up to me and gave me a tight squeeze. I could feel the pain seeping from his chest. True, he had had problems with Shanice, but I guess no one wanted to see a loved one serve time in prison.

"I'm sorry for everything," he murmured and then walked out.

Satchel gathered her things and met me at the back. The reporters were waiting for her outside the courtroom doors. She gave her spiel as I kept walking out the front doors. It took her close to twenty minutes to wade through the press. When she stepped from the last courthouse cement stair, Satchel took a deep breath. She looked around the area for me, so I immediately sent her a text indicating I was watching her from the coffee shop across the street. She peered across the street and began strutting across the pavement. She was back. The last few weeks, there had been no strut in her step, but on this day I saw her stride pick back up. She walked in and took a sip of my coffee.

"At least she's not getting the death penalty or life in prison," were her first words.

"Did you think they would give her the death penalty?"

"The DA was going for life, but you never know. I feel good about everything."

"Me too."

"How are you holding up?" she asked.

I simply nodded and sipped my coffee. Satchel mentioned having to go see Shanice later, and I asked to go with her. As expected, she said no, but she did arrange for me to see Shanice in the visitors' room. I knew they would soon move her to the federal prison, and I needed to see her before she left.

I was only allowed ten minutes to see her, so I quickly got to the point. Shanice had nothing to say this time. I didn't have anything to say, either; I just wanted to give her something. I went in my purse and pulled out the three pictures of her and Carl.

"I'm not sure if you want these, but . . ." I handed them to her.

She looked at them and clinched her lips extremely tight. I didn't know if she was about to break down into tears or become enraged, but then a single tear fell onto one of the photographs. She took the pictures, turned, and began walking away. Suddenly, Shanice turned back around and said, "Tell Adrian, he is going to get his. I'm going to make sure of it."

After uttering those words, she disappeared. I didn't know what that meant, but I was not going to be the bearer of bad news. I grabbed my purse and left.

Chapter 12

Fancy Panties

2 ounces vodka
2 ounces pink lemonade
4 ounces Brut champagne

Stir the vodka and pink lemonade in a glass filled with ice. Add the Brut champagne or sparkling wine until full, and serve in a collins glass.

By Tuesday morning I'd made peace with the idea of sleeping with the virgin bidder. I wasn't proud of it, but I honestly couldn't turn down that kind of money. Carl's mortgage payment was due, and I'd used up his savings paying off final hotel bills. I had around six thousand dollars left to my name and no job. If this house didn't sell, it, too, would end up in foreclosure. Therefore, Thursday morning I went to the doctor and had a checkup. They'd arranged for everything. As I suspected, my hymen was long gone, but the doctor probed and prodded, and reached the verdict that I was indeed a disease-free virgin.

This was still a hoax, because there was no proof.
However, somehow it was working, so who was I
to judge. What I wanted was the Rolodex of men
who bidded on this type of thing. I had a piece of
swampland to sell them.

On Thursday, I went shopping for lingerie. Not
that I cared about this weirdo who would pay
thousands to have sex with me, but this fiasco with
Carl had changed me. I'd become a skeptic like
Satchel; I no longer believed in princes on white
horses or fairy-tale endings. In fact, I trusted no
one, and worse, I'd started planning what I could
get from people before they figured out what they
could get from me. I'd become an opportunist
overnight. If everyone in the world was out for
himself, why should I be any different? Satchel
lived this way. The only people she trusted were
my mom and me; everyone else was a coin toss.
My dad used to be in that category, until he left
my mom for some other woman. I forgave him,
Satchel never did, but now I was seeing things
through her eyes.

I walked around several exclusive lingerie shops,
but I wasn't motivated to buy one single pair of
panties. I didn't have that sexy panty swish like
most women. So I went to the Jockey outlet as a last
resort. I fumbled through the racks and saw a new
line of microfiber, boy-cut panties that guaranteed
no panty lines. I figured, what the hell. I could be
a little daring as long as the crotch was still cotton.
I purchased two pairs, and as soon as I got home
and showered, I tried on one. They fit perfectly,
and the guarantee was on point. There wasn't one

panty line. I rubbed my bum and embraced the new me in my sexy new panties. With my hands on my hips, I stared at my seminude body in the full-length mirror. I felt sexy and confident. Maybe Satchel was right, and there was some link between cute panties and self-assurance.

"I am hot!" I said to myself.

But, hot panties or no panties, the real question was, would I be any good in bed? I was about to find out.

Satchel still didn't believe I'd put my virginity up for bid, and I figured that was best. If she actually thought I was going through with this, she'd tie me down in the house for at least three weeks, or until the whole thing blew over. I nervously approached the lobby of the W Hotel. Mei had called me thirteen times that day to make sure I wouldn't back out. The last three times, I didn't answer the phone. As I entered the lobby of the W, Satchel called. She teased me about my "fake" date and said that he could be a slasher or serial killer waiting to gut me. I could feel her cynical sense of humor slowly working its way back into her body. I laughed at first, but then I started thinking about her comment. What if she was right? I sat in one of the plush lobby chairs and called Mei.

"Do you and your Mafia crew do background checks on these men?" I asked.

"Kind of. Why?"

"What if he's a serial killer?"

Mei laughed and said that had never happened, and that I was crazy. She insisted that everyone knew where the party was taking place, and there was no way he could get away.

"That won't help once I'm in a bunch of tiny pieces."

Again, she laughed and offered to come watch. I smirked and hung up. Looking at my watch, I saw I had only about thirty minutes before my bidder got here. My heart was racing as I went to the front desk and got the key.

I walked into the suite, which smelled sweet, like freesia, and placed my things down. I didn't know what to do, so I turned on the television. My legs shook, and then my whole body began to wiggle. I used the bathroom and then washed my vagina immediately afterwards. I wanted to be as fresh as possible. I went back to the bed area and prepared myself. I unbuttoned my blouse to expose the top of my bra, crossed my legs, and positioned my body against the head-board. Ten minutes later, I had to pee again. My nerves were working overtime. Therefore, I did the bathroom routine once more and washed off my clitoris. When I came out of the bathroom, there was a knock on the door. By now my heart was beating out of my chest. I slowly opened the door, only to see Cole standing on the other side.

"I told Mei, I was okay. Why did she send you over here?" I snapped.

Cole shrugged his shoulders and walked in the room. I looked at the time and saw I had about eight more minutes before my bidder was going to be here, so I told Cole to hurry with his speech. Cole didn't seem to care as he plopped on the edge of the bed and looked at the television.

"You have to go. He should be here in a minute," I declared.

"You shouldn't do this," Cole retorted.

I only laughed. "Oh, it's going down. Now, you have to go."

Cole didn't budge. Finally, I sat next to him and explained how this money was going to be good for all of us. No, I didn't have any intentions of sharing my cootchie money with Cole, but I needed him to leave. Still, he wasn't moved. I was starting to get upset.

"You cannot be here when he comes. I know you don't agree, but we can talk about this afterwards," I said.

Cole pleaded with me. "Izzy, this is not you. This is not the girl I know. It's not right, and you shouldn't let this money govern you like this."

I couldn't help but laugh. Cole was tripping. "Cole, baby, it's over forty-four thousand dollars. That's one thousand dollars forty-four times. For what? For one night of sex. I don't care anymore! I saved myself for my husband, and look what that got me. I was cheated on, left in debt, and laughed at. I'm tired." I collapsed on the bed. I looked over at him and tried to be as sincere as I could be. Yes, I was still having doubts, but his being here didn't help. "I just want to come up like everyone else. You have to understand." Just then there was a knock on the door.

I grabbed Cole's arm and pushed him to the other side of the suite. "Go out that door. I'm serious. Stop playing." I shooed him out the door, took a couple of deep breaths, and opened the other door. Mei came rushing in. She searched the room.

"Where is he?" she said.

"He's not here yet," I answered.

"Where's Cole?" she said.

"Oh, he just left." I opened the adjoining door, and Cole was standing in the center of the room. Mei walked up to him and smacked him in the face. He quickly lifted her petite frame in the air. She fussed and kicked in the air.

"What is going on?" I asked, trying to break the two of them apart. Finally, Cole lowered Mei to the ground, but he still had a grip around her arms.

"This asshole bid on you," she said.

At first I didn't get what Mei was saying, but then I saw the fury in her eyes.

"You mean he's my bidder?" I asked.

Mei gave an irritated nod, and at that moment we both turned on Cole, beating him in the chest while yelling and cursing. He fought off the best he could, but we took him down. Mei held his legs as I sat on his stomach.

"How could you?" I asked.

"I didn't want you doing this. I thought that you would reconsider, so I figured it wouldn't matter," he admitted.

"No, no, no," I said repeatedly hitting him in the sternum.

"Hit him again!" Mei ordered.

Cole lay there and took his beating before speaking again. "I'm sorry, but for real, Izzy, how were you going to do this? It was a stranger. You always talked about how much virginity meant to you."

"That doesn't matter anymore, Cole. Carl is dead. Who am I saving it for now?"

"Yourself," he whispered.

I slowly moved from atop him, but Mei continued to hold his feet and give him an ornery stare. I sat beside Cole and gave a heavy sigh. "You just don't understand. I always thought my virginity made me stand out, made me precious. But no one cares, Cole. People don't care if you're a virgin or if you're a slut."

"I care," said Cole.

"No, you don't," I countered. "Before you knew I was a virgin, I recall you saying that you would never date a virgin. It'd be too much work for no payoff."

Cole recalled saying that and tried to save face. "But, I would marry one, and I still respect you."

"You know what? It's not even about other people anymore. It's about me. In my eyes, it's lost its value, and I really need the money," I said. Just then I realized that Mei had said they checked the account. "What about the money? Mei, you checked the account, right?" I asked.

"This asshole hacker got into our site and created a fake account after getting the information from my computer," replied Mei. "When the money never registered, we took a look at the bidder's ID. It was your address listed, with an ID name of longpoleCole."

"Hey, that's what I call you, Cole," I blurted out. They both looked at me. It was obvious they were wondering why I would call him that. I quickly went on the offensive. "That's really messed up, Cole. Here I am, thinking I'm worth forty-four thousand, and it was you all along."

"You're priceless," he said, trying to comfort me. "I know you guys see the humor in this."

"No, Cole, we don't," I said firmly. "I really needed that money."

"Me too," added Mei.

Cole apologized again.

I turned to Mei and said, "Maybe we can put my name back on the list and say something went wrong."

Mei shook her head. "You've been marked. Once your bid closes, you can't go back on. You can be a virgin only once. It doesn't matter if something happened. They know your face."

I slapped Cole in the chest again. "See what you did? I've been marked."

Mei, who was sitting at Cole's feet, began to furiously kick the bottom of his heels. Finally, Cole had enough. He stood up and spoke. "Enough of this hitting me! I was looking out for you. Izzy, I obviously care more about you than you care about yourself. I don't even know who you are anymore. Mei, you're insane. I'm sure you'll find another virgin. Sorry. I'll pay for the room." Cole walked toward the door.

Mei and I sat on the floor and stared at each other. Neither of us could believe Cole had messed up this money. I was truly heated. I'd never been so close to a lump sum of money like that ever before, and yes, losing my virginity was a huge sacrifice, but it was one I was willing to make. Maybe I had changed. Hell, a lot had happened, and life changed people. This didn't make me a bad person. I glanced over at Mei and could see her mind spinning.

"Remember that group of girls you spoke to about saving themselves?" she asked.

"Don't even think about it," I said before she could finish.

"Oh, it's already thought about. I'm getting another virgin, and you're going to help me."

After the bungled virgin bid, I was in a sour mood the rest of the weekend. Cole stayed clear of the house, which he knew was best. I didn't take a single call from Satchel, because I knew she would only laugh and continue to swear the whole thing had been made up in the first place. Shanice was still downtown but was going to be transferred to a federal prison within two weeks. Satchel still refused to let it go. She insisted Adrian had had something to do with it. There had been no cameras in the hotel rooms or the hallways of the Shelby, only in the lobby, and Satchel had reviewed those tapes over and over again. We tried to piece together the link between Peyton and Adrian, but we couldn't. I figured Peyton was the only man Carl had trusted. Who knew what he was supposed to do with that insurance money, or why he would make up some story about a child. Insurance companies weren't allowed to divulge the names of the beneficiaries on policies. Satchel said that since it was a murder case, Peyton had probably felt it was necessary to say something just in case it came up. Making up the story about a kid would justify his not giving the money to me or Adrian.

Now that the case was over, Satchel had paid Keith a visit. She'd wanted to ask him questions that she had had no time to focus on during the trial. In their meeting, Keith detailed his relationship with Marley and Adrian. He admitted to asking Marley to start a fight with me, but he said he'd had no idea I would be carrying marijuana. Satchel was now free to tell him about the deposit slips, but as suspected, he insisted that Carl had been paying him for detective work. He said Carl had still had him doing work, although Warren said he'd been fired. However, when Satchel asked him about Carl having a son, his answer was surprising. He said yes, but he gave no details. Satchel said he was very frank in answering that question and acted like it was common knowledge.

Adrian, on the other hand, said Keith was full of shit. He insisted that his brother did not have a child and that Keith had only said that to keep Satchel chasing a loose end. Adrian was convinced that Shanice had purposely killed Carl, and that she'd thought she could get off. He also maintained that Keith had been very upset when Carl had questioned him about the bribery, and it was possible Keith had still done it, but since Carl was our only link, it could never proved. Satchel knew deep down that someone was getting away with murder, and it was killing her.

I beat Cole home that evening and was hoping to be asleep when he got there. No chance. He arrived about twenty minutes after me. He hadn't said anything to me since the bungled virgin deal, but I knew my friend. He wasn't going to let another day pass without any communication. Before he put his things down, he knocked on my bedroom door. I opened it slowly, and he charged in. Cole took me in his arms and kissed me. He backed me up to the edge of the bed, and in the next few seconds, we were kissing on the bed. My head was swimming; it all had happened so quickly. I tried to take breaths in between the lip-locks.

"Cole, please don't," I gasped.

He stopped kissing me and lifted himself up off my body. However, when he looked me in the eyes, I started kissing him again. This time the kiss was more passionate. Cole removed my blouse and then my bra. He was ravaging my body. The comforter and sheets were tossed all over the bed. I was nervously excited. I quickly took off his shirt while trying to kiss him. I bumped my head on his chin, but it wasn't going to deter me from this moment of passion. I got his shirt off and rubbed my hands across his bare back. I quickly moved to his belt buckle and then his pants. We were down to our underwear, and his hips were grinding into mine. I didn't have a moment to even think about this being my first time. It was happening faster than I thought. He glanced down at my under-wear and spoke.

"I like your panties."

I beamed. "They're fancy," I said before lock-ing my lips around his again. Like teenagers, we made out on the bed for close to fifteen minutes. I was ready. I slipped off my underwear and used my feet to attempt to remove his. He assisted, and now we were both naked. Cole jumped up, ran to his room, and came back quickly with a box of prophylactics. My heart was racing so much, I thought I was going to pass out. My breathing was irregular, but I didn't care. I was about to do it. He started kissing me again as I tore open the box. Then Cole moved down toward my breasts and my stomach. He rubbed his chin across my Brazilian wax.

"I like this, too," he said, with a smile. He kept nuzzling my clitoris. But I didn't feel comfortable with him going down on me.

"I haven't showered," I commented.

"I don't care. I like the scent of day-old puntang."

Well, that was a disgusting statement; and truthfully, it almost made me sick. How much day-old puntang had he tasted? I pulled him back up to my face, but I didn't want to kiss him anymore. I was slowly losing the desire, so I figured I had to just do it, or I was going to quit altogether.

"Here," I said, handing him the condom. "Put it on."

Cole kissed my neck and then tried to kiss my lips, which were closed.

"No more kisses," I said. "Let's just do it."

Cole put on the condom and wiggled his penis around my opening. With him still on top of me, I looked down to see what the problem was.

"You okay?" I asked.

He nodded and kept playing with his thing. He stroked it, rubbed it, shook it from side to side, but it was not growing.

"Just let me go down on you," he said.

I hopped up. "Then I have to shower."

Cole sat up, frustrated. "You're ruining the moment."

"What? Your dick is ruining the moment. I'm fine."

Cole sucked his lips and said, "This doesn't ever happen to me."

I gave him a look of disbelief. We stared at each

other, and then I began to chuckle. "Day-old puntang?" I asked, with a curious expression.

"Yeah, it's natural," he said, as if his statement could be justified.

"Well, I think your little friend down there likes fresh puntang."

Cole rose and walked into his room. I was a little disappointed, but instead of following him, I jumped in the shower. When I came out, he was watching television. I plopped on the couch, beside him, and put my head on his shoulder.

"I'm still mad at you," I said.

"I figured that would help the passion," he responded, with a chuckle.

We sat there a few more minutes, and then I asked him, "Cole, are you really attracted to me, or is it the virgin thing?"

He turned to face me and smiled. Cole took my face, lifted it to his, and gently kissed my lips. "You are so adorable. Of course, I am attracted to you."

"I don't want to be adorable. I want to be sexy."

"Adorable is sexy."

I smirked and looked away. He, once again, turned my face to his.

"Izzy, I've had a thing for you since day one. Do you remember what I said to you when we first met at Applebee's?"

I began laughing. "Yes. We were filling the ice bin, and you said, 'Now that we've broken the ice, how about we sleep together?'"

"It sounds so much cornier coming out of your mouth," he replied.

"No, it doesn't," I assured him. "You are definitely a cornball."

We both laughed. Cole walked in the kitchen

and returned with a piece of pie. As we ate, he spoke to me in an unfamiliar fashion. One I hadn't ever heard from him.

"Izzy, you are a class act. You value yourself so much that you decided to wait. What makes that precious is that no one does that these days. It's more than just a tight pussy. Women don't care about sex anymore, so men don't care about it. I remember when we first talked about you being a virgin, and how you lit up, knowing that no one in the world would have what your husband would have. You talked about yourself like a gift. That's some special shit. . . ." He continued to talk, and I took in every word. "I'm really sorry about the bid thing. I just didn't want you going out like that. And, maybe I was a little jealous. I always looked at you as someone I could marry. But I never thought I was good enough."

"How could you say that?"

"I saw the men you dated. They either were rich or looked like models. I'm neither."

"I didn't purposely go after those guys."

"I know. It's just what you attracted. You have that kind of aura. Those types of guys know they have the pick of the litter, and you're a top pick," he said, with a smile.

At the end of his speech, Cole kissed my cheek and scooted a few inches away from me. I thought about his words as he placed his hand on top of my hand and caressed it.

"Thanks," I said.

"You're welcome."

I laughed and pushed him farther away. "But that whole speech didn't keep you from trying to sleep with me."

"Once you decided you were going to do it, I figured I should be the one. Hell, I've put in the most time. I knew you before Carl."

"What about being precious?"

"I'm a man. Precious or not, I would tear that ass up."

I let out a loud chortle. "You got to get it up in order to tear it up," I said, pointing at his crotch.

"That doesn't ever happen," he reiterated forcefully. "I'll show you. Come here."

Cole playfully leaped for my body, but I got out of the way and ran into the kitchen. He cornered me by the fridge and cuddled me in his arms. He planted tiny pecks all over my face.

"So now what?" I asked him.

"I want you to take me serious. I like you, Isabelle."

"I think I like you, too, Coleman. But it's too soon. I can't think about getting into a serious relationship right now."

He kissed me one more time and agreed to wait. At least until we both felt it was right.

Chapter 13

Baby Mama

2 ounces pineapple juice
1 1/2 ounces 99 Bananas banana schnapps
1 1/2 ounces Stolichnaya strawberry vodka
1 dash grenadine syrup

Shake the ingredients in a cocktail shaker with ice. Strain into glass on the rocks, and serve.

My sister was officially depressed. Not only had she lost the case, but she honestly believed that Shanice had been tricked. The thought of her spending time in prison was eating Satchel alive. I had to talk to her. We met that morning and had breakfast. She said Shanice was doing fine, all things considered, and that she was still begging her to look into Adrian. Shanice continued to insist that he'd been involved. She begged Satchel not to stop looking for clues. Satchel had made a promise, and now it was haunting her.

We went over everything one more time, and I admitted that I was starting to believe that maybe

Shanice was guilty of more than a bad joke. I asked Satchel to simply consider it, but she wouldn't.

"I know people," she said. "I didn't take Shanice's case because of the money or because of your deal. I took it because when I talked to her, I saw the truth. Yes, I've taken cases when I thought my client was guilty, but this was not one of them."

"Fine. What do we do now?" I asked.

"I don't know," Satchel said, placing a few bites of French toast into her mouth.

"I need a job," I told her. "I met with the Ciel guys, but that place won't be open for another two months. The house hasn't sold, and I have to pay the mortgage."

"I'll help you with that while you look for a job. Whatever happened to the old man who wanted to buy the house for his daughter?"

"Normandy. He wanted to sleep with me, remember?"

"Oh yeah. By the way, was the virgin crap really true, or was that just some scheme Mei told you about?"

"It was real," I told her.

"What happened?" she asked.

I didn't want to hear her berate me about it being prostitution or about Cole coming to my rescue, so I just replied, "Couldn't go through with it."

My sister smiled and caressed the top of my hand. "I'm proud of you."

"For what? I lost the hotel, and I was no help to you with this case."

"First of all, you're not a lawyer or a detective, so the case was not your job. Secondly, you didn't lose your mind. This would have taken down most people. But you handled it all so well."

Inside I was shining bright. My sister's view of me had always meant a lot. I'd spent most of my life trying to make her proud.

"I know I teased you about the virgin thing, but you know I'm jealous, right?" she asked.

"Really?" I said, with a grin.

"A little. I mean, I don't know any virgins, none over eighteen. So that means my little sister is one in a million. I don't know a million people, but you get my point. And, now that this virgin thing has catapulted you into the tabloids, it's kinda like your calling card. That's cool."

"I almost slept with Cole," I blurted out.

"What!"

"Long story short. He kissed me one day when I was under duress, and ever since then, there's been this strange sexual tension."

"With Cole?" Satchel said, with a bewildered look in her eyes.

"Yes, with Cole!" I reiterated. "Don't say anything, because I might like him."

Satchel hunched her shoulders and pretended that the thought of it made her nauseous. We giggled about it and finished breakfast.

I went by the Shelby that Monday morning and parked in the empty lot. I walked to the front door and saw the padlock with chains. It was so embarrassing. Everyone knew what that meant. I was praying that the public would come to the conclusion that no one had wanted to take over the business after Carl's death and so the hotel had closed, or that it had been sold to another company, which hadn't moved in yet. I wondered if Carl was looking down on me, and if he saw this as a huge disappointment. I then speculated why I even cared about Carl at this point. This was all his fault.

I kicked the door and yelled, "This is all your fault."

Adrian walked up behind me. "I hope you weren't speaking to me."

I jumped, startled by his presence. "What are you doing here?" I asked.

"Same thing you're doing here."

We both took several steps back and looked at the building.

"I should have helped you save this place. I'm sorry," said Adrian.

"I should have let you sell it. I'm sorry, too."

Adrian and I fell silent as we looked at the sign on the door.

"Think my brother's mad at us?"

"Who knows?" I responded. "Who cares? We have to just go on with our lives."

"What are you going to do now?" he asked me.

I shrugged my shoulders and motioned toward him, silently asking the same thing. His stare was as blank as mine. We continued to stand in the vacant lot and look at the building.

Finally Adrian spoke again. "I swear I didn't kill Carl."

"The trial's over, Adrian."

"Yeah, but I know you still think I did it."

"That doesn't matter."

"Yes, it does. It matters to me. I do a lot of shady shit. Everyone knows that. I never really worked hard, and I always relied on my brother to take care of me. And I've dabbled in a little illegal activity every once in a while, but I'm not a murderer."

"Adrian, I know you were stealing money from the hotel."

"I was going to pay everything back. Carl knew I had a problem, and he helped me out. Sometimes he used hotel money to do so."

"I don't want to talk about it anymore."

Something in my gut was saying Adrian was telling the truth. I had the same truth feelers as Satchel. But I didn't want to feel that. I wanted Adrian to be the bad guy; everything pointed to him, and it just made sense. But as I looked into his eyes, I saw only sorrow. Adrian then pulled out his checkbook.

"What are you doing?" I asked.

"I owe you some money. It's not fair for me to keep all the insurance money, especially since I didn't help with the funeral costs and you let me stay in the house."

"Why are you being so nice?" I asked. This was the new Izzy. The old me would have smiled, given Adrian a hug, and assumed he was a good guy, after all, but no more. Adrian was up to something. "Did you talk to Peyton?"

"Uncle Peyton? No. Why?"

"You know he came to town."

"What was that old drunk doing? And why didn't he come to the funeral?"

"Said he was out of the country."

"That bum's never been out of the country his whole life. He's probably never left the East Coast," Adrian replied.

"Well, that bum . . ." I stopped midsentence. I was about to tell Adrian about the insurance policy, but I knew that would tear open an old wound. "Well, that bum said hello."

Adrian rolled his eyes and wrote on the check. "Ndeeyah got a job at the Marriott, and we can continue paying rent at the house if you let us stay there."

"That's fine. I plan to use that property as collateral to buy my own house once Carl's place sells."

We lingered and looked at one another. It was like saying good-bye to someone you'd sat behind all year in school. You hadn't really talked to that person, but for some odd reason, you were going to miss seeing them.

"So, I'll see you later," I said.

"Yeah, take care. I'll mail the payments to you, unless you want to pick them up."

"You can mail them. That's fine."

Adrian walked to his car, which was parked around the side, and I strolled to mine, which was parked in the front. I glanced down at the check and read the amount, five thousand dollars. Maybe his guilt was getting the best of him. I didn't care. I needed that money, so I quickly went to the bank and made a deposit.

Later that day, I drove back by the Mail Boxes Etc. I hadn't paid the amount due, so I wasn't sure if I still had access to the box or not. I placed my key in the box and opened it. Nothing was in there. I walked over to the counter and questioned the clerk about the box and the bill. She said that they would hold all mail until the bill was paid.

"So there is mail?" I asked.

She shrugged her shoulders and went back to work.

"Hey!" I yelled. The woman turned around. "I'm not done talking with you. I need to see if any mail came to that box."

The woman made a face, slowly turned, and went toward the back. A few moments later, she came back with two letters in her hand. I reached for the mail, but she snatched her hand back. "Are you going to pay the bill?"

I was perturbed. But I had just received five thousand dollars from Adrian, so I assumed the $122.00 bill wouldn't kill me. Besides, if I paid it, I could continue intercepting mail for this mysterious person until I figured out who he or she was. I pulled out my checkbook while the woman at the counter asked if I wanted to update my records. She looked in the computer and pulled up Carl's account. She finally handed over the mail. The first letter was an orthodontist bill; the second was a pack of discount coupons for Sears. Both pieces of mail were addressed to a Kainda Suthma.

"Kainda Suthma?" I said aloud. I had never heard of anyone by that name. Maybe there was a mysterious baby mama out there. Carl's name was on the account, so it couldn't be an old key, but there was no letter detailing an escrow account. There probably was some random child out there that Carl had taken taking care of. His entire life had been a secret. Why would this be a surprise? I took the mail and left.

I put in a few applications at several bars that day, but no one was hiring. I didn't want to work at a restaurant or a nightclub, so my choices were limited to sports bars and high-end bars. Cole wasn't as particular; he got a gig working at Verve, a club downtown. He had tried to get me to apply there, but I wasn't quite that desperate yet. Bartenders at nightclubs were disrespected entirely too much for me to deal with. Mei got a gig working at a country club. She said they needed more help at the bar there, so hopefully she'd be able to put me down.

That night Cole and I decided to take in a movie. I hadn't been to the movies in so long. Carl hadn't liked going to the movie theater, and I normally worked at night and handled personal business during matinee hours. We couldn't decide on what to see. While we were breezing through a movie site on the Internet, Cole saw the mail I'd laid on the table. He picked it up, thinking it was his.

"Kainda Suthma? Who's that?" he asked.

"I wish you could tell me."

"Sounds African," he said.

"It sure does."

I hopped up and flipped through several pieces of scratch paper on my desk. I found Ndeeyah's phone number on one of the pieces and called her, but she didn't answer. I scrolled through Carl's phone, but I didn't see anyone with that name, and there was nothing with that name on it in his stash of papers. Cole and I went to the movies, but as soon as we returned, I pulled out the phone book. There was only one listing for a Suthma in the book. It was an Ira Suthma. It was late, so I made my calls the next morning. Ndeeyah was first.

"Hi," she answered very pleasantly.

"Hi, Ndeeyah. I have a question for you. Do you know anyone named Kainda Suthma?"

Ndeeyah was quiet for a few seconds and then replied, "Not that I can think of. Why?"

"I think she was a friend of Carl's, that's all. The name sounds African. I thought you might know her."

"Oh," she replied.

"You know anyone by that name who worked at the hotel?"

"No," she said.

"Okay. Thanks, anyway." Ndeeyah and I hung up.

I followed up that call with one to Warren. He knew no one with that name. He said that there had been no one on payroll by that name, so once again it was a dead end. Ira Suthma had a thick Middle Eastern accent, and he didn't know anyone by that name of Kainda Suthma, either. My only chance at finding this woman was to stake out the Mail Boxes Etc. Sure I wasn't working, but that place had twenty-four-hour access. I didn't have that kind of time. I went online, searching for that name, hoping that she'd have a MySpace or Facebook account, anything. Satchel said it was a dead end and told me to give up. But just like she couldn't let Shanice's trial go, I couldn't let this die. If Carl had a child that was ten or eleven, he'd be in school, but school records were more secure than bank records. Plus, I didn't know the child's first or last name. I grabbed Peyton's number from my purse and called him, and as I'd suspected, the number was no longer in service. If there was a child out there, he was never going to get that money, for sure.

After three more hours of searching, I gave up. It was late afternoon when I got a call for a job interview at the country club. They wanted to see me as soon as possible, so I threw on my clothing and headed toward Gwinnett. With traffic, it took close to thirty minutes to get to this place. I was perturbed and spoiled. I lived in the city, and Ciel had been ten minutes from my house. If I were to get a job out here, I'd be in traffic every day. By the time I got to the interview, I no longer wanted the job, but I really had no choice. I couldn't sit back like a fat rat and not work. That money Adrian had given me was not going to last that long. The interview went well, and they wanted me to work a party that weekend. I was hired as a temporary bartender. It was a start.

When I returned to the car, I called Adrian and left him a message. "Hey, Adrian. Do you know a Kianda Suthma? I think she's Carl's baby mama. Call me back."

During our last talk, he had insisted Carl didn't have a child, but maybe he knew this woman. At least that would put an end to some of the mystery.

Around one that morning, Satchel gave me a call; she was at the police station downtown. She wanted me to meet her there and asked if Cole could bring me down there. Cole and I were still night owls from all the years of bartending, and luckily, he wasn't at work that night, so we hopped in the car and drove downtown. Satchel was waiting for me out front. She walked me to an officer's desk, and there I saw Ndeeyah sitting in the tiny chair. She had scratches, scrapes, and a swelling black eye. She was giving a statement to Detective Crooms. From what I overheard, she and Adrian had gotten into a fight. I quickly pulled Satchel aside.

"What is going on?" I asked.

"Did you call Adrian this afternoon?"

"No, oh yeah, I did. I asked him about Kianda Suthma."

"Well, look no further," Satchel said, pointing to Ndeeyah. I was confused. "Her full maiden name is Kianda Ndeeyah Suthma." My mouth flew open.

"She had a child by Carl, or is it some mistake?"

"No, apparently she and Carl were together."

"So where's the child?"

Satchel motioned toward their son.

"Oren? Oren is Carl's child? Oh my God! Did Adrian know?"

"According to Ndeeyah, he found out the week of Carl's death," Satchel explained. "Ndeeyah said he was so enraged that he killed Carl. She covered for him, but after the call today, she insisted that he come clean. She got scared and said she was going to confess, and that's when the fight started."

"Oh my God!" I shrieked.

"She already made her official statement, so I thought you should know," Satchel added.

"Where's Adrian?"

"In the hospital, in surgery."

"What?"

"He took four stab wounds to the chest."

"Ndeeyah stabbed him?"

"No. Oren did."

Just then Oren rushed over to his mother and embraced her tightly. She embraced him as she continued talking to Detective Crooms. I was flabbergasted. Satchel was trying to contact the judge to give him the latest news. She was praying that Adrian made it out of surgery so that she could put him behind bars. I was in such shock that I couldn't move. When Satchel got off the phone, she walked over to check on me. I was still in a daze.

"You okay?" she asked.

"I think so. How did Adrian find out? Peyton said Carl's son was ten or eleven. Oren's what? Eight?"

"Forget about Peyton. Oren is Carl's son. Ndeeyah thinks Keith told Adrian, but she's not sure," said Satchel. "Ndeeyah said he just came home and questioned her, and she confessed the truth to him. Next thing she knew, he came home and said he'd killed Carl."

I watched Ndeeyah rise and slowly walk toward me. Her eyes were filled with tears. "I'm sorry," she said. "I should have said something, but I was so scared."

Keith walked up to her and read her her rights. She was going to be placed under arrest for accessory to murder. She'd told on herself, and I wasn't sure how this would play out, but Keith was putting on the handcuffs. Satchel's phone rang; she spoke for a second and then hung up.

"Adrian is out of surgery. We won't be able to see him until tomorrow," Satchel announced.

Just then Oren shrieked, "No! Where is she going?"

"Mommy's gotta stay here tonight. Okay baby? You go with Isabelle," said Ndeeyah.

"Me?" I questioned.

"Oh yeah," said Satchel. "That's the main reason

I called you down here. She wanted you to keep Oren."

"Why me?" I asked.

"She doesn't have any family here, and he is your husband's child."

"No. I can't keep him," I whispered.

"Well, I can't, either, and he can't stay here," Satchel pointed out.

I glanced over at a tearful little boy watching his mother being placed behind bars. I really didn't have a choice.

"Who's going to keep him if they go to jail?" I whispered again.

Satchel shrugged her shoulders and handed me Ndeeyah's keys. "You can take him by the house in the morning to get his things."

Satchel walked over to Dective Crooms, and I looked at Oren. Her case was solved, and I was playing stepmommy/auntie to this little boy, who had just stabbed his daddy/uncle almost to death. I was in the pit of dysfunction. I rushed back over to Satchel. "Shouldn't he go see a counselor or something?"

"He can't go tonight," she exclaimed. "Just take him home, and we'll figure everything out in the morning."

I walked over and asked Oren if he was ready to go. He didn't say a word; he only rose and followed me to the lobby. Cole had fallen asleep on the bench, so I woke him up. He gave Oren a puzzled look and then looked at me.

"I'll explain when we get home," I assured him.

Chapter 14

Death Shot

1/2 ounce Opal Nera black sambuca
1/2 ounce tequila

Pour the Opal Nera into a shot glass. Over a spoon, add the tequila, and serve.

Satchel and Detective Crooms went to see Adrian the next morning. He looked pitiful, according to Satchel. His chest was bandaged, and he had several tubes feeding in and out of his veins. He was conscious enough to know that Satchel was in the room, but not enough to do much reacting. I wanted to go, but this visit was official police business. Plus I was still baby-sitting Oren.

Detective Crooms sat by his bedside and spoke. "Hi, Adrian. How are you feeling?"

Adrian rolled his eyes in the detective's direction but didn't speak. The detective told him why they were there and said that they needed to get a statement from him.

"Statement for what?" Adrian whispered.

"A statement about what happened. We took your wife's statement, and we need to compare it to yours," said Detective Crooms.

Adrian sat up in the bed and looked at Satchel, who was standing by the door. He was in obvious pain when he positioned his head on the pillow and readjusted his torso.

"Are you able to speak with us, or shall we come back?" asked Detective Crooms.

"I'm fine," Adrian murmured.

"Okay, well. Can you tell us what happened?" asked Detective Crooms.

Adrian cleared his throat and began. "Isabelle called me and said that my wife was the mother of Carl's child. When I questioned Ndeeyah about it, she admitted it was true, and I went crazy. We started arguing, it got out of control, and when it became physical, Oren saw me on top of his mother and grabbed a kitchen knife and stabbed me. That's what happened."

"So when did you find out about Carl and Oren?" Detective Crooms quizzed.

"Once I heard the phone call, I questioned Ndeeyah. That was yesterday morning," said Adrian.

The detective looked at Satchel, who was taking notes. They both gave Adrian a peculiar look.

"What?" Adrian asked, observing their expressions.

"There is a conflict between your account and your wife's statement," Detective Crooms informed him.

"What did that lying bitch tell you?" Adrian asked, very agitated. He rose up in bed.

Crooms pulled out his notepad but then said, "Maybe we should do this in a few days, when you are feeling better."

"No, I want to know what she said now. Did she tell you that she hit me first? Did she tell you she had plenty of opportunities to tell me that was not my son?" By now Adrian was yelling, and the machine attached to his tubes started to beep.

"Calm down, Adrian," said Satchel.

"Did she press charges? I knew she was going to press charges," Adrian yelled. His temper was raging, and nurses began rushing into the room. Satchel rushed to the bed, asking one more question just before they were asked to leave.

"Did you know about Oren before yesterday?"

"No!" Adrian yelled. "How would I have found out?"

"Keith?" said Satchel.

"What! Keith knows about this?" Adrian raged. After that the nurses asked them to leave. Adrian was so upset, he was rattling the bed.

Satchel and Detective Crooms stood outside the room, looking at each other. They weren't sure what was going on, and it wouldn't be until Adrian was doing better that they could get a full statement and possibly understand what had occurred.

I took Oren to his house to grab some of his clothing and toys. We walked inside, and Oren went into his room. I waited in the kitchen at first and then walked down the hall to Ndeeyah and Adrian's bedroom. There was broken glass on the floor and a broken lamp lying across the bed. Items were strewn about the room, and it was obvious a fight had erupted here. Oren came to the door and spoke softly.

"Mommy and daddy were fighting in here."

He hadn't said anything to me since we got to the house yesterday. I was surprised to hear him speak.

"I know, baby. Sometimes mommies and daddies don't get along."

"Daddy called Mommy a whore. He said it really loud over and over again."

Suddenly my phone rang. It was Satchel, informing me that Adrian's statement didn't match.

"I think you should talk to Oren. He seems to know what happened. We're at the house now," I said.

Detective Crooms and Satchel agreed to meet me at the house before meeting Keith. I went into the kitchen, looked in the fridge, and poured some lemonade for Oren and myself. I explained to him that Satchel and the nice man from yesterday were going to ask him some questions. He shrugged his shoulders, went back into his room, and started up his video game. I sat in the living room and waited for Satchel. Thirty minutes later Detective Crooms, Satchel, and another detective showed up and called Oren into the living room. As soon as Oren saw Detective Crooms, he pulled on my shirttail and whispered, "You said the nice man was coming. He's not nice. He took my mommy away."

"I know, but he's protecting your mommy, so it's okay to talk with him," I said. Oren shook his head and headed back to his room. "He doesn't want to talk with you," I said, pointing to Detective Crooms.

"Maybe he'll talk to me," said the other man, but Oren didn't turn to acknowledge him. He continued to act as though they weren't in the house. The three looked at me as though I could do something about the once gabby, now silent little boy.

I walked back in Oren's room, knelt by his side, and said, "Oren, do you want your mommy to come home?" Oren nodded yes. "Well, then I need you to tell me what happened again. Just like you did a minute ago."

Oren looked at me and sighed. "I was in my room when Daddy came home. Mommy was in the kitchen. He said he had to talk. Then I didn't hear anything. Then Mommy came running down the hall, and Daddy was calling her a whore. She kept saying, 'This is your fault. This is your fault.' I looked out my door, and she hit Daddy with the lamp. Then he started choking her and yelling louder. I yelled for him to stop, but then I saw the knife Mommy dropped on the floor, and so I picked it up and stuck Daddy with it until he got off of Mommy."

We were all standing there in shock as Oren conveyed the details of the quarrel. Oren looked at me for any sign of approval. I smiled, and he slowly nodded.

"What happened next?" asked Satchel.

"Daddy started bleeding, and Mommy took the knife from me. Mommy called nine-one-one," said Oren.

"Did she say anything else to your dad?" asked Detective Crooms.

Oren nodded. "She said he was in trouble and we were going to the police."

"That's it?" asked Satchel. Oren nodded his head. "Very good. Thank you. You've helped your mommy a lot."

Oren gave a tiny grin and rushed back to the living room.

The four of us stood in the room and stared at each other. We began putting it together. We were sure this tied into Carl's murder, but how?

"Keith!" Satchel shouted. "We have to talk to him."

Detective Crooms said, "I'll call and make sure he's still at the station."

They left, and I helped Oren pack the remainder of his things. When they got to the station, they called Keith into the room and questioned him about when he learned that Oren was Carl's son. Keith admitted that he had found out Carl had a son when he was doing his investigation. He stated that he hadn't known who the son was.

"How did you find out?" Detective Crooms asked. "And why didn't you mention it?"

"I asked Carl about an insurance claim, and he said it was for his son, and that's why Adrian wasn't the beneficiary. And why would I mention that? So what? He had a son."

"His son is Oren Trace, Adrian's son. That's why it's a big deal!" Satchel yelled. "Some investigator you are."

"Why are you coming down on me?" Keith muttered.

"Because I don't believe you," Satchel shouted. Finally, Detective Crooms asked Satchel to leave the room. At the same time, she received a call from Adrian's lawyer, telling her that she wasn't allowed to visit his client anymore unless there was probable evidence of his wrongdoing. She told Detective Crooms about the call.

Meanwhile, I was at my home with Oren. He'd finally warmed up to me and wanted us to play video games. I told him I was no good, but that Cole was great, and he should play with him. At first Oren made faces, but after Cole egged him on and threatened to kick his butt at basket-ball, Oren agreed to play. I heard Cole and Oren in the other room, having a great time. This brought a little smile to my face. This little boy had just had a traumatic two days, and yet he was able to smile and laugh by doing something as simple as playing a video game.

"Oh, to be a kid again," I whispered.

Cole called me into the room. I walked in, and he motioned toward Oren. He was pulling paper out of his book bag, but in his hand was a very odd object. He was tugging at it when I called out to him.

"Oren, what are you doing?"

"Trying to get the top off this crayon," said Oren.

Oren handed the "crayon" to me. Only it wasn't a crayon; it was a wax bullet.

"Where did you get this?" I asked.

"From Mommy's car. It was on the floor," he said innocently. Both Cole and I froze while staring at each other.

"You know what this is, right?" I said to Cole.

Cole nodded slowly. "Is it real?"

"If you're hunting elk, it is."

I ran so fast to grab my cell that I was light-headed by the time Satchel answered.

"I . . . I . . . am with Oren, and he pulled out something that he thinks is a crayon, but it is a bullet, a wax bullet," I said. "He said he got if from Mommy's car."

"You've got to be kidding," said Satchel. "Can you bring it down here? I'm still at the station."

Cole and I rushed Oren to the car and sped down to the police station. Once again, Cole had to wait in the lobby. This time Oren waited with him. I handed the bullet, wrapped in a paper towel, over to Detective Crooms. Satchel looked on. "He said he found it in his mommy's car," I repeated.

"Oh my God!" Satchel murmured. "She did it."

Detective Crooms called the other detective over and sent the bullet down to the lab to check for fingerprints. He told Satchel she could go into the adjoining room and listen as he questioned Ndeeyah. When Detective Crooms walked into the interrogation room, he first asked Ndeeyah if she wanted a lawyer.

"Why? Do I need one? I already told you guys what happened," she said openly.

"Well, we have two problems. It's your husband's word against yours, and we found a wax bullet in your car."

Ndeeyah's eyes became enlarged. "Are you saying Adrian is setting me up for this?"

"I'm saying, do you want a lawyer?" Detective Crooms repeated.

"Ndeeyah's breathing sped up as she stood and paced the small grey room. "I don't have a lawyer. Adrian uses this guy, but—"

"Is his name Thomas Guy?"

Ndeeyah nodded.

"Adrian's already called him. He won't be able to represent you both. It's a conflict of interest," Detective Crooms informed her.

"So what should I do?"

"If you waive your right to a lawyer, then I'd start by telling the truth."

Ndeeyah began to sweat, and then came the tears. "Just find me a lawyer," she said. "Just find me a lawyer."

Satchel called and got Ndeeyah a lawyer, and Ndeeyah sat in the room with him and spilled her guts. She was frightened and panicky. While this was going on, Satchel and the other detective took one more look at the hotel lobby tape and discovered that Ndeeyah had been working the day of the shooting and that she'd left the front desk two times: once for ten minutes and once for thirty. When she returned the second time, she seemed distracted. They awaited her confession, which she gave willingly.

"I used to confide in Carl about Adrian's gambling and wasting of money. This led to a friendship and then a love relationship. We carried on an affair for a few months before I became pregnant. Carl didn't want me to have it, but I don't believe in abortion. I decided to have the baby and stay with my husband. I know it was wrong, but I didn't want to lose everything. Carl didn't want me, and I knew if Adrian found out, he would leave me, and I didn't have anyone or anywhere to go. I had no choice."

"Everything was fine until Carl hired Keith, who found out my real name and then discovered my relationship with Carl. Keith was doing as much investigating on Carl as he was on Adrian. When Keith found out, he started blackmailing Carl. This went on for a year, until Carl couldn't take it anymore. Carl said that he wanted to come clean with everyone before he got married. He was going to end things with Shanice and tell Adrian that Oren was his son. I'd heard Adrian and Shanice talking about her joke, and at first, Adrian didn't believe she was going to do it, but then he realized that she was. He went to tell Carl, but then Carl fired him, so Adrian figured it was just the exposure Carl needed. I checked Shanice in at the hotel that day, and she had no idea that I knew. But after she left her room to eat, I went to the room and replaced two of the wax bullets with real ones."

By now, Ndeeyah was bawling. She just kept apologizing and saying she had had no choice. She couldn't go back to Kenya, and she couldn't lose everything. She had begged Carl not to say anything, but he was convinced it was what he had to do. Satchel diligently went to work on changing Shanice's verdict in light of the new evidence. She was able to get a hearing two weeks from the day of Ndeeyah's confession.

No one had even considered Ndeeyah to be the killer. All of this explained the nature of Ndeeyah and Carl's relationship. They'd been hiding this secret for eight years. Ndeeyah wanted to know how we had linked her to Carl, and Satchel told her about the insurance payment from Peyton. However, we weren't sure if Peyton was going to make good on his promise to her. She asked that if he did, I make sure Oren was taken care of and not punished for her foolish mistakes. She seemed sincere, but most people did once they got caught. Truthfully, she was going to let Shanice go down for a murder she'd committed. Though she didn't pull the trigger, she had planned and plotted the death of her child's father. No one was going to give her an ounce of pity.

Detective Crooms had suspected Keith of several bad dealings but could never prove anything. He and the other detective agreed to keep Ndeeyah's confession under wraps for a couple of days. That night I think both Satchel and I slept peacefully for the first time in months. However, by morning I was filled with angst. I wanted Keith to admit he'd been blackmailing Carl, and I was going to use my newfound skunk scent to do so.

Chapter 15

Sneaky Bastard

**2 ounces Midori melon liqueur
2 ounces Malibu coconut rum
2 ounces Dole pineapple juice
1 ounce blue Curaçao liqueur
1 ounce vodka**

Mix the Midori, Malibu, pineapple juice, Curaçao, and vodka in a cocktail shaker. Shake well. Pour into highball glass. Sit back and enjoy.

I hadn't talked to Mei in a few days, not since all the chaos with Oren and Ndeeyah. However, she came to visit me that next day, bubbling over with excitement.

"I got another virgin, and she's a sister," Mei confessed.

"One of your sisters, or one of my sisters?" I asked.

Mei pointed vigorously at me. "I got her from that group of girls you went and talked to."

"You're out of control."

Mei followed me around my place, trying to convince me to go into this ordeal with her, but I was totally against it. It was then that she realized that Oren was in the living room, playing video games. She pointed at him. I couldn't say anything about Ndeeyah's confession, so I simply replied, "Baby-sitting."

Satchel called shortly after, and I had to meet her downtown, so Mei hung around while I got dressed, and then we both left.

Adrian was supposed to come home in a couple of days, but until then, I was playing Mommy. Oren was a sweet child, very quiet. I often found myself staring at him, looking for Carl's features. I saw them plain as day. This made me wonder what our child would have looked like. I knew that Oren was going to go back and live with Adrian; thankfully, the state hadn't raised a stink about that. But I knew that I would have an active part in the rest of his life, and this brought me joy.

All the way out the door, Mei rambled on and on about her new business venture. She was determined that this was going to be her new line of business. She hadn't really considered it before me, but now that she had witnessed the money potential firsthand, Mei was determined to corner the U.S. market. My friend was officially going to be an Internet madam. I could do nothing but laugh. She surely had the personality for it, and if she could get away with it, more power to her.

I asked Cole to watch Oren for the day, and at lunch Satchel and I talked about everything.

When I left her, I called Keith and asked him to meet me at Fox Sports Grill. Keith didn't know why I wanted to see him, but he agreed to come, and when he arrived, I didn't inform him that I knew about the blackmailing or the confession. I knew Keith was shady, so I knew this would work. When he came in, I laid it on the line.

"Keith, I know about Carl's son. He told me. He also told me that you know. I need help, police help. Carl's uncle, who is a drunk, was the beneficiary of this insurance policy. He's supposed to set up some escrow account for Carl's son. The policy is worth five hundred thousand."

"Oh really?"

I could see Keith's wheels turning. I really put it on, batting eyelashes and all. "Is there any way you can use your police influence with the insurance company? I know if they think Peyton was arrested, the policy would go to the second holder, which is me. I would gladly compensate you for it."

"You're asking me to break the law?"

"Come on, Keith. You're no angel," I said, with a wink. "I'll cut you in on the money and whatever else you want." I leaned in and caressed his arm. Keith started shifting in his seat. He didn't know how to take my flirting.

"Okay." The word rolled slowly off his tongue.

"Is there anything I can do for you?"

Keith looked around and leaned in. "Are you really a virgin?"

Bingo. I knew I'd seen curiosity in his eyes that night he came over. If I could just convince him that I was willing, ready, and able, Keith would be putty in my hands.

"I am. But that doesn't matter to me anymore. It has gotten me nowhere in life, and I'm ready to come up. Why? Have you ever been with a virgin, Keith?"

"Not that I know of."

I simply smirked and looked away.

"So what are you saying?"

"What are you saying?" I asked, tossing the question back at him.

"I want half," he said.

"What? Forget about it. I was hoping we could make a deal, but I'll just figure something else out." I leaned away from him, looked at the menu, and changed my entire tone. "I heard the bayou shrimp and pasta is really good here."

"What about Satchel? What would she say if she knew you were here?"

"Satchel doesn't care about you. Not in that way. Let me worry about Satchel. She won't even know. That is, if we are talking about the same thing."

"I've always been attracted to you, Isabelle."

"I know. That's why you touch me every time you greet me. I'm not stupid. So are you going to help me?"

Keith gave a few sighs and looked around again. I guess he was so used to spying on people, he assumed someone was spying on him. "So what's up?"

"You know what's up, Keith. I don't want to play games. I look at this as a business deal. You help me, and I will help you. Besides, it's time I get this virgin monkey off my back. But promise me you won't say shit to Satchel. For real."

"I don't buy it. Why are you asking me?"

"Because you're the police. If I had a badge, I would do it myself. And you're the only cop I know that . . . well, that would be willing to work with me."

"Let me think on it."

"Fine."

I ordered my plate to go, and by the time it came, Keith said he would call me. I prayed he fell for it.

He called an hour later and asked if we could meet at eight, but at eight fifteen, he called and said that he was running late. I flipped on the television and drank a Sprite while I waited. I couldn't believe how calm I was about the whole thing. It was like a relief, a saga coming to an end. I waited an additional hour, but I didn't hear from Keith. He wasn't answering my calls, either. Close to ten, he finally called and said that he was on the way. He apologized for his tardiness but said that he had been unexpectedly held up. By now Cole was home, so I told Keith I would have to meet him at his house.

When I was leaving, Cole, of course, asked where I was going. He noticed I was dressed up and assumed I had a date.

"I'm going to meet Satchel," I told him.

He grabbed me by the waist and kissed my cheek. "I've missed you. You've been very preoccupied lately."

"I know. I should be better next week. Promise."

I hurried to leave before he asked anything else. I hated lying to him, but right now it was all I could do.

* * *

I arrived at Keith's house in twenty minutes, and he was there waiting. He was strutting around in his jeans, with his shirt off. He pulled me into his grasp as soon as he opened the door. He leaned in to kiss my cheek, but I moved out of his way.

"This is not a date. This is business," I reminded him. "By the way, how do I know that you will do what you say you will? Maybe we should wait until after you talk to the insurance people."

"You don't trust me?"

"Not really. But I know you are just as hungry for money as I am. So if you don't talk to them, no one will get the money."

"One more time. Are you really a virgin?"

I rolled my eyes and replied, "Yes, Keith, I am."

"Wow," he replied. "Well, after tonight, you won't be able to say that." I showed very little enthusiasm. "Cheer up," he said.

I gave him a look as though I'd just tasted something bad and then replied, "Let's just get this over with."

He rose and led me to the bedroom. On the way there, I explained that I would probably get scared and want to chicken out, but that he should not listen and should keep going no matter what. I was determined to complete this task tonight, and I really needed that money. I told him about the debt and everything. We got to his bedroom, and I looked at his king-sized bed.

"Did you change your sheets?" I asked him.

"Since?"

"Since the last time you had sex?"

"I changed them two days ago," he replied.

I walked over to the bed and slowly sat down. "I don't want to kiss," I said.

Obviously irritated, Keith plopped down on the bed and retorted, "Anything else, Izzy?"

"I know you were blackmailing Carl. He told me you were shady. This is why I came to you."

"I wasn't blackmailing Carl. He was simply paying me to keep certain information under wraps."

"It worked." I paused and then continued. "I swear, it's about the come up. I never really understood that before all this shit. Now I do."

Keith kept giving me suspicious looks. I was talking too much, and I didn't want to give myself away, so I shut up and kissed him. Yes, I didn't want to kiss at first, but it was the only way I knew to really convince him. Keith crawled on top of my body and removed my shirt. He kissed my neck and then my breasts. It was utterly disgusting. Keith worked down to his boxers, and I was in my panties, the cotton white ones. I surely wasn't wasting my fancy silk ones on this fool. He tried to remove my underwear.

"Stop, stop," I said. But he kept going. "For real, Keith, stop. I can't do this."

Keith covered my mouth with his hand and snatched my underwear practically off my hips. His large hand muffled my yells as I wiggled uncontrollably. I realized that he wasn't going to stop; he was going to go through with it. All of a sudden, Satchel burst into the bedroom. She walked over to the bed, carrying a revolver. She aimed it at Keith, and then at me.

"I knew you were up to something," Satchel said.
Keith immediately jumped off me.

Still aiming the gun, Satchel walked over to the stereo and cut off the music. "Izzy, how could you? I told you how much I cared for him, and I told you we were getting back together."

I said nothing.

Satchel then pointed the gun at Keith's chest. "An hour ago, you said we could work things out, and now you're in bed with my sister." Satchel truly seemed hurt. I tried to ease out of the bed. "Be cool, Izzy. Don't you move. I got more words for you."

"This is not what you think. Tell her, Isabelle," Keith implored.

I didn't say anything.

Satchel had a possessed look in her eyes. She then moved close and aimed the gun at Keith's dick. "What would you say if I told you *I* changed the bullets in the gun? I knew what Carl was doing to my sister, and I wasn't going to have her be made a fool of her entire life."

"What? No, you didn't," he said.

"Wanna take your chances? Wax, real, real, wax?" said Satchel. She moved the gun closer to his penis. Her possessed look became an absolutely crazed look.

"He was going to rape me," I yelled.

Keith twisted in my direction and quickly defended himself. "What? No! We had an agreement. I told her that I would talk to the insurance people, and she offered to have sex with me. Tell her about the five hundred thousand."

"So you blackmailed my sister into having sex with you?" Satchel yelled. She cocked the revolver. "She told me you blackmailed Carl. I should have believed her, but no, I believed you. I was such a fool."

Keith was so confused. He didn't know what to say. "No. Carl was a different situation," he sputtered. "He didn't want anyone to know about his son. He paid me willingly. Izzy wanted to have sex. Just stop pointing that gun at me. Are there real bullets in there?"

Satchel winked at him and gave a partial grin.

"Fuck you!" he yelled.

Satchel pulled the trigger and hit Keith in the groin. He bent over in agonizing pain. She then looked at me with sorrowful eyes.

"Izzy, how could you?" Satchel said again, but I still said nothing. Finally, Satchel spoke again. "How could you wear those damn white cotton panties when you knew this was going down? Get your clothes on."

I quickly hopped from the bed and grabbed my pants and shirt. Since Keith was still in agony, Satchel walked over and handcuffed him to the bedpost. I walked over and cut off the video recorder hidden by the stereo. Satchel called Detective Crooms and told him to come to Keith's house, and Keith finally saw the wax splattered on his boxers. Once the officers got there, Satchel explained to them what happened. Of course, she didn't mention it was a setup. One of the officers began reading Keith his rights. He was taken in on attempted rape, blackmail, withholding evidence, and apparently, a couple of other naughty deeds that had nothing to do with me. With my heart still beating overtime, I hugged my sister, who handed the revolver to one of the officers. Satchel couldn't even look at Keith as he was being hauled off. She and I had to go to the station and give official statements of everything that had happened, and I eventually dropped the attempted rape charges.

This was the true story. Satchel stopped by Keith's around eight to say she wanted to get back together. She held him up a couple of hours so that when he called me, I could say it was too late and that Cole was home. I then purposely told Keith we would have to meet back at his place. By then, Satchel had had time to plant the video recorder and hide. It worked perfectly. Yes, the plan was entrapment, but Keith had given additional information that was going to be used against him. Keith Carson might not have to spend time behind bars, but he would surely be barred from the police and could no longer harass me, Satchel, or even Adrian.

After we gave our statements, Satchel and I went to IHOP to grab a bite to eat. We sat down and ordered two large sweet teas.

"I'm proud of you," Satchel said.

Just then my phone rang. It was Cole. He was concerned about my whereabouts. It was close to two in the morning. I told him I would be back in a couple of hours. He was still up and hungry, so he decided to join us at IHOP.

We sat quietly for a minute, and then I asked Satchel a question. "Were you really falling for Keith, or did you just say that?"

Satchel looked out the window and huffed. She finally murmured, "For the first time in a very long time, I allowed myself to give in to the feeling. I really did care for him. After all, he was fine."

"Hell yeah, he was fine ass Keith Carson."

We both laughed. I talked to her about Mei and her virgin prostitution ring, and caught her up on the latest between Cole and me. Over pancakes, my sister and I returned to normal. In the last two months, my life had turned upside down and back around again.

Chapter 16

Happy Ending

2 ounces Absolut Mandrin vodka
4 ounces club soda
2 splashes cranberry juice

Add the vodka to the club soda. Mix in the splashes of cranberry juice. Garnish with a lime wedge and enjoy!

In lue of the new evidence, the judge reduced Shanice's sentence at the hearing. Instead of second-degree murder, the charges were lessened to accidental homicide. She would come up for parole in five years. Ndeeyah was found guilty of premeditated murder and received life. However, since she wasn't the trigger person, she could be paroled in twenty-five years.

I wanted a vacation so bad, but I had to remain in town because I was on six months' probation for that stupid possession charge. It all worked out, though, because while I was doing my probation time, I got an interesting call from Jonah.

He was very thankful to Satchel for having the courage to believe in his sister. He'd discussed matters with his father, and they were speaking to the bank about purchasing the Shelby. Jonah wanted to know if I was interested in running the place. I told him no, but that I was sure I could find someone capable. I was, however, interested in managing the bar inside the hotel. I even had aspirations of purchasing it one day.

One month and two days after that call, the Franklin Group bought the Shelby. I'd already spoken with Warren about running it, and Mr. Franklin had an executive staff he was putting in place as well. We renovated the bar. It was now one thousand square feet, with sleek flat screens, modern furniture, and a black marble bar top. The back of the bar had blue back lighting, and we stocked everything from top-shelf liquors to Pabst Blue Ribbon. It was perfect. I was appointed the manager. Mei and Cole were my designated lead bartenders. Everything was ideal. Occasionally, though, I still looked around corners, thinking Keith was going to pop up and come after me for what we did to him. But I refused to live in fear. Plus Mei was the Chinese Mafia queen. With one click of the button, she could probably have Keith picked up, shipped to Mali, and doing slave labor for the rest of his days. It was good to have friends in high and low places.

Peyton did what he was supposed to do, and Oren was set. Once he became eighteen, he'd be practically a millionaire. Even Adrian got himself together. He stopped gambling and was taking care of Oren. Though we couldn't hire Adrian as a manager, we found a position for him as head of security.

Cole and I were still dating, but abstaining, which was much more difficult now than it used to be. We talked about taking our relationship to the next level but wanted to wait until our one-year anniversary. We were going to Bermuda. I'd come to realize that friends most often made the best love relationships. They knew your journey, and when you lost your way, they sometimes were the only ones who could help get you back on track. That was what Cole did for me. His adoration and respect helped me relearn how to respect myself.

Emerson said, "Whatever games are played with us, we must play no games with ourselves."

That was my new creed.

I was still Izzy the virgin widow, and some chick asked about writing a book on my life. As we were thinking up titles, I came up with the perfect one, *White Cotton Panties*. I knew it was going to be a best-seller.